MANIFEST DESTINY

Zachary Daniel

MADE FOR SUCCESS

Made for Success Publishing
P.O. Box 1775 Issaquah, WA 98027
www.MadeForSuccessPublishing.com

Copyright © 2022

All rights reserved.

In accordance with the U.S. Copyright Act of 1976, the scanning, uploading, and electronic sharing of any part of this book without the permission of the publisher constitutes unlawful piracy and theft of the author's intellectual property. If you would like to use material from the book (other than for review purposes), prior written permission must be obtained by contacting the publisher at service@madeforsuccess.net. Thank you for your support of the author's rights.

Distributed by Made for Success Publishing

Typeset by Nord Compo

First Printing

Library of Congress Cataloging-in-Publication data
Daniel, Zachary
    Manifest Destiny
    p. cm.

LCCN: 2022910262
ISBN: 978-1-64146-744-5 *(HDBK)*
ISBN: 978-1-64146-745-2 *(eBOOK)*
ISBN: 978-1-64146-746-9 *(AUDIO)*

Printed in the United States of America

For further information contact Made for Success Publishing
+14255266480 or email service@madeforsuccess.net

Chapter 1

There's an unsettled nervousness before committing an act you know is wrong. The mind is sharp and focused while adrenaline courses through your body, ready to push you past your limits.

I enjoy that sensation and thus welcomed it as I sat patiently on the park bench. It was time.

She emerged from behind the hedges, jogging from the south side of the park. She was a couple of minutes late—perhaps her coffee took longer this morning. I gazed down at the rumpled newspaper by my side. September 21, 1995. A single glance at the headline had me cursing under my breath.

OPEC RAISES PRICES.

My daily commute was already taking a chunk out of my wallet, but apparently the turban-wearing extremists wanted a little more.

She took a sharp turn by the fountain at the center of the park. Perfect, she was on her normal route. Sweat began to bead at my fingertips, and my chest tightened.

It was now or never.

I pulled the hood of my black sweatshirt over my head, departed the bench, and began trailing her. The sweatshirt was a gift from my father when I made the high school baseball team. Two sizes too small now, it gave me a slim runner look.

Swinging past the playground, my anticipation built. A wave of anger buried deep within me began to emerge as the feelings of being buckled over a baseball field bubbled up from my subconscious.

The park was nearly empty, with only a few morning walkers passing by the pavilion near the opposite side of the park. The dawn housed a calm silence that was only interrupted by the occasional rustling of the leaves or the chirp of a bird. It was almost perfect, but after today, it would be forever tarnished. However, it was a burden I was willing to bear.

Keeping my eyes open for anyone outside their usual routine, I closed the distance between us, and when she rounded the corner toward the forest trail, I knew we were alone. Her pace was quick, and I forced myself nearly to a sprint to shorten the gap.

As we entered the grass cushioning, the trail began to narrow until great oaks hugged the path. The branches arched high above, only letting slivers of light illuminate patches of the route. Fallen leaves in various stages of decay covered the trail, and the noise made from their trampling interrupted the quiet of the jog and left colorful crumbs in their wake. With her headphones on, my movement behind her was silent and unsuspected.

She ran in athletic attire, wearing a skin-tight white vest with matching sweats and running shoes. She held a small plastic water bottle in her left hand. Half-empty now, the contents sloshed violently inside. She had terrible running form, especially for someone so experienced. Her arms flailed wildly instead of purposefully and in sync, and her choppy motion held no rhythm, no balance. Her blonde hair was tied in a ponytail jostling side to side with every stride. I focused chiefly on its movement, for within a few steps, I would be able to reach out and grab it.

I was ready to strike. I steadied myself like a lion before the pounce.

"*Now!*" my mind screamed, and I lunged for her. Diving, I catapulted myself onto her, swiftly covering her mouth with my right hand. She lost her balance from the weight of my body before her legs caught themselves, tripping her and forcing us both to the gravel. We landed hard and skidded for a few feet. The small rocks and dirt embedded in my arms and knees, but the pain from the abrasion was masked by adrenaline.

Her face absorbed the brunt of the fall. The dirt smeared on her cheeks, turning crimson as the wounds beneath began to bleed. As she struggled against my grip in an effort to break free, my hand was dislodged from her mouth, and she got out a short, piercing scream before I was able to recover. The echo of her scream seemed to carry into the ensuing fight.

I soon established myself on top and used my weight to subdue her. With my knee pressed against her back, I reached into my backpack for the duct tape. I started the tape on the left side of her mouth, extending it across when suddenly, I realized I couldn't tear the tape.

Her movements were violent, and she was trying desperately to throw me off. I needed at least one hand to keep her secure. After a desperate struggle to sever the tape, I became panicked that someone would appear behind us on the trail at any moment. My hands were perspiring at a faster rate than I could wipe them off on my shirt.

Every neural impulse was fixated on finding a quick answer. Her mouth had to be taped shut, but I couldn't risk her squirming free for even a second. My frantic neurons suddenly recovered, and I knew what I had to do. I wrapped the duct tape rapidly around her head, allowing the roll to simply hang after the fourth rotation.

Within a minute, I had carried her struggling body out of sight of the trail and tied her to a tree. Other than a few scrapes on my arms and legs, it couldn't have been scripted better.

Deep breath. Now comes the hard part.

I watched her struggling against the restraints, yearning to break free, but I knew there was a slim chance of that happening. The knots were sailor knots, a type my father taught me back in Boy Scouts, and not easily undone. Nonetheless, she fought, but her efforts were fruitless, and her mumbled screams through the duct tape were futile.

There was a calm feel to the forest. The leaves bristled in the slight breeze, and for the time being, it felt as though we were the only two on earth. I eyed her as I started my monologue.

"Why did you do it, Nancy?"

She shot to attention but didn't respond. There was no use playing dumb now.

"How do you go home to your family at night? What's the dinner conversation? 'Hey, Sam, could you pass the potatoes? Oh, let me tell you about the elderly woman I murdered today.'" Her eyes darted towards me. I couldn't tell if it was because I knew her son's name or the crimes she committed. Either way, the stare was deadly.

"You must be surprised I know so much," I continued. "I mean, you couldn't possibly believe that you could keep this up forever." She was still silent.

"How's the husband? Ever thought about offing him? C'mon, Nancy, don't tell me you never considered cashing in that life insurance policy on him." Now I was reaching, but her eyes told me I was probably right. They possessed such an unremorseful cruelty that it sent a small shiver down my spine.

She was mumbling now, and I knew I needed to hear her last words. Everyone deserves to have that final say, no matter the crime. I handed her a small pen, fitting it between her hands, and tossed a pad of paper on her lap. Immediately, she started writing.

Meanwhile, I put on a pair of thick latex gloves, always orange, because it was my favorite color. Then I pulled out the syringe, an 18-gauge needle to be exact. When she laid eyes upon it, a fearful dread overcame them. She squirmed as if she could retreat into a safe haven. It was odd. She was a nurse and worked with needles all day. They were even her weapon of choice, yet she recoiled at the sight. Although I couldn't say I wouldn't be doing the same given her situation.

While I waited for her to draft her parting words, I took a seat against a sturdy oak facing her. I cleared away the shriveled leaves that had fallen to forge a spot on the dirt floor. I took in a deep breath, letting the cool fall air prick the inside of my chest. Releasing the excess, I watched my breath dance away into an invisible mist. The thought of how we took such a gift for granted and how quickly it could be taken away brought a sobering calm. I felt the anxious anger momentarily drift away.

A short grunt indicated she was finished. I rose from my resting spot and took the pen and pad from her, examining it. Short... very short for a last confession, and shallow, unapologetic, without a hint of remorse. I scoffed at her last words: *"Do you know who my husband is? Whatever you want, he can get it for you; just let me go."*

"You think this is about money?" I was chuckling now. "C'mon, Needle Nancy." I fancied my nicknames. "You murder six patients without remorse and expect no consequences? Whatever sick fantasy you were fulfilling, I hope it was worth it."

I had gloves and a needle as planned. I then took a moment to examine the scene. After noting the area was secure, I grabbed my tourniquet and, rolling up her sleeve, wrapped it tightly around her frail bicep. I made sure to softly explain the procedure, which I suspected she knew all too well herself.

"Now, Nancy, you know what this wonderful drug is?" I flashed her the syringe as I located a large vein on her arm. "In about five to ten minutes, your heart will stop beating, and you'll die. Now, I'm not sure if you're religious, but I suggest making peace with God or whatever higher power you believe in."

I moved my attention back to her arm. She resisted when I tried to locate a vein but relented once I became more forceful. She squirmed as I injected the potassium chloride into her arm. I had combined it with a painkiller to neutralize the pain—no need to be barbaric. As I withdrew the needle, she relaxed, staring ahead as if in another world. Maybe she was making a last plea to her maker, or perhaps her thoughts were with her family.

I had always been curious about what a person's final thoughts were before death. Perchance there was a great secret to life that can only be realized in its last moments. I would know one day, but not today. No, today, only Nancy Papperman knew. The wife of Steve Papperman, a successful banker, and the mother of 7-year-old Sam. She was a stay-at-home mother who only recently started back in the workforce, working twice a week as a CNA in a nursing home. She had frequent spa appointments, an addiction to shopping, and ran the neighborhood gossip like a talk show. I doubt that she would be missed by many outside her family. Through my investigation, I had failed to come up with many redeeming qualities and wondered if anything I said even registered with her.

"Nancy? You know this would have never happened had you not euthanized those people. Unfortunately, you did, and the law may not have caught you, but I have." Her gaze didn't avert from the distance she was staring into.

I may have gotten in the last words, but they fell flat, sounding like guilty justification or boasting as they left my mouth. I cringed.

We sat there in silence. It was a silence similar to a graveyard. Whenever I visited my father's gravestone, the quietness of the cemetery felt different than anywhere else.

I averted my attention to the woods of Cyrus Park. My favorite park would never be the same, for me or for others. There was no doubt that the northern Trenton community would be shaken by today's events.

Suddenly, her body language changed. It started slowly as her head began to drop, and her face reached a ghostly pale. The spark in her eyes dimmed like the filament in an old light bulb, flickering every few seconds like a revival was imminent. Her body seemed to recede into its hollow self. Life had left her.

Her passing left me with an uncomfortable lack of satisfaction. I did not expect to feel empowered killing her but rather for avenging those she had murdered. I simply had to. Had I not caught her, my own mother might have been next.

Chapter 2

When I admitted my mother to Saint Christopher nursing home two months ago, I had my best friend Chris, who worked for the NYPD, run a background check on the home. He found a recent rise in deaths. Not unusual or suspect at first glance, but after more digging, he discovered that most of the deaths were first reported by Nancy Papperman.

She had begun working at the establishment six months prior, about the time that the death toll rose. I told Chris I was just curious and I wouldn't worry as it was almost certainly a fluke, but I knew. Oh, I had more than an inkling that there was something more occurring, and I refused to let my mother reside there without knowing all the facts.

I began a little detective work of my own by following her during my "sick" days. I learned Nancy's schedule fairly easily; she was a creature of habit. At night, I would sift through her garbage, looking for anything that could aid my efforts. You can discover a lot about someone through what they throw away. It took me quite a while to connect the dots, but I noticed an unusual amount of bleach being discarded. After some research at the library, I discovered it was the main component used in the production of potassium chloride. She would just slip that drug into a patient's veins, and within a few minutes, they were dead. Quiet, clean, and unsuspecting. A tiny part of me was impressed by the ease of her operation.

Despite the evidence, I was initially skeptical that someone of her apparent intellect was capable of synthesizing such a compound. Though, upon patching up my bio of her, I re-evaluated my assumption. School records indicated that she was one of the top students in her class and had even applied for medical school but was rejected. She was plenty capable.

Other than her killing "hobby," she also appeared to be cheating on her husband with a man named Finger, a teacher at her child's school. Definitely could've picked a man with a better name.

None of the investigation would have been possible without my longtime best friend, Chris Stanky, who was practically a brother to me. Back in high school, people had a field day with his name. See, he was not so much unlike me. We attended the same schools growing up, and his father died of a stroke a month before mine was murdered in a robbery. The tragedies were the cornerstone of our bond.

As a teen, I struggled to find purpose and happiness while grappling with major depression. Thankfully, Chris and I had each other to lean on for support and thus were inseparable. We shared all our problems, hardships, and successes, and it made life bearable. Nothing could replace our fathers, but at least part of the void could be filled with each other.

Growing up, my father was God in my eyes; he did no wrong. He worked hard as a carpenter for a local business but always had extra time to spend with me. He was the one who developed my baseball skills throughout my childhood. He was the most loyal Mets fan I knew and made me promise if I ever made it big, the only team I would play for would be the Mets. He loved baseball, and at least twice a month, we would head to Shea Stadium and catch a game.

Arriving an hour before the game, we would settle into our seats: section 327, row 6, seats 10 and 11. One hot dog with brown mustard, a Dr. Pepper, and a bag of peanuts were all we needed. It was our little slice of heaven. During the game, in which the Mets normally lost, my dad would share some wisdom or joke about some funny-looking patrons. His favorite, though, was exploiting my gullibility. One time, he had me believing that every sip of Dr. Pepper had a different flavor. Subsequently, every gulp was followed by, "You're right! That one *did* taste different!"

Truth was, it didn't matter if the Mets won or lost. They did a lot of losing back in the day, but my father and I always managed to have a great time. I cherish those memories. Things had been so much simpler.

"*Snap!*" A twig broke nearby, and I was jolted back into reality. My head spun as I scanned the woods. A squirrel bolted up the trunk of a nearby tree. Seeing the innocent trespasser, my heart returned to my chest. I needed to get moving.

I turned my attention to Nancy, who lay in front of me. Pale, cold, not so powerful anymore, but her eyes held an eerie, unyielding gaze. I quietly cleaned up my supplies, removed the rope and duct tape, and undressed her to remove trace evidence. I felt guilty leaving her naked, which added an element of humiliation to her death, but the risk of getting caught superseded her dignity. I hesitated to remove her diamond earrings. Her family deserved to have something of hers to remember. Leaving them behind, I stuffed everything into my backpack and made sure to comb the area one last time for any trace left. Once satisfied, I quietly slipped back onto the path from which I came.

Chapter 3

Nancy was the first person I had killed. I never set out with the purpose to kill, but for serious offenders, it seemed the only fitting punishment.

I pulled into the driveway and sat a moment. The radio DJ started up a Styx song as I let my body sink back into the leather, and my mind slowly drifted back to the last time I'd heard the song.

The original sin that set me on my path occurred on September 21, 1978. The memory played vividly in my mind.

I had just made the varsity baseball team as a freshman and had been at a typical afterschool practice. They were mostly made up of scrimmaging, batting practice, and simulated scenarios. I liked my teammates for the most part, but with the age gap, I had trouble fitting in. The hazing and purposeful exclusion on account of that difference didn't do much to help.

We were in the middle of a scrimmage. I had just rocketed a double to the right-field corner and proudly held second base. I was leading off second, inching ever closer to third. The pitcher was eyeing me up and down, debating whether to try for a pickoff. No doubt he wanted to. The best pitcher on the team had just given up a double to the freshman, and his pride must have been a little bruised. I could sense the shortstop creeping up behind me. I wiped my hands together, letting the dirt from my batting gloves settle in a dust cloud. I was taunting him, but despite a few tense seconds and a couple of stares, he started his motion forward.

"Nick, can you come over here for a minute?" my coach yelled from the dugout, effectively stopping the game. What could possibly be urgent enough to warrant stopping the game? He could've at least waited until the inning ended. The pitcher whirled around, letting out a heavy sigh. I reluctantly began to trot across the infield.

"Got lucky," the pitcher sneered as I passed. Had we kept playing, I would've shown him that luck had nothing to with it. Nonetheless, I probably earned myself a surprise hazing sometime in the coming days.

On the other side of the fence, I saw my dad's friend Officer Luke Murray standing next to Coach Reisch. Fear began to grip my chest, thinking that somehow he had found out about the drinking party I had participated in last weekend. My terror only persisted for a few fleeting seconds as the long look on his face told me it was something different, something worse. He looked at me with a sorrow that was puzzling.

His clean pressed dark blue uniform absorbed the rays of the hot fall day, and the reflective gold badge displayed proudly on his chest radiated sunlight back into my retina. Squinting, I turned my gaze down toward the ground. He was shifting his weight back and forth like he was uncomfortable. *Maybe it's the heat*, I thought.

"Son," he began with a heavy sigh. I lifted my head, looking for eye contact to perhaps provide a glimpse of where he was going, but his eyes were looking anywhere but me. They darted first to the left, then upwards, then down. All the while searching for words, beginning and starting his sentence three times before finally spewing forth his pain.

"Someone broke into your house this afternoon. Your father came home for lunch and, well… eh… em… the intruder stabbed your father in the chest. He died on his way to the hospital. I'm sorry."

And just like that, my world stopped.

"What? But… no-n-no, you're lying!"

"I'm sorry." He leaned in for a hug, but I collapsed to the field in utter disbelief. The crippling came at the hands of a sentence so unfathomable that replaying the words in my head no longer made sense. Once my paralyzed mind confirmed that it was all real, I started sobbing. I mean, I blubbered like I never had—or have since. I lost control.

A few teammates tried to console me, but I had already receded within myself. They didn't know what it was like. They all had fathers to go home to. Fathers to play catch with, to watch sports with, to grill with, and to cheer on the team with. Fathers to give them advice about girls, to teach them how to become a man, and to teach them how to love. To cherish every moment spent with them. To have such childlike glee when around them, because when you see them, you see what you want to be. That part of me died on that field that day, a part I will never recover, the best part.

At that point, practice had ended, and Officer Murray ushered me into his car to drive me to my mother, who was waiting at the hospital. On the way, he had tried to console me, but I was gone—zoned out, numbed into the abyss of my subconscious. I was sad and angry, but mostly scared. Scared that I had lost my life and that I would never be able to regain it.

Chapter 4

The phone rattled violently, startling me from the groggy state of my morning. I snatched the phone off the system. Holding it to my ear, I heard a familiar voice echo through.

"Ahh, I got a tip about a terrible accountant, real lazy. You got one of those there? He's not the best looking either, and a Yankees fan of all things." A crackle started on the other end.

"Chris, you think you're so clever, don't you? I should call your precinct and tell 'em you've been stealing doughnuts again."

"Oh, hardy har har, how original."

"Well, you keep putting those down, the wife might start looking a bit south of the state line, if you catch my drift."

Chris blew right past the remark. "Speaking of the wife, her and the kids are just getting over the flu. It's been a mess."

"Sounds like you need a drink and some bad company."

"It's like you know me or something."

"Well, hey, I gotta run to the office soon. How about dinner and a few drinks tomorrow night? Mulberry's at eight? I'll see you then."

"I'll count down the hours… wait, Mulberry's agai—"

I smashed the phone on its console. I wanted Mulberry's, and I knew Chris would convince me to try somewhere new if I hung around too long.

Chris and I tried to get together at least once every other week. We used to get together more often, but a couple of years ago, he had packed up and moved his family to New York City, where he had received a job offer as a sergeant in the 23rd precinct. He hated the daily commute, so the decision was a no-brainer. Along with that, he had never been too fond of Jersey anyway.

Chris moved here from New York when he was eight, and he's missed that city ever since. I had asked him once why he missed New York so badly. Our past wasn't a subject we usually dwelled on.

He told me that when his father was alive, they used to go on adventures all over the city. Whether they were out looking for food, folk, or just the weird, there was never a dull moment. His father used to call it "America's America." On the surface, the city is rough yet so alive. You just have to view and harness it in the right way. His father showed him that reality, and he wanted to show his kids as well. That was a fair enough explainer to me.

I took a sip from my mug, breaking my obliviousness to the time on the clock. I scarfed down a banana between the sips of joe, then proceeded to the office to coast by with another mundane shift. After the dull day, I settled down at one of my usual watering holes to unwind with a couple of drinks during happy hour.

Once I sat down, I ordered a drink. Taking my first sip, I felt my shoulders slump and the tension melt like butter. There was nothing like Captain and Dr. Pepper. Taking another sip, the heavenly mixture tickled as it went down my throat. The bubbly warmth when it hit the stomach was unrivaled. I let out a smile and a deep breath for the first time all day. I sat with my drink and enjoyed the last few minutes of the *Happy Days* rerun that played overhead.

It wasn't too long before I made it back to my apartment. Once there, I kicked back with another drink, wrestled the TV tray over with my leg, and whipped out a deck of cards from the side pocket of the recliner. I shuffled quickly, fumbling on the bridge, and then dealt out my spreadsheet. The slick cards spewed out quickly, and 28 of them later, my solitaire setup was complete. It was my favorite card game, and even though it always frustrated me, the game regularly consumed my late nights on the weekday. I would come so close to beating it but was left just a couple of cards short. I would've rather not even come close. This time was no different, and as I realized defeat, I took another swig of my mixer.

The drink fleetingly reminded me of the first time I ever avenged someone. I had been seated at a dive bar 14 years ago to the day, mulling over my drink and seething with anger. No other day of the year gets me so distraught. At that point in time, I had been an angry young adult still consumed with my father's death. The resentment had been building for three years and was at a breaking point.

The bar was called Rails. It was small and known for its cheap drinks, hence the name. The night wasn't too busy. I was a regular, always getting a drink or two and watching the rest of the patrons. That night, the bar held the usual crowd… except for one bunch towards the end of the bar. They were obnoxiously loud and were getting stares while they shouted and hollered for some inane reason. They took up the whole far side of the bar, except for a scrawny college-aged student nestled amidst the group. He looked out of place and seemed to be doing his best to ignore the brutes behind him, focusing his attention instead on the football game broadcasting overhead. I caught him wincing a couple of times, likely attempting to ignore the yelling or the occasional crude joke.

As the night went on, he started getting jostled around. At one point, a drink was spilled on him without so much as an apology from the drunks. A couple of times, it looked as though he was about to speak up, but he held his tongue. That was probably a smart choice.

He caught the bartender's attention for another drink, upgrading from his beer to some sort of mixer. I didn't blame him. He needed something stiffer. Right as he reached for the glass, another jolt from behind threw him forward, causing his drink to spill on the wood bar top. The sigh that proceeded summed up his night. The bartender quickly rushed over with a napkin and made apologetic eye contact, topping off his glass. I knew he was about to say something, and I pleaded in my mind for him not to. *Just leave while you're somewhat ahead*, I thought.

"Excuse me, guys," the man said, "would you mind calming down a little?"

In a matter of seconds, a nuke exploded at the end of the bar. The group looked shocked. There was a befuddled disbelief among them, and everyone looked around for some indication of how they should react. After a couple of tense seconds, the largest of the group stepped forward. I decided Bruiser was an appropriate name. He looked the part of a bar drunk that's itching for a fight, someone that, for motives unclear to me, craves the beatings they dish out to the unsuspecting.

"I will calm down if you step outside with me and my friends and apologize," Bruiser sneered, edging closer and closer to his victim.

At this point, the young man realized what he was getting into, but it was too late. He had little choice in the matter. It was either quietly step out and take his beating or cause a scene that would probably end much worse. I felt bad for the kid. He sighed and nodded, already looking defeated. Getting up, he slammed his drink for the last ounce of courage, then slumped out of the bar, followed by Bruiser and his friends, who were jeering and cheering the whole way out. A small group of us took notice of the situation and snuck outside for what was sure to be a beat down. The participants in the fight readied themselves in true comic goon-like fashion. One guy was stretching his calves, another one was talking to himself, and a third guy put on gloves. After about 30 seconds of this nonsense, Bruiser took the circle for the little audience.

"Listen, kid; I will give you one chance to be the bigger man and pick up our tab for the night. I think that would go a long way as to settling this misunderstanding," he sneered as he looked around in mocking glee.

The college kid meekly replied, "No, thank you."

Then *thud!* He socked Bruiser smack in the nose. My jaw dropped, and at once, it felt as if the air was sucked out of the entire circle. Bruiser staggered back slowly, reeling from the surprise attack. He covered his nose, and his friends stood wide-eyed as blood dripped out between his fingers and down his face. The crimson liquid was an indication of his mortality.

"Thud!" Another strike, this one to Bruiser's stomach. He buckled over in pain, collapsing to the pavement. Then the college student broke loose, kicking Bruiser ferociously. The fierce kicks unleashed unexpected power and emitted a mean mashing sound. He got in three to the ribs before Bruiser's friends swarmed him. After the quick start, the college student was overpowered. Two restrained him, locking down his hands as he thrashed violently against their control. Their restraint let the third assailant start to get strikes in. A heavy gut shot forced the air out and left the college student gasping. He was getting beat but given the numbers advantage, his resistance was impressive.

The cronies wailed mercilessly on the kid until Bruiser finally resurrected. I had barely noticed his slow rebirth. By now, the blood had soaked into his shirt and the Red Sea that was his friends parted, exposing his defeated victim. Embarrassed and outright pissed, the fire in his eyes would have melted glaciers.

"Step aside!" he yelled, staggering over towards the group. His friends parted further and revealed a limp young man, bloody and curled up.

"You're done, kid."

As expected, he mercilessly wailed on the college student. Blow after blow landed without restraint. I had never seen someone beat so badly, and the longer the onslaught went, the more disgusted I became. The other onlookers' faces were a mix between horrified and mesmerized. Why was no one doing anything? I could feel my anger coming on tenfold. How could we all let this happen?! This kid was just trying to enjoy his night. He didn't ask for this. This was an injustice, and Bruiser was just going to walk away from it. I couldn't let him.

Sirens arose from a distance, breaking the sound of fist on flesh and scattering those in the circle. I kept my eyes on Bruiser fighting through two of his friends, running the opposite way. He wasn't going to leave my sight. He moved like a rather nimble bear and wasn't easy to keep up with. Intramural basketball hadn't done me any justice, and I found myself gasping for air before the second block. After three blocks, his movement slowed to a slight jog and then gradually declined to a speed walk. He was tired. His wheezing was audible from half a block away.

As my strides closed the gap between us, I was certain he couldn't hear my approach over his own heavy breathing. I watched the greasy assaulter saunter down the side street, no doubt a smug look on his face, enjoying his escape. My anger rose to a blistering level. It started deep and rose until it encompassed me. Uncontrollable but euphoric; alarming, yet invigorating. The empowerment was intoxicating. No one deserved to get away with a crime so heinous, and I was not about to let it happen.

Turning down an alley behind a closed food bank, I saw my opportunity. Bruiser, still breathing heavily, had little idea of what lurked behind him. I took a deep breath, focusing on the back of his sweaty mullet skull, and then with the weight of my body behind me, struck him in the base of the head, resulting in his dramatic fall to the ground. I barely hesitated before following him to the pavement. Wailing punches ensued. He put up some fight, but nothing I couldn't handle. His hands were more of an obstacle than a defense. *Left to the head, right to the chest, head, head, head.* I was putting all my force into the blows. Bruiser's head sounded like a splatter against the pavement. My anger from the last three years was released with every blow. It was liberating. *Smack. Smack. Smack.* My dad's killer was beneath me, absorbing the pain he caused me.

Before I realized it, he was lifeless on the ground, his face mutilated—if you could even call it a face anymore. It was so swollen and bloody that it looked more like a skinned pig after throwing it in a beehive. He was breathing, though, thankfully. I stood over him for a long minute, mesmerized by what I was capable of. Never had I acted with such maliciousness. There was a latency between the time it took for my bewilderment to turn to disgust.

I sulked out of the alley and walked to a convenience store down the block. I left my jacket, splattered with blood, outside and did my best to look a bit less like a madman. Using their pay phone to call the police, I informed them there was a beaten man in an alley nearby. After I hung up, I stood at the phone for a minute, still confused over what I should be feeling. I held the phone by my side like I still had calls to make.

"You all right, kid?" The clerk's voice caught my attention, his backwoods accent a complement to his unkempt look. I hadn't even noticed him.

"Yeah, I'm sorry. Just a crazy night," I said, barely glancing his way before heading to the back fridge and grabbing a familiar six-pack. Checking out, I could feel the cashier's eyes bead down upon me. His slow checkout pace built a mounting anxiety. I needed out of there.

Outside, I hustled to my car, which was only a couple of blocks from the bar. I made sure to take an extended route to avoid any confrontations with the cops, who assuredly had responded to my call by then. I opened the car door to sit down, placing the beer next to me. I took a second to sink slightly into the firm seat, then laid my head against the steering wheel. I finally took a deep breath and relaxed, letting my emotional guard down.

The rush of anger I had felt a short while ago now saw a new emotion, and at first, I tried to hold it back. Just sniffles. A few tears. My teeth were clenched so hard, my jaw would surely break if they slid apart, and my eyes shut tight like a dam holding back an ocean. I resisted for a few moments, but it was inevitable; the reservoir broke, and I began sobbing. The tears poured down my cheeks like a swift current on the rapids. The salty taste reaching my tongue only added to the disdain of my own tears. My nose drained its slimy waste to the back of my throat, pooling in a sticky, gooey mass that I forced down, knowing its texture would haunt me.

It was the first time I had cried since my father's death. The emotional reserve culminated in a euphoria as the pain that had built up in the dark of my soul now poured out in waves. In the midst of my breakdown, I turned on the radio to some classic rock, and the melodies struck a chord. The rivers turned to streams, which turned to trickles, which eventually gave way to a smile. A smile that felt genuine. Over the radio, "The Grand Illusion" played. I could feel the music, the words, the meaning, and I invited the track to lull me into introspection.

I couldn't fully comprehend why I cried or had such disgust for myself, yet I still felt enjoyment for avenging the college kid's beating. I suppose I was comforted knowing that the person I hurt had hurt someone else. So, what did that make me? A vigilante? Or perhaps I was just as bad as Bruiser? I pushed the thoughts aside before they dampened my mood. That was enough for the night. I fired up my 1970 Dodge Challenger and headed home to enjoy my amber nectar.

That had been the spark that ignited a furnace inside me. I knew from that first night, this pattern would continue whether I intended it to or not. So, I made a pact with myself. Every year on the date of my father's murder, I would punish an individual who committed a crime by committing that same crime against the offender. It felt right to have that purpose. It felt helpful. I had intoxicating dreams about becoming a hero, avenging victims of crimes who had been denied justice. The kind of justice that I was never able to find for my father's death and vengeance that should have been brought upon the assailant. Sadly, as often happens with grandiose intentions, the reality was much, much grimmer.

Chapter 5

I pulled up to Mulberry's just a sliver before eight. Being punctual was important to me. I knew Chris would show up a few minutes after, but it didn't bother me much. I would normally just sip my drink and browse the talent until he showed up.

Mulberry's was a local joint that had trouble deciding whether to be more of a family place or a bar. For us, it was a good blend—not too rowdy, but good cheap drinks. Inside the establishment, Mets memorabilia covered the walls, which was probably why I liked the place. The owner used to play Triple-A ball in the Mets farm system; he never could let that dream die. Sometimes he would make rounds at the tables to share baseball stories with customers. Either he rubbed pants with one of the greats, or he was having the season of his life and almost got called up. Not to say they weren't interesting stories, but I thought he needed to give it a rest and let the past go.

I was seated by the host at a two-person table situated near the far end of the bar. The waitress was pretty cute and couldn't be older than her early-20s. Her pinstripe dress and baseball jersey complemented her figure, and I'm sure she got generous tips.

"What would ya like to drink, sir?" She flashed a smile my way, and it made for a nice first impression.

"Um… Let's see. How about Captain and Dr. Pepp—"

"Ohh, I'm sorry, we only carry Coke," she interrupted.

"I guess that's fine," I mumbled. *What a disappointment.* "Say, whose jersey you got there?"

"Hmm." She twirled around, trying to see the name on the back. The uniform was none other than Nolan Ryan, the legend himself. But the puzzled face, the fact that she needed to even look at the name, told me she was clueless.

"I'm not sure." She sounded impatient. She probably had other customers to charm and more tips to make. Hell, I was going to tip her nicely. Before I got the chance to enlighten her on Mets baseball, she scurried off to the bar to put in my order. It stunned me that she didn't know who Nolan Ryan was. My dad and I used to worship him, even after he left the Mets. Some of the relics on the wall looked to be from the owner's childhood collection. A picture showing him in the middle of a swing during youth baseball caught my eye. It was baffling to me how he got so much enjoyment out of reliving that every day, and to think, his family was probably subjected to the ritual also.

The waitress brought me my drink swiftly. I watched her dodge between packed tables in the effort to deliver my order. I thanked her, but she was nearly gone by the time I had gotten the words out. I wasted no time sipping the potent concoction. A little too stiff for the first one, but I could manage. I eyed the entrance of the bar, and sure enough, a couple of minutes late, Chris hustled in. He looked the role of a cop—about 6'3" and 240 lbs. It was an intimidating frame if you didn't know him. On the inside, however, the guy was one of the softest I'd ever met. He was loyal to a fault. He was honest and had a calm, friendly demeanor that radiated off him.

Tonight, he wore a black blazer with blue sweats and a white undershirt. He notoriously dressed himself terribly, and if not for getting married, the outfit tonight would have been much worse. Nevertheless, he took pride in his attire. As long as he was happy, appearance mattered little. He scanned the restaurant for me, his head weaving back and forth. I put up a half-wave, and his eyes finally caught mine. He shuffled over, carefully avoiding the patrons in his way.

"I'm sorry. Wife wanted to hear about my day before I drove down," he apologized.

"Aw naw, no problem. You're only 15 minutes late. That's actually early for you." He shook his head and chuckled in defeat as he got settled in.

Scanning the menu and not finding anything too appetizing, we both settled on a burger when the waitress approached. While she collected the menus, I asked him if he had any decent stories from the week. Being in the NYPD, he normally had plenty to offer.

He laughed and flashed me a look like I wasn't going to believe what he told me. I noticed the waitress had lingered collecting our menus and was now fixated on Chris. I could tell she wanted to eavesdrop, but the busy tables pulled her away.

Leaning in like it was a government secret, he started a story about a paranoid schizophrenic who lived on the streets. The guy used to be a money guy, but the illness had taken hold of him in his 30s. He had been successful, with a wife and kids, until the condition gripped his mind, and he descended into madness.

"Everyone hears 'paranoid schizophrenic' and thinks a murderous maniac, but this guy had never harmed anyone before and he had been on the streets for eight months," Chris explained. "His only fault was carrying garbage bags full of rats and talking to himself, so the officers usually left him alone. Then on Tuesday, you see, witnesses saw him stab a man in a rat costume outside a pest control storefront. Unprovoked, he just dropped his bag, screamed, and assaulted the man." He nodded his head as my face surely resembled a look of disbelief.

"It created quite a panic in the city as the 5 o'clock news aired the story immediately. A stabbing in broad daylight on a busy street. Well, it had folks worried. I had the brass breathing down my neck the second after I got wind of the story. Fortunately, some local cops knew his usual stomping grounds, and within a couple of hours, we had located him in an abandoned warehouse. Then…" His voice trailed off in suspense. He shook his head like he couldn't believe the story he was telling.

"Then, I kid you not, they discovered hundreds upon hundreds of dead rats, just rotting in the place. Dried blood stained the floor, and there were so many flies it looked like a black, buzzing haze. It reeked like nothing you could ever imagine! Piles of rat carcasses, each in various stages of decay, with magots and fluids pooling to create a discolored mucous. Even some of the veteran officers couldn't hold their lunch. And there, in the middle of it all, sat that crazy bastard, calmly holding a deceased rat and talking to himself in his own little world. It's a little fascinating to me how the human brain works—that a reality so sickening to us could be so normal for him."

Chris then explained how he talked to a psychiatrist at Bellevue Psych Hospital. The doctor explained that the man thought rats were spies who would turn him into the government, and when he stabbed that person on the street, he saw him as a rat spy and not a person.

"That was his reality," Chris explained, "and he was just acting upon what made sense to him. We couldn't charge him because he was legally insane, so he will just remain at Bellevue until he is deemed capable to stand trial."

I looked at him speechless.

As if on cue, our burgers landed in front of us, the white saucers steaming. Both Chris and I exchanged glances, indicating the story should've waited until after dinner. I gazed down at a rather delicious-looking burger embedded in a mountain of fries, and all I could think of were those damn rats. Judging by Chris's face, he was having similar thoughts. With neither of us hungry anymore, we made small talk and nibbled at our food. After pounding a few drinks, the conversation turned more serious.

"Hey, Nick, uh, I was wondering how you've been doing lately. This time of year is usually pretty hard for you, and well… yeah." Chris asked this every year, but never as an empty gesture. He was always genuinely concerned.

"Oh, I've been alright." I tried to pass that off as a suitable response, but Chris had cracked guys plenty tougher than me. He just waited, stone-faced, until I provided him with a real answer.

"I think about him a lot, but there's nothing I can really do about it. I just can't stop thinking about him. It… it makes me so angry." My fist had curled up. "I was always curious about who did it, you know? What I would say to him. I've thought of a million things I would say, but if I actually did ever see him, I don't know if I could find the words." I took a long sip.

"All these years, I've had an image of what the guy was like. Some mangy-beard, strung-out druggie. A younger gritty man with fair skin and the eyes of a shifty fox. One who long ago abandoned his conscience for a thirst of money and misery, leaving destruction in his wake and recharging off the memories of his victims."

I glanced up and knew I had caught Chris by surprise. "Or who knows? Maybe I'm completely wrong, and it's a woman… or an alien!" I was just trying to ease the tension now

"Oh, wow, Nick." Chris shifted uncomfortably in his seat. "Here I thought you didn't have an imagination." The third Coke was settling in. "See, when my father died, it was easier knowing that no one was responsible, and there was nothing that could've been done. But you, man, that uncertainty is something I'm not envious of."

Over the years, Chris seemed to put his father's death behind him, forgiving God and refusing to speak about it negatively. He was strong but also had the help of closure.

Right then, an idea crept into my head. Almost instantly, I became excited by the thought. Closure. Maybe that's what I needed.

"What are you smiling about over there? Probably imagining me in a bikini or somethin', ya perv." Chris wasn't immune to the booze either.

"Chris, you work in law enforcement."

Instantly, he began to applaud my observation.

"No, no, I'm serious here. What I'm gonna ask is a huge favor, and I completely understand if you don't want to, but…" Chris leaned in uncomfortably close with wide eyes, and I shooed him away back into his seat. If he kept this up, he was going to get on my nerves.

"What if you could help me out by looking into my father's murder again? Perhaps they missed something the first time, and well—"

Chris shot up his hand, then lifted a finger to give himself a moment.

It was a lot to ask from a friend, even one like Chris. He paused, looking toward the ground for what felt like an eternity, deep in thought. He only interrupted his stare with sips of bourbon, which would transition him from one pose of contemplation to another. The suspense was killing me. My face was stone-cold serious, but the excitement inside felt like a child on Christmas morning. It was one of those ideas that should bring anything but excitement, but I couldn't help but be giddy at the thought.

"Okay, I'll help ya," Chris conceded.

In my mind, angels came down and sang *Alleluia* at our table. I was ecstatic, showing my jubilation in the form of a fist pump.

Chris continued, "I will do all I can. Now, the case happened in New Jersey, which is outside my jurisdiction, but it was so long ago, I won't be stepping on toes if I poke around a bit. I won't make any promises for results, but there is also a new DNA technology we've been starting to use that wasn't around when your father was killed."

He started explaining the process. Basically, everyone's body has a different blueprint, and now they have the technology to read that blueprint and match them together from a crime scene through body fluids. It was like Sci-Fi. Chris said it was the biggest thing to happen in law enforcement since fingerprints. The problem with DNA was that it was still in the very early stages, and it would be difficult to run a scan for me if needed. I told him we would cross that bridge if we came to it. I thanked him profusely, though he shrugged it off. We then turned our attention to the neglected burgers.

The burger was actually really tasty when I wasn't thinking about rats. The bun was toasted golden brown with just enough crisp from the lettuce to offset the soft, juicy beef. The brown mustard I requested was just the "icing on the cake," as they say. It brought a slight bite that complemented the seasoning in the patty. The fries were average, rather salty, and not as crisp as I would like, though overall, I was pretty satisfied.

The dinner conversation turned to his family. Chris had a wife, Sandra, and two sons. One was 6 years old, named Damion, and the other a 4-year-old named Joey. He told me they both wanted to be Yankees one day. Stuffing my face with fries drenched in barbeque sauce, I informed him that if they were smart, the Mets should be the team they strive for. He knew my obsession with the Mets, but he was always more of a Yankees guy. I couldn't blame him, though. The Yankees were always in contention, while the Mets struggled to put together a decent team. Either way, it was nice to hear his kids were interested in baseball.

Finally, we finished up our drinks and decided to call it a night. I left a generous tip, and we promised to get together soon. Chris said he would check into the case and get back to me as soon as he got anything relevant. I located my vintage Challenger before giving one last thanks in the form of a hug and parting ways in the parking lot.

The fresh, cool night air brushed against my face as a slight smile appeared. I thought I was within grasp of what I desired most… Oh, how wrong I was.

Chapter 6

My apartment was situated in a rather upscale area near the center of Trenton, New Jersey. It wasn't a sprawling place by any means, but three times the size of what I could find in New York at the same price. I had the money for New York—and a love for the city—but I wouldn't have some of the luxuries I had here. Not to mention the commute would bring regret with every trip. The apartment boasted modern furnishings and was very tidy, almost to the point of emptiness. I was never one for much décor. A few years prior, the space had been even emptier. The incident that led to that, as jarring as it was, opened my eyes. It started how most regrettable encounters occur: with a woman.

I had been spending my evening at a local bar. It was a Friday night, so the crowd was young. I wasn't old, but I had a few years on most of the patrons. I had dressed up a bit that night, hoping to catch someone's eye. It just so happened I did, from a girl named Lucy. I had seen her around once before. She was a bit short but curvy, with silky brunette hair cascading down her back. She provided quite the eye candy for any man, but it was her smile and face with its raw cuteness that really drew you in. No doubt she saw eyes pop when she walked into a place.

I had been playing with a half-empty glass of some ghastly mixer while alternating my attention between the TV and those around the bar. I couldn't resist stealing a glance at her every time I turned my gaze away from the baseball game. She seemed to be alone, although it was tough to tell with the slew of guys that approached her with wide-eyed confidence—none of whom stayed for longer than a couple of minutes. When the plan they'd been cooking up and the confidence they had been slamming down foiled, they would return to their batch of friends, who would laugh or berate their fallen companion before buying him another drink. She watched this routine with amusement, knowing full well what she was doing. I desperately wanted to approach her but knew the chances were slim. After another thwarted attempt from a bar patron, she swung around, letting her hair whip wildly.

Our eyes locked from a few barstools away. *She caught me*, I thought. I froze momentarily before smiling. "Not too big, but not without interest," I told myself. Hopefully, she didn't see the sheer panic behind the expression. My heart throbbed, and I could feel the violent pulse from the back of my throat.

She returned a warm and seemingly sincere smile that was like crack. Butterflies started to churn with the love potion already in my stomach. I didn't want to get ahead of myself, so the infatuation was tapered, thinking that the smile was probably just friendly. But to my surprise, she began to move from her seat. Anticipation set in. *She could be coming over here.* Swirling my drink and looking up at the scoreboard, I wanted to seem unassuming. I said a silent prayer, hoping the empty seat to my right was her destination.

I sensed her cozy up in the empty seat beside me. Attractive girl, decent buzz. I waited a few seconds, mulling my drink and watching the scoreboard. I had a few fond memories during high school of my sis trying to give me pointers about girls. My dad had a few that he shared while at the breakfast table, but my sis insisted I never take his advice. "Be a little weird, but confident," she would say when I sheepishly entered her room, asking how to get noticed by my crush. I could tell Lucy was looking at me. Time for some old-style charm.

"Excuse me? Lucy, isn't it? What would you say to a drink?" I asked candidly.

"Oh, I would love one, but I never accept drinks from strangers."

She is flirting with me.

"Good to know. My name is Nick Jacobs, my favorite fruit is an orange, I enjoy a good foot rub, and I think movie popcorn is overrated. So now you know my deepest secrets. What's your drink?" The giggle and the shine in her eyes told me the quirky wit paid off. Her eyes wandered from me to the ceiling, contemplating her answer.

"Strawberry daiquiri, and my favorite fruit is a banana… and you're crazy about the popcorn." Her emphasis on banana with a long pause while staring directly into my soul had my perverted mind racing. It also caused immediate choking on my drink. I tried to hold the glass to catch the dribbling.

"Oh wow. Not like that." She nervously laughed and handed me a napkin.

"Like what?" I scrunched my face tight. "Here I go sharing my most personal details, and the most I get to know about you is that you like bananas…" I shook my head.

She looked at me puzzled, the hamster wheel spinning in her head as if I didn't just share the same thing.

"Well, how's about this," she leaned in as though to whisper, "I never tell people, but I have six toes on my right foot."

I shot up straight and turned away, calling over the bartender,

She grabbed my shoulder with her left hand, "No, no, I was just kidding!" I turned back to her.

"I can't believe you would just leave if I had six toes." Her tone was judgmental and disapproving.

"Leave!? I was just calling over the bartender for a couple drinks!" A sly smile formed to meet her embarrassment. I wasn't usually this quick on my feet, but I was letting the liquor do the talking.

I could tell she probably had never paid for a drink in her life, so when I called the bartender over and asked him for a Captain and Coke and a strawberry daiquiri, both parties probably thought I was paying. When he checked her ID, I noticed the name read Celia and asked her where Lucy came from.

"Oh, I hate the name Celia. Everyone calls me Lucy." At the time, it sounded fine to me.

"Are these both on your tab, sir?" the bartender asked.

"No, they're separate."

His head shot to the left, and he gave me a puzzled look. Then, uttering an uneasy okay, he glanced at Lucy. She appeared just as surprised as the bartender. A girl like her expected free drinks, and here she was paying. She probably didn't even have any money on her. I turned my attention back to her.

"Listen, Lucy, how 'bout we make a wager?" I suggested with a sly smile. She nodded her head, eyes bright and curious.

"See the dartboard over there?" I pointed to the other end of the bar where a lone dartboard stood. "For whatever number you hit, I will pay the dollar amount for drinks. You get two tosses: one warm-up, and one that counts."

The proposition had her a little confused at first, but the game finally registered, and her excitement grew as she grabbed my arm, pulling me over to the machine. As I was dragged through the bar, a huge smile was painted on my face. The rejected suitors were probably filled with jealousy, wondering how I had managed what they couldn't.

Once over at the machine, a rather nice electric one with plastic-tipped darts, she grabbed two darts and, wasting no time, threw her practice one. It hit the metal outside the dartboard and landed on the bar floor.

"Looks like I have a cheap date tonight," I laughed.

She gave me a smile and said, "Ohh, just you wait." Watching her eye up her target, I had low expectations. She squinted one eye and made shadow movements to imitate the trajectory. After the routine, she let her money-dart fly, and lo and behold, it stuck. That was surprising enough, but in our rush to inspect it, we saw it lodged in the triple 17.

"Yes!" she screamed before starting a little victory dance for the bar. I hedged the jubilance with the horror my wallet faced. I couldn't believe her luck. I wasn't worried about her hitting anything substantial, especially after the first toss. Triple 17s, though? What were the f-ing odds?

"Well," I conceded, "you definitely surprised me. Nice throw. You, Lucy, have $51 to work with tonight. For my sake, hopefully you're a lightweight." I was still looking at the dartboard in disbelief. Finally, she broke the trance, embracing me in a hug and leaning in to whisper that she would make my night worth it. The sexy tone sent a shiver through me. Hell, after that, I would have given her my account number as well.

We made our way back to the bar stools, enjoying the drinks and each other's company. She was a really cool girl with an adorable laugh. To my good fortune, she was also interesting and intelligible. I was taken aback by the depth of what she had to say. She also enjoyed baseball, though she was a Pirates fan.

We talked at length about the sport, arguing about our favorite teams and news around the league. She worked as a registered nurse at a hospital in Pittsburgh and was only up in Trenton to visit her mom.

We laughed and joked the whole night as the bartender continued to feed drinks our way. Anyone watching would have thought we had known each other forever. It was one of the best times I had ever had on a date. I could've spent days talking to her, and I hoped that we could continue the fun after they made last call at the bar. We finished our drinks and headed out to my car, as she seemed in no shape to drive herself home. She was still speaking articulately but was losing her balance and leaning heavily on me. When she saw my car, I knew she was impressed.

"Nice car! A 1970 Challenger." She slid her hand along the hood and bent down to get a better look at the body. "Looks like a 325. What a ride." This girl knew her cars, too. *Damn.*

We walked around the car, my arm draped around her. Her shoulder prodded my chest. Asking her on a second date was on the tip of my tongue, but I wanted to be sure of the timing, and it never felt right. Every few seconds, the process repeated. I told myself that it was the perfect moment, and my mouth followed by opening, my eyes turned to her. However, my posture suddenly became awkward and uncomfortable. Then… nothing, the words dangling in my throat. Frustration followed my cowardice, and I would vow next time to finally follow through.

Once I opened the door for her, I finally found the words.

"Say, I had a really great time tonight, and I was wondering if I could see you again sometime soon. I have a feeling that you'd enjoy that, too." The words hung suspended in the air, helicoptering with awkwardness. I had been so relaxed and casual the whole night, but now I was vulnerable and serious. The change in tone added to the uncomfortable feeling as it left my tongue. It wasn't my smoothest line, but I was hoping for a yes. I was really into this girl.

She paused for a moment before asking, "Is the night ending?" She sounded confused.

I fumbled for a response. The redirected question had caught me off-guard.

"I mean, I thought so. I was going to drop you off at your place. I wanted to be sure you were safe getting home."

"Well, I could be safe at your place. If you don't mind, that is," she said, flashing me that smile.

No, I did not mind in the slightest. I only responded with a grin and a door slam. I sped home, showing off all the horses in the engine. I had gritted teeth and a deviant grin as I powered past blocks at breakneck speed. Intoxicated, a beautiful woman by my side, and one hell of a car to finish the trifecta. I could have conquered the world that night.

Once arriving at my place, we wasted little time finding the bedroom. Her hands slowly moved lower, seductively, nearly causing a premature episode.

Hopping into bed, she was electric, simply insane. She was dominant in that she was in control but strangely made me feel in charge and manly. She could've been lousy in the sack, and I would've still wanted her. It was just the icing on the cake.

Concluding, we collapsed, sweaty and breathing heavily on the bed like a steamy scene from a motion picture. Taking a moment to gather ourselves, laughter emerged from us, slightly out of ecstasy and partially out of exhaustion.

"Wow," she said, "I was surprised you kept up."

"Me too. You were unbelievable," I replied. We took a few more moments, allowing the perspiration to dry and absorb into the fiber of the sheets. When our breath returned, she rolled to get up.

"Any wine in this place? I'm looking for a nightcap." Even in the dark, I could feel her playful smile.

"Ah yes, I believe there is a bottle or two on the rack in the kitchen. Glasses in the cupboard above the corkscrew in the drawer next to the dishwasher."

"I'll be sure to get you one, too." She said as she headed towards the kitchen. I relished her figure passing in the shadows on her way out. She came back a short while later with two glasses of red wine—not my favorite, but I would manage. We sipped, laughed, and cuddled the rest of the night. At one point, we drifted asleep. It was the perfect evening.

Morning arose with a bright light emanating from the shades. I was met with the sun and a pounding headache. When I rolled over and looked to my side, I noticed I was alone. I felt the covers where she should have been. Was it possible I had been dreaming? Well, for one, there were two glasses of wine on my nightstand, so I knew that last night was indeed real. However, the kitchen and living room showed no sign of her. I was rather disappointed because, after such an amazing night, I had hoped for a second date. I hadn't even got her number. The discouraging prospect of what that meant sank in as I slumped back to my room.

But something felt off, something other than the splitting headache and foggy thoughts. The light coming from between the shades was bright. What time was it? Locating the clock on my nightstand, I saw it was four in the afternoon. How had I slept that long? I needed some coffee. Normally, my apartment was pretty bare but walking toward the kitchen, it felt like it was lacking any semblance of character. That's when I saw it: my wall of paintings was gone. There were four the night before, and now the wall was completely bare. Through the denseness that was still my hangover, it sank in; she must have stolen them from me! Of all people, of course, this would happen to me. In a daze, I scoured the apartment, looking for what else could be missing. Unfortunately, I found that I was also missing my Rolex watch and coins from my collection.

Unbelievable. We have a perfect night, then she drugs me and takes my stuff. "Irate" put my mood mildly. Not only did the woman of my dreams vanish, she fucking stole from me! Fuming, I thought about calling the police, but what good would that do? I had no phone number, address, or car description, and even her name was fake. I had nothing, nada, zip. Plus, I was rather embarrassed.

Passing the rest of the day with TV and frozen pizza, I moped around the apartment. The mundane laziness became such torture, I reluctantly decided to go out to the bars. I was pissed, I was hurt, but mostly, I felt stupid and naive.

Once out, I ordered a drink, and the bartender asked for my ID. I fumbled with my wallet, and in the process, it clicked. The name on her driver's license said Celia! The light bulbs in my head flipped on. I had my lead. The prospect of finding her started to come to fruition right there on the barstool. But the idea of what I would do when I actually found her, well, that came from a much darker place. She claimed to work at a Pittsburgh hospital, of which there were many, but it couldn't be that hard to locate, could it? I prayed that she had lied about her name, but not her story. Something told me that between the few drinks and the fast-paced conversation, she would have let the truth slip through.

I took off work the following week, citing a much-needed vacation—a vacation to Pittsburgh where I would hunt down the thief Celia. It might have been a tad delusional to think I could find her, but I wasn't about to forfeit my stuff without trying. Besides, it was fun. My cover was a private investigator. (Chris had taught me a couple of techniques he used to coerce suspects.) I visited each hospital and, working some Nick magic, I was given a list of hospital staff more times than not. It was a relief but also alarming how easy it was. There were two hospitals that refused, but I gambled she wasn't employed at either. I had found three people named Celia. Of those, only one was a registered nurse.

Bingo. I had her. Maybe I had chosen the wrong career. The next obstacle was the schedule. Simply asking worked the first time, so I thought I'd try it again. Waltzing into St. Agnus Memorial Hospital, about ready to turn on the Nick charm, I spotted the same lady who had given me the employee list.

"Hi, miss, it's me again. I was wondering if you could give me Celia's work schedule. She's an RN," I said politely.

"I'm sorry, but we can't help you anymore. It's against policy. If you don't leave in a timely manner, I will be forced to get the police involved." The abrupt response was rattling. She didn't even raise her eyes to look at me.

I gave her a hurried goodbye and walked out the doors rather quickly. As I scurried back to the car, I contemplated turning her in to the police, but after a brief consideration, I decided against it. My father's birthday was in two days.

Since the easy route failed, the only way possible would be to trail her from work. So, I sat in my car with a clear view of the employee exit, waiting for her to leave. It was a tedious wait, but it would all be worth it. When I got hungry for lunch, I made a quick run to a food stand in a grocery store parking lot across the street.

Munching on a hot dog and peanuts, I counted the minutes, and time dragged to a halt. One hour, two, three, five, six. I began to think that maybe she didn't work today.

Then I saw her. At first, I wasn't sure because she looked different with scrubs on, but once I saw her face, I knew my efforts had paid off. Three rows away, she started her car, a dainty BMW. I thought she would have had a different ride for a car enthusiast, but oh well. She was completely clueless to my presence and peeled out of the parking lot. I began to trail her a good distance behind. For once, I wished I had a different car since the Challenger had a tough time blending in. I almost lost her a couple of times when I got unlucky with a red light, but the 350 horses under the hood quickly eroded the gap. We pulled into a cluster of apartment complexes, and she took a right into a complex called Meadow Down Stables. *Who comes up with names like these?* I started to slow and watched her enter the building. I rolled over to a spot across the street and waited to see which lights turned on. Second story, second room from the left side of the building.

I had done it. The odds had been against me, but a little wit and a lot of luck culminated into grade-A investigative work. A celebration for my success was in order.

I departed and searched until I found a local park. I really had a fancy for parks; they were relaxing yet liberating. But there was something else about a park that I couldn't place.

By the time I parked, it was late in the evening, and the park was rather empty. I reached for the glove box, pulling out a hand-rolled Nicaraguan cigar and my eight-ball lighter. I set out to find a bench. Near the center of the park, there were a few clustered together. I picked one and settled in. After cutting it, I carefully lifted the large stogie to my nose, letting the scent of the cigar roll around my nose. Putting my mouth to the cigar, I opened my lighter, and out popped a glorious flame. Lighting the end, I breathed in deeply, letting my lungs fill quickly, followed by a slow exhale that allowed the scent to linger around me. I didn't smoke often, only on certain occasions, but I deeply enjoyed the practice when the time arose. I continued to puff the cigar down, savoring the rustic pepper smoke that engulfed me and watched as a couple of cars, each with a few teens, parked on the road.

The teens popped out and wandered down a trail, disappearing behind the trees. The late-night rendezvous was undoubtedly for a smoke, rolled with something a bit more potent than my cigar. The thought of it brought me back to my adolescent years. After my father died, I had a tremendous amount of tension and built-up anger and anxiety. One evening, a friend offered me marijuana to relax a little. I had been offered before, but this time, it was my choice, not peer pressure pulling the strings. I like to think I have control over my actions. I obliged, and I have to say, I enjoyed it. Connections, feelings, and problems I had never seen came forth, and the music! Oh, the music was something else. I enjoyed the high while it lasted, but by the end, I wasn't sure how I liked it. Smoking a few more times made me realize it wasn't for me.

I ground the cigar in an ashtray as I headed back to my car. The day's events had me exhausted. A nearby Super 8 motel promised to be a place to rest my weary eyes. It wasn't what people called five-star, but it did the trick.

After a calm sleep, I woke up to a sunny September 21, 1991. For $28 a night, the mattress wasn't bad. It was a blustery autumn day, and I was feeling excitement and anticipation for the upcoming events. I had all the confidence in the world that everything would go as planned. When she left work at 9 p.m. yesterday, I figured she worked the 1 to 9 shift. So, I rolled up near her complex at about noon and waited. The radio was blasting rock tunes, and a cup of black coffee kept me company.

At about 12:45 p.m., she pulled her car out of the complex. Her scrubs were on, so it definitely wasn't an errand. I waited until she passed, then cruised into the parking lot, finding a place close to the door. I approached the entrance casually, making it only a few feet away before realizing how short-sighted I was. In order to get into the complex, I needed a key. Dumbfounded and pacing in front of the door between the narrow sidewalk leading up to it, I weighed my options. I was so consumed in my thoughts I barely noticed a resident walk out of the complex. I quickly lurched to grab the door behind him, trying not to draw attention.

"Oh, hey, you new here?" he asked. Halfway through the door, I was caught a little off guard.

"Uh, yeah, just moved in on the second floor. Left my key at the office and had to stop back to get my presentation. It's been quite the morning." My reply received a smile and a welcome. We made a quick introduction with a friendly handshake.

"Say, is that your car right there?" He pointed to my Challenger. I nodded proudly.

"That is one sick ride." He walked around to the side, examining the body.

"If it would be alright with you, maybe sometime we could take a spin? I'm sure it roars when you open it up." He had a thing for cars, too. Jeeze, did only car enthusiasts live here?

"Of course! We'll talk, but I have to run." I barely made out what he said before I slid through the doorway.

I headed up the stairs and looked for the second room from the left. "Apartment 224," I said out loud as if I was leading a search party. I still retained my lockpicking skills from my teen years, which I had refreshed on my motel door the previous night. I used to pick locks regularly to trespass in abandoned buildings. I was quite the delinquent during those years.

I removed a simple lockpicking kit from my backpack and prayed no one left their apartment in the next minute. It only took about 30 seconds till I heard the glorious click, and I was in. Hustling inside and locking the door behind me, I scanned the apartment. Not drabby, but certainly not somewhere I would consider living. She had a standard queen bed, a couple of dressers, a La-Z-Boy, and a television, but everything else seemed out of place. She had Persian and bear-skin rugs, silk sheets, and an elegant gold mirror. The décor must have been stolen goods from her victims. I felt so cheated standing amidst it all. The fact there were so many others made me a little sick. I felt sorry for all those guys, but I was about to set things straight. Starting in the bathroom towards the back of the apartment, I came across her jewelry stash, which, of course, had plenty of watches, tie clips, and rings. I thought I saw mine, but as I reached for it, the door lock of the apartment jingled.

Fear gripped my chest as I stared into the mirror. Who the hell was here!? Where could I hide? I whirled around to scan the room, but my foot caught the bag and sent me into a disoriented free fall. My head slammed into the ceramic tile of the tub. The withering blow barely registered before the door flew open with a shuddering bang. Reflexively, I rolled into the tub, taking my bag with me and pulling the curtains halfway to conceal me. I could barely make her voice out as she began to scold herself for forgetting her ID badge. Numbness in my head was giving way to searing pain, and blood began to gush from the gash.

Just as I was certain she was about to leave, her footsteps turned toward the bathroom. Each step thundered louder than the last as she approached, my head throbbed harder and harder. I tried my damnedest not to breathe as the echo brought her closer, but each exhale ricocheted from my chest cavity like an explosion. My heart was jumping out of my chest. Sweat poured profusely from every cavity, and warm streams of blood dripped unabated down my face.

"God, my hair looks like crap," she said, pulling out a comb and giving it a run-through.

My mind was screaming. Huddled in a fetal position, clutching my bag, I was teetering on passing out. I pleaded with God to make her go.

Seemingly satisfied, she put the comb down and briskly left the apartment. As I heard the door close, I started gasping for air. Feeling my lungs re-inflate never felt so good. I still felt my heart pulsing, daring to break out of my chest. I gave myself a moment to pull it together.

Slowly emerging from my hideout like a G.I. in a bunker, I crawled over the bathtub ledge onto the ceramic floor. I laid my dazed and beaten body prone on the cold tile until I opened my eyes to see blood pooling beneath me. I shot up, ripping a nearby roll of toilet paper off its hinge. I held it to my head while I peeked into the tub. It looked as though someone got their organs harvested in the thing. Pulling the roll away to find it soaked halfway confirmed the severity. I turned to the mirror, bloody roll in hand, and faced my reflection. A gnarly finger-length gash oozed from my forehead. I took the liberty of washing my face in her sink and using her bath towels to stem the bleeding. Surely, she would wonder how a burglar managed to injure himself. A few first aid supplies from the medicine cabinet later, I was back in business. The wound wasn't done bleeding, but the bandage held up. *I can get stitches later*, I reasoned.

I first recovered my watch from her jewelry box. It was almost identical to the one my father once wore. A platinum Rolex with gold trim inlays and initials on the band. It meant so much to him, potentially even more than any of his baseball memorabilia. I wore it every day as a constant reminder. I found my paintings in her closet along with a few others and my coins on her dresser. Then, I turned my attention to the jewelry box again. Just before I reached to open it, the transgression I was committing hit me. I should be wearing gloves. Bringing out a pair from my pocket, I wiped off every surface I touched and scolded myself for being so careless.

I emptied the box and left only a single earring for her. Oh, how that would sting. To think the person who robbed her was so thoughtful and calculating as to leave one earring for her to curse. Every time she saw that earring, it would reanimate the violation she felt when she first realized what had happened.

While salivating over that image, I started to compile other contraband from the rest of the apartment. I discovered a couple of expensive mink coats and pulled them into the hallway, grabbed a fancy leather suitcase to pack some of it in and rolled up the Persian rug. I also snatched an antique wall clock and more clothes on my way out. Just enough to have an impact. I wasn't going to rob her of everything.

The headache was starting to dull thanks to the pain medication I found in the cabinet, and with a sigh and a smile, I strutted from the exit like I owned the joint, loot in tow.

On the way back, I took a detour by a homeless shelter on the outskirts of Pittsburgh to donate what I stole—minus my belongings. I had no use for most of the stuff, and I had no desire to risk selling the goods. The front desk attendant was hesitant when I dropped off the spoils. I should have considered how suspicious and odd it looked, but she accepted the load nevertheless. I left knowing that the majority of the expensive things would be sold by the residents, and the staff might even keep a few things for themselves. Still, it brought me joy knowing that I had at least helped one person. Perhaps I had an impact on them.

Chapter 7

A few days had passed since dinner with Chris, and I became preoccupied with what he might have dug up on my father's case. I tried to keep my mind away from speculating by fixating on work. I was an accountant for a small New Jersey law firm called Wolfsheim. There were only two partners, a couple of part-time paralegals, and a secretary. I was the youngest in the firm by 15 years. The business was aged, drab, and not making much money, but no one gave a damn. The partners hardly landed the big money cases because competing with the large New York firms never worked in our favor. There was never much to do there, so I was liberal with my time off.

As the partners saw it, I could have as much time as I liked. Either I was there, got paid, and did little to no work, or I wasn't there and didn't get paid and roughly the same amount of work would get done.

For me, it was a perfect fit. It was relaxed, easy, and the pay was inflated for what I did. Only a year into working for the firm, we had landed a huge case that was way out of our league. There was no way our small outfit was the ideal choice to handle a case of that caliber, but we worked around the clock for months to retain it. Normally, litigation of that magnitude would have been handled by a large New York firm, but one of the partner's friends was the plaintiff in the suit.

The plaintiff was suing a neglectful owner who chose to build new upscale apartment complexes instead of fixing the problems with the old ones. While we poured over testimonials and photo evidence, it was alarming how dire the situation was leading up to the disaster. The complex's decrepit state was criminal. Mold, poor plumbing, broken fixtures, faulty heating, and rat infestation—the complaints and violations went on and on. Most were serious problems, but the gas lines were pressing. At 110 years old, they were long past needing replacement and were leaking into the building for months. Despite complaint after complaint, there was never any indication the problem would be fixed. Most tenants couldn't afford to move and were essentially trapped there. After weeks of pleas and demands, the owner scheduled a repair over the weekend.

On the Friday before the lines were to be inspected, and most likely condemned, one of the leaky gas lines led to an explosion in the apartment complex. The blast rocked two apartments on the first floor and one on the second. Both lower units were vacant at the time, but the second floor was not. The apartment that belonged to our plaintiff contained his wife and newborn son, and the blast killed them both while he was at work. The resulting fire engulfed the rest of the building, but all the other residents were evacuated safely. We won the case, but the victory wasn't much of a consolation for the father. I couldn't begin to imagine losing one's entire family that way. And though no amount of money could bring them back, we fought for every last cent.

In the end, our side settled with Iscariot Properties, which had complexes all over the country, for $22 million, $9 million of which was a commission for the firm. Even after subtracting the enormous cost of litigating the case, the partners were set, and they handed out generous bonuses to the staff. Raises followed that year. I became grossly overpaid, but the owners seemed to care little as we were keeping busy from the publicity generated by the case.

As for the man who lost his family and home, he spent his money traveling the world. He sent us postcards over the years, and it seemed as though he tried to put the past behind him. The last postcard was from Sweden, where he informed us he met someone who taught him to love again. It read, "I've learned to live with the demons and bury the hate I have for them."

The phone rattled on its console, breaking up the monotony of my typically boring day. I reached for the jittery plastic.

"This is Nick Jacobs, accountant at Wolfsheim and Company. How may I help you?" A chuckle greeted me at the other end.

"Nick, that you? You sound so official." It was Chris, of course.

"Yah bet your sweet ass, it is. What can I do you for?"

"Well, not so much what you can do for me as what I can do for you. I got a little update for you. Remember how I told you I would look into your father's case?"

I immediately put down the invoice I was handling, swallowing hard.

"So, I did a little digging." He paused as if looking for confirmation that he should continue. I had my ear pressed tightly against the receiver. What could he have possibly found? The killer? My silence must have been an invitation to divulge.

"And, well, your father was stabbed once in the chest. There did not appear to be a struggle in the house. The only items stolen were cash and your father's Rolex…" His voice trailed off

"Okay," I said. "Is that all?" I felt a mix of impatience and disappointment.

"Hold your horses, Nick. Gimme a second." He took a moment to collect his thoughts.

"See, they investigated this guy called Alvin Dupont. He got busted for a string of robberies in that area. Unfortunately, he swore he had nothing to do with the murder, and there was no evidence linking him to the scene. The murder weapon was a kitchen knife, and although there were no usable fingerprints, two different blood types were recovered from the weapon. One, presumably your father's, and the other unknown, but most likely from the assailant. They could only identify the blood type, which was O-pos. Coincidentally the same as Dupont's, but also the same as 40% of the population. That was back then. Today, we can go a step further."

He went on about using DNA analysis on the unknown sample and that he would need DNA from a suspect to run an identification match. Back at the time of the murder, DNA hadn't been discovered, but since it was available now, the case could progress.

"The technology gives us a possibility of finding the assailant," he said. That last sentence lingered in my ears, ringing as though an echo in a long-abandoned dungeon. There was a chance.

I was hanging on to every sentence. My heavy breathing had condensed on my hand, and I wiped the moisture on my pants. I was already consumed by the news and the potential of finding my father's killer, but by the same token, I was also a bit discouraged there were no concrete answers—only leads. My hope rested with this Dupont bum. Either he did it, or he had useful information to share.

"Where is this Dupont guy now?" I asked.

"Already ahead of you."

Chris really did his research. "He bounced around prisons for a while, mostly for petty theft. His current stint is at Rikers." I could hear his deep inhalation from the other end of the line.

"Though, Nick, I have a feeling he didn't do it. With no history of violence, it's rare to see someone like him escalate then de-escalate, but it's possible."

"Well, I'll find out soon enough," I said.

Chris went on to tell me that he could have the lab in New York run the comparison, but he would need five samples to run against for accuracy. He suggested I make a stop at a local pharmacy and pick up sample swabs and plastic bags to preserve the DNA. Then, with a bit of luck and some of my charm, I would need to persuade Dupont to volunteer a saliva sample. He paused to enthrall me with his wisdom.

"Now, if you can't get the sample with his blessing, don't do anything drastic, Nick. There are other avenues."

Chris offered to volunteer his, his wife's, and one of his kid's for comparison also. After thanking him profusely, he warned me that I better know what I was doing. He wanted to help me but would pull the plug if he didn't think my mind was in the right place. I heeded his warning, hung up the phone, and paused a few moments to get my mind in the right place. A minute later, I dialed the number to Rikers.

After a hold time that consumed nearly my entire break, I finally reached a secretary. Posing as an amateur journalist, I asked for an appointment to visit Alvin Dupont. I wanted to ask him questions about his life for an article I was working on. She didn't seem to care what the excuse was and penned me down for the following Wednesday at 5 p.m. She informed me that Alvin had the right to refuse, but I knew he wouldn't pass up the opportunity to talk about his crimes and possibly make the paper. I thanked her, put the phone down, and reclined in my chair.

Suddenly, another rattling phone call came through. I answered with my usual introduction but was interrupted.

"Hey, Nick, it's me again." Chris was back on the line. "Well, I'm a few days behind on the paper, but apparently, Nancy Papperman was murdered. I just thought I'd call you about it because, if I remember right, she was one of the names that kept popping up at your mother's nursing home." He didn't sound suspicious, and he wasn't questioning me, but it was worrisome that he even made the call. I couldn't decipher his angle.

"Oh yeah, she was," I replied, hinting at a vague naivety in my voice. I tried to sound slightly surprised and even paused ever so slightly to try and indicate I was searching my memory for the name.

"I think I remember seeing that, too. She was the wife of that famous banker, wasn't she?" I asked incredulously. "I don't know what to think about it. It's pretty sad, I guess."

"Okay, yeah, of course, I never thought anything like that, I just uh… well really I'm not sure. Guess I just found it interesting and called to tell you about it. Sorry to bother ya, bud. Get back to not working. Talk to you soon."

A deep sigh left me as I settled the phone on its console and tilted back in my seat. I was certain he suspected nothing, and why would he? With that said, Chris was blessed with good instincts, part of what made him such a great cop, and it wouldn't take too many connections to start suspecting something. It was definitely noted.

Despite those concerns, I barely gave the conversation a second thought after my workday. Arriving home from work with carry-out Chinese in hand, I saw I had a message on my machine. My sister had called, wanting to have lunch the next day. I quickly dialed her number, and she answered on the first ring.

"Hello?"

"Hey, Anita, it's Nick. How's it going?"

"Fine," she answered, but her tone was excited. "Nick, you know I prefer Ann."

"I know, I know," I admitted sheepishly. "I just like Anita better. Dad always called you that, and it sounds so much better than boring Ann."

"Well, sue me for a boring name, but until then, let's keep that cutesy name stuff in the past."

Fair enough, I mouthed silently into the phone.

When I took her up on her offer for lunch, her voice must have jumped an entire octave. I was beginning to wonder what was up, as it was rare that my sister and I visited outside of holidays—not because we had any rift between us, but we were never too close. She had even rougher teenage years than me and battled drug addiction for a stint. After my father died, she got help and has been clean ever since. She was now successful, married, and had a son named Will. Her husband was a successful marketing executive and raked in the big money with overseas deals. Eleven-year-old Will was quite the kid, and it was a shame I only saw him a few times a year. He had hazel eyes, shaggy brown hair, was slightly on the chubby side, and had a personality that could warm even the coldest individual.

She suggested a small café down the corner from her house, and I obliged. We had eaten there once before, and it wasn't bad, but it wouldn't have been my first choice. It's the kind of place that rich housewives from the neighborhood frequented. Overpriced and low on options, every menu item sounded unnecessarily fancy. In anticipation of an unfulfilling meal, I planned to grab something from McDonald's and eat it on the way. Before the phone conversation ended, my sister asked if I wanted to join her and Will at the Wild Springs amusement park on Saturday for his birthday.

"Of course. That sounds like a blast," I blurted. "I wouldn't pass up that opportunity."

"Oh, thank you. That would be great! I was worried you wouldn't want to. Will will be really excited. Nate has a business trip to China, so he can't make it; plus, I'm not much of a roller-coaster person, but I thought you would be."

In all reality, her inclination was far from the truth. I dreaded the steel traps dating back to my childhood days of visiting the parks with the family. The only way I rode coasters was when my dad coerced me on them. Only then would I venture onto those twisted deathbeds. That was when I was young, though, and I counted on at least still being able to tolerate them, or it would be a *long* day.

After hanging up the phone, I smiled. My week was shaping up. I then returned my attention to the Chinese food—sesame chicken, fried rice, and egg foo yung. I wondered if Asian people ate like this all the time. They couldn't; they were usually so skinny. Either way, their food was heavenly. I reclined in my La-Z-Boy with food on my lap and reruns of M*A*S*H in front of my eyes and dozed off shortly after.

Chapter 8

As Wednesday approached, uneasy feelings emerged. Short bursts of adrenaline and anxiety would flare up when I thought about what this meeting meant for the investigation. If this Dupont guy didn't volunteer his DNA sample, there was nothing I could do about it. The investigation would hit a dead end, and I would be back at square one.

Tuesday had me laying restlessly in bed, unable to sleep. Scenarios churned in my head, and trying to fight off my imagination proved frivolous. I tossed and turned, hoping I could lull my restless mind asleep, but I couldn't. Somehow, I managed a little sleep before I woke to the sound of my alarm blaring.

I had made certain it was extra loud when I turned it on the night before. It was a big day, after all. When it blared, the typical grogginess was nowhere to be found. The anticipation for the day had me up from bed and headed to the kitchen in seconds. I prepared a large batch of coffee, not out of necessity but out of habit. I only bought premium-brand coffee and, for the most part, drank it black. I never understood people who put in creamer or got fancy drinks at coffee shops. That just wasn't real coffee to me.

I sat at my table, munching on a bowl of Lucky Charms and washing it down with a fresh brew. It probably wasn't the best combination, but I had gotten used to it. Since I was a kid, I had eaten cereal plain, but something was tugging at me as I ate. About halfway through, I decided to reach into the fridge for something different—milk. I hadn't had that blend of cereal and milk in as long as I could remember. I thought it tasted like soggy manure as a kid, and Dad always ate his plain, too. To my delight and surprise, the breakfast staple was pretty enjoyable. This was going to be a welcome mix-up to the morning. And to think I had suffered without that sweetness for so long.

Scraping the bowl of the last rainbow marshmallow, I rehearsed my cover story in my head. Using my real name was a must because I needed to show identification, but I would claim that I was dabbling in amateur journalism and was recently assigned to do a piece on robberies and the criminal mind. And what better way to write the story than to interview a career thief? The story sounded surefire to me. As a further explanation, I would tell him I did a little research on crimes in my area and saw Alvin Dupont's name came up frequently for theft. Searching for him, I soon saw that he was here in Rikers. If he questioned why, which I was almost certain he wouldn't, I would divulge that I wanted a life-long criminal that did not just have one big robbery, but many smaller ones since that was often the norm among them.

Of course, he would love it. Spilling details about crimes and the litany of injustice brought upon him would be a delight. I would pretend to vigorously take notes, ask him about subjects I didn't care about with the hope that our connection would be strong enough by the end of our meeting that he would volunteer a saliva sample. I'm sure he would be apprehensive, but if I explained the new DNA process and that a friend from The University of Pittsburgh was researching a link between theft and DNA coding, I might sway him. It could explain why Dupont was so inclined to steal, after all. Then the moment of truth. It was futile to predict what his response might be. All I had was hope.

I finished my last drop of coffee and glanced at the clock. Time for an excruciatingly long day at the office. I told the partners I had to leave work at 1 p.m., making sure I had plenty of time for the drive. I couldn't be late. Of course, the partners had no problem with me leaving early, seeing that I would probably finish my work by noon. After the drive to the office, time screeched to a halt. Every minute crawled by, and each hour felt like five. Luckily, some billing landed on my desk around 9 a.m. At least that kept me busy for an hour in between the daily monotony. The billing was for a client whose case we lost, and I almost felt guilty that we got a commission off it. I never thought our firm was very good. We didn't always get the best results for the clients.

And while I understood little about the justice system, I witnessed it fail on a regular basis—especially in a certain case.

It happened about eight years ago. I had been working in the firm's accounting department for about a year, and after we won that huge settlement, we were given more and more opportunities with large cases. One such case slid across our desks that got the whole firm riled up, especially me. The case was from a young woman by the name of Atina Rodgers, who lived alone with her son Hahn. She had a rough go of it, working two waitressing jobs just to make ends meet. She wasn't sure what was closer to the breaking point: her bank account or her sanity.

However, she got a lifeline in the form of a customer, "a man in a nice suit," as she described him. He was really impressed with her charisma and asked if she had any experience as a secretary. She only had a stint at a summer internship in high school, but he still suggested she interview for an office assistant position at his business. He owned apartment complexes and was looking for help. Atina was flattered but unsure. It was typical that customers would make a pass at her, but nothing like a job offer had ever come out of it. She said she would think about it. But after she got stiffed by her last table during a 16-hour day, her mind was made up.

At a high-rise apartment building in downtown Manhattan, she met the man for an interview at his office on the 22nd floor. She had never been in a building so tall and started to become nervous to the point she was going to be sick. Ushered in by an attractive assistant, she couldn't even greet him before he embraced her in a hug. "Atina, I've been waiting for you." He took his place behind an ornate desk. Taking a seat across from Mr. Bates, his large gold nameplate on the desk, he asked her what she thought of the place. She began about how it was very impressive and that she was honored to have an opportunity to prove herself. He then started peppering her with personal questions. Her past, her current job, what kind of movies she liked to see. They talked briefly before she mentioned her child, Hahn. At that, Mr. Bates interrupted her to point out the window toward a construction project down the block. "That's my newest building, set to finish in two years. It will be almost twice as tall."

"That will be quite a feat," she told him. She remembered how much Bates said he liked her.

"We have to get you here. You would fit in perfectly; I mean, look at you." He started to bring on some harder questions about her experience in office settings and how she would respond to different situations. The questions were tough, and it was daunting. She had cursory experience in an office but had never interviewed for a position higher than a waitress. It was intimidating. Toward the end of the interview, the line of questioning turned personal again. He asked about a boyfriend.

When she awkwardly answered she didn't have one, without breaking his gaze, he told her, "I just like to know my personal assistants well. We spend a lot of time together." It was an uncomfortable moment that hung in the air until he transitioned into pay, which was almost twice what she made waitressing. She almost tuned out at the mention of the pay, thinking of the burden that much money would take off her. He continued, "The only caveat is you have to live in the building." It was an odd stipulation at first, but it would make sense soon enough.

He explained that personal assistant matters came up at all hours, and he needed her at his beck and call in case they needed to place an international call or deal with emergencies. When Atina said she couldn't possibly afford the place, Bates laughed and waved his hand, stating they would provide the apartment. Atina was beside herself. This was her opportunity to provide the life she wanted for Hahn. She knew there must have been serious competition for the job, but she hoped her impression lasted.

Sure enough, three days later, she received a call, and by the next month, she was all moved in. Hahn hadn't wanted to leave his old school, but Atina assured him he would make new friends and that they would have a better life.

The first month went by easy enough. She was overwhelmed at times, but Mr. Bates was very accommodating, even delegating some of her responsibility to another secretary. With the new pay and free room, she was putting more in Hahn's college fund than she ever had and was even able to spend a little on herself.

Then, late one fateful Friday night, Atina heard a knock on her door. She opened it to find Mr. Bates in front of her. He appeared disheveled with glossy eyes and an untucked button-down. He asked if he could come in. She obliged, despite how weird his visit was, and moved aside as he walked by and stumbled into the kitchen. He started flipping through cupboards.

"What are you looking for?" she offered.

"Any booze in this place?" he retorted.

She moved to the cabinet above the stove but warned him that she thought he had enough.

"That's a funny way to talk to your boss." His voice rose as he poured a small glass of vodka. At this point, she became extremely uncomfortable.

"We can have a short talk in the other room, but then I need to get some sleep, and so does my son. He has a soccer game early tomorrow." She tried to compromise but made it clear he needed to leave soon.

Bates's attention turned to the boy's bedroom. "I'm gonna wish the little guy luck tomorrow," he slurred, then strode toward the door.

"No!" Atina nearly yelled and grabbed at his swinging arm. Bates's head snapped toward her, and anger arose in his eyes. "Let's just talk in the other room. He needs his sleep," she said firmly, attempting to distract and de-escalate the situation. Her grip on his arm tightened as she led him to her bedroom.

Once inside, he began to kiss her, the vodka still heavy on his breath. She started to resist and pull away, but that only made his grip tighter. His mustache bristled alcohol fumes up her nose as his dry rotting breath left a terrible taste in her mouth. When he reached for her pants, she swatted his hand and thrust him away. He didn't like that. He came back to her immediately.

"No," she pleaded as he pushed her to the bed, his weight pressed upon her. He kissed her neck and then moved to whisper in her ear. She felt the heat of his breath and cheap patchouli cologne choked the air around her.

"I brought you into this company because I thought you would do great. You can't even handle a fraction of the work. I was going to fire you last week, but I thought I would give you a chance to prove yourself. It would be sad if tomorrow were his last soccer game." He brought his face to hers, and Atina's fear turned to horror. Hahn. She closed her eyes and brought her lips up to his.

"Good girl." She could feel a shadow of a smile creep onto his face.

"No, no, no," she mouthed as he thrust upon her. She imagined Hahn at his college graduation ceremony, beaming with a diploma that would open more doors than she could count. A dimpled smile as he took photos with his classmates and promised to keep in touch. He would be able to do anything with his life; make himself truly happy.

The image faded away as Bates let out a loud grunt and rolled off her. She lay frozen until she could hear labored snores coming from beside her. Trembling as she walked to the bathroom, she wept under the stream of the shower. She had to do this for her son. She had to stay strong for him.

For the next month, there were no late-night appearances from Mr. Bates, though it didn't stop her from dreading every Friday and Saturday night. She shook in her room, praying she didn't hear a knock. When he announced that he would be out of town one weekend, she nearly shouted for joy. Then, on the fifth weekend without a visit, the door rapped at midnight. Atina winced, and sheer terror shot through her. She felt like she couldn't breathe.

The knock came again, this time louder. Maybe he would go away, maybe he would think they were out of town. Then there was a rap so loud it shook the apartment. She sprinted over to the door and opened it.

"What took you so long?" He looked down at her.

"Bathroom" was all she could muster while staring at his leather shoes. He lifted her chin to his glossy eyes.

"You are so pretty when you're shy." He reeked of whisky and sweat, just like her father.

Her father had abused her during her childhood, often sneaking into her bedroom during evenings when their mother worked nights. In the morning, he would give her brother crude advice about girls. "Women love the chase, they just don't know they want it." Her brother would nod in acknowledgment, absorbing knowledge from his idol. The sickening practice led her to the numbing appeal of drugs. Eventually, getting pregnant with Hahn saved her life.

After Bates's third visit, she began to have a few drinks every weekend night, but it barely helped. She started leaving the apartment on the weekend until a comment about the absences anchored her back. Before long, a few drinks turned into a bottle of wine. She soon developed a sense of self-loathing and disgust towards herself. She felt she wasn't even good enough to be an office assistant and had to sleep with the boss just so she could cling to a job. The animosity mounted until she couldn't show her face around the office without having a buzz going. Whenever approached by Mr. Bates, she cowered, absorbed by fear and shame in his vicinity.

Then, one day, Bates told her they knew she was drinking on the job and that she was being terminated. She had to be out of the apartment by next month.

After a two-week binge and blowing the small nest egg she had left, she was picked up for prostitution. The short stint she served was enough to have her son taken away, and when released, she was beside herself. She saw our advertisement after being dropped off by the complimentary bus the jail provided.

What I felt for Atina was beyond professional; it was personal.

Being passionate about the case and winning it were vastly different, as we soon found out. This Bates character had a couple of phenomenal lawyers and a cache of money to throw at our small firm. After officially filing suit, the firm was drowned in paperwork, and the partners worked their asses off to dig themselves out of it. It was busy enough that some remedial duties bled over to me. Perhaps in a slightly unethical grey area, I wanted to help in any way I could. Atina and I bonded personally during the case, and I needed to see justice.

After about four months, we had built a relatively solid case but were unsure if it could stand up in court. The defense was going to argue that the relationship was consensual and that Atina was an untrustworthy substance abuser. At a pre-trial hearing to determine whether our case was to proceed to a jury trial and what evidence might be admitted, our side presented and tried to establish the uneven power dynamic as well as show that Mr. Bates tied sexual encounters to continued employment. Sitting in the back of the courtroom, I was optimistic and fully expected the trial to be heard. In front of a jury, however, the emotional hammer would be too much.

When we finally turned it over to the defendants, they attempted to twist everything, portraying Atina as a subpar parent who entered a consensual relationship with Mr. Bates and that on their first sexual encounter, Atina initiated the engagement with a kiss and never said no. They painted a picture of a woman who became disgruntled when she was let go because of her job performance. Then, out of revenge and desperation for money, she drummed up this ridiculous and unsubstantiated charge. I saw her wipe away silent tears while sitting beside the partners. I couldn't believe my ears. I was sickened, but they had every legal right to construe the truth in the way they did.

Then it took a turn for the worse. The judge rambled on that there was no "concrete" evidence the relationship was not consensual, and all the evidence was circumstantial as to the charge that employment was linked to sexual acts. Therefore, he was dismissing the lawsuit unless the plaintiffs had anything more. A request for an extension by a member of our duo was quickly reprimanded by the judge. I could tell from our partners' frantic tone that the case was in danger. As the partners explained later, they couldn't believe what had just happened.

Our partners were livid with outrage and pleaded with the judge to reconsider. Their interjections fell on deaf ears, though, and the rap of the gavel was the official silencer. The judge ruled in favor of the defendants and threw out the case. It was a sucker punch to the gut. Atina turned to the partners as the judge started to leave, asking what happened as if she were in denial. The partners sat quietly in their chairs while the courtroom filed out, perhaps building up the courage to confront her with what had just transpired. They all finally rose and approached, fatally wounded, a look of grave disgust on their faces. She started to break down and scurried to the back of the courtroom to me.

"He's right; I kissed him," she said, trembling. I grabbed her shoulders to console her.

"He forced you. You said no."

"Only once at the beginning. I never told him to stop." She looked at me, eyes blurred. "I was never clear."

I was beside myself. "Shh, shh. You did nothing wrong." I squeezed her tightly.

"We're sorry," the older partner Aron started. "We did everything we could to win, just came up short. We would like to pay to put you and your child up for a couple of months, though."

Atina's eyes shot up for a brief second and accompanied a quick smile, "Thank you very much." Then her tone shifted. "But what about the other months? What will give my child the best opportunity to live once I run out of money? I trusted you. I put my son's life in your hands, and you failed us. You said we had a good case!"

Her words stung. The firm didn't owe her anything, but they still felt responsible for her and her child.

"I'm not sure, Ms. Rodgers, and I'm sorry we cannot help you further," Aron said.

Kayla, the other partner, simply nodded and stared ahead. We all slipped out of the courtroom to endure a painfully silent ride back to New Jersey.

I was irate. There was no excuse for this. A despicable, slimy excuse for a man held her hostage and preyed on her desire to provide for her son. I couldn't think of a more perverse ploy. Then he hid behind his lawyers and money, avoiding the consequences. I was not about to let them completely get away with it. The wheels started turning, and the plot began to hatch. I yearned to rectify the transgression and racked my brain for solutions. There were many options to choose from, but I finally settled on the one I deemed most viable. I needed Mr. Bates alone. It didn't matter that the plan I formulated had a high chance of failure; this was personal. He deserved it. Looking back, blind hatred fueled that need to avenge more than almost any other, and it almost cost me.

I began a surveillance campaign. He was a busy man and often operated inside his offices or weaving his way through a crowded downtown. Getting him alone was key, but I became increasingly skeptical that could be achieved. Eluding all eyes in New York was no easy feat. His large skyscraper in downtown New York presented too much security. The only solution seemed to be to make my move on his commute to or from work. After his workday, he headed straight home with no exceptions, but it was on his way to work that I saw my opportunity.

He liked to walk to work and stop at a small bakery on his way to the office. Precisely at 6:55 a.m., he strolled into Mama Bee's Bagels as part of his daily ritual. He ordered the back leftmost poppyseed bagel, a milk, and a packet of cream cheese. I couldn't imagine how I could possibly get him alone at the shop. There were cameras, customers, and staff in the vicinity.

Then the thought shifted. What if I had a chance while he was on the walk to the office? In that case, I would have to get him off the street voluntarily. The problem with that was creating a scenario in which he wanted to be alone. It took a couple of days to brainstorm an idea, but the wheels started turning after I saw a cycler get off his bike and puke in a trash bin. Poison. It was an idea so perfect I knew I had found my option. I would arrive in the bakery before him, poison his bagel, and then trail him until he had to step out to puke. He would rush to some back alley behind a dumpster, and that would give me the chance I needed. It was beautiful.

I took a week off work and began to scout out every detail. Purchasing a ski mask and an airsoft gun with cash, I spray-painted the orange tip to make it look like a real handgun. I ran over my route and had every detail synced up except where he was going to stop. Along the way to his work, there were a plethora of alleys, with about half providing suitable intervention points. I was fairly confident that he would stop before he reached his offices, which was perfect because I wasn't keen on this going down in the lobby bathroom.

The substance that would induce his vomiting was rather potent. I found the concoction in a book at the local library and tried it myself first. It worked like a charm, to say the least, and I had an iron stomach.

"Hit me with your best shot da-da-da-dun!" my alarm jolted me awake at 3 a.m. Pat Benatar provided a fitting song for the day as I rushed out of bed. I had to get a move on, so I grabbed a banana and hit the road. Stopping by a local convenience store, I picked up the day's paper. The date was September 21, 1987, and the headline read "SOVIETS PERFORM NUCLEAR TEST." I scoffed at the bold letters, of course. I had grown up despising those commies. My father used to advocate for nuking them before they nuked us. Efforts from my mother to talk him down would just aggravate him more.

As I drove to the Manhattan bakery for my rendezvous with Mr. Bates, I couldn't help but think, *What if this went wrong? Was I ready for the consequences?* The thoughts frightened me slightly, but thinking of Atina and Hahn fueled my crusade, soon overtaking my fears.

I pulled up to the quaint bagel shop at 6:40 a.m. It was quiet on the sidewalk outside as I rubbed the vomit-inducing chemical on my right index and middle finger. It was odorless and, for the most part, blended in with my skin with perfect camouflage. I took one last deep breath to collect myself, pausing to reflect on what I was about to embark on. Slowly approaching the entrance while replaying everything one last time, I pushed in the door and waltzed in. It was a small shop that smelled like heaven. A clear counter and a display case ran the length of the store with two registers on either end. The cases were lined with delectable pastries with a smell you could nearly taste. The space was partitioned with wood shelving, each holding another variety of delicious treats. Different candies and sweets filled the store, with a lone fridge holding pre-made cakes in the corner. I could have gorged myself, but I had a job to do.

I first paced around for a minute, examining the wide selection, and then moseyed on over to the display case facing the counter while pretending to be deep in thought. There were two workers that I could see: a young preppy girl, who looked to be in her early 20s, and an elderly lady who I presumed to be the store owner and main baker. The aroma from the fresh doughnuts she brought from the kitchen lured me to her end of the counter.

"Hi, miss," I started, "How much for a bagel?"

"One dollar, young sir," she responded.

"Hmm. I'll take one of the poppyseed bagels then." I pointed to the backmost left one with my finger.

"Excellent choice!" she exclaimed, reaching with wax paper for the treat. I hoped my gesture influenced which bagel she snatched; otherwise, I would be buying a lot. To my luck, the old bird picked right. Grabbing it, she handed the bagel over the counter to me. I reached with my right hand to grab it, and as I touched it, I pretended to change my mind.

"Uhh, on second thought, I feel like being a little fat this morning. How about a doughnut instead?" She paused, bagel in hand, then smiled and said "all right." I noticed she put the bagel back in the same place, the back left.

I let out a sigh of relief. "Sorry, ma'am, I couldn't make up my mind." She nodded and smiled. I started toward the doughnut section of the display case. Just then, the younger girl spoke up.

"Mom, we should get rid of that bagel. It went over the counter." I halted midstride. Panic surged through my body. Shit,

I was so close. That skank. What could I do if they took the bagel away? The older lady hesitated. She seemed torn between listening to her daughter, who no doubt was right, and taking a hit to her pride, seeing as she was being corrected in front of the customer. I held my breath for a tense moment, then decided I needed to make an excuse for her.

"I only touched the wax paper, not the actual bagel, if that makes any difference," I suggested and held my breath. Fear gripped my chest. Blood pumped with such force I thought my arteries might burst, and I felt like my voice came out a bit shaky. The daughter shrugged and obliged. A wave of relief washed over me. All as planned. The elderly woman finished grabbing my doughnut and rang me up for $1.05. I paid in cash and thanked her for her patience. It was the best dollar I ever spent.

I enjoyed the treat from the comfort of my car. The outside of the doughnut was fried enough that it was crisp and a little greasy, while the middle remained soft, dissolving in the presence of my saliva. The frosting was generously applied, but not so much that it overpowered the sugar dough. Mama Bee knew how to make a damn fine doughnut.

As I enjoyed my treat a storefront down, the man of the hour pulled up exactly on time. I was so focused on my treat I barely noticed him walk past me. He was in and out shortly, presumably grabbing his usual bagel. I watched him devour it on the walk. I trailed him a good distance back since the streets were sparser than I had anticipated. With the major variable of my plan past me, I walked down the street on a high.

About 10 minutes later, I noticed my stomach becoming upset; a deep nauseous sensation came on that signaled puke was soon to follow. Over the next five minutes, the urge became stronger until I was certain I would have to duck off the street.

That's when it dawned on me that I never washed my hands after touching Bates's bagel. When I ate my doughnut, I still had the substance on my hands. The epiphany cascaded into a frantic turmoil, churning my already fragile stomach. I wanted to scream at my stupidity. Things were coming unhinged.

It took him two more blocks to finally pull off, and that moment couldn't have come soon enough. I held the vomit in the best I could, but I knew as soon as I let it go, it would be like a fire hose. Bates mercifully pulled to a stop behind a dumpster halfway down the alley. I waited until he stumbled behind it before I raced around the dumpster across from him and collapsed on all fours. The puke projected like a cannon, and I swear it flew at least 10 feet. The acid from the vomit coursed through my throat like hot sandpaper that left me gasping for breaths between bouts. At the intermission of each vomit session, I would momentarily taste the acidic sugar concoction, and its foulness caused me to shiver. It felt amazing to let it out, but every time I thought it would end, even pleaded for it, it still kept coming. Even when I couldn't possibly imagine my stomach having anything left, I still managed to spew contents and fluid. My throat burned as though someone coated a cactus in gonorrhea and rubbed it against my esophagus. When it all subsided, I looked over at Bates. His face was flush. Murky saliva drained from his mouth and even after repeated spitting and gasping, dribble still clung to his lips. The expulsion of the bagel lay on the ground in front of him. He looked as defeated as I did. His eyes caught mine; he was in thought.

"Hey, didn't I see you outside Mama Bee's?" he asked, his breath short.

"Yeah, you did," I confessed.

"Well, that's the last time either of us goes there. That was something else." A scowl settled on his face.

I simply nodded, mirroring his reaction. He was dressed in an expensive black suit with a white vest and tie. Glasses and a tie clip were among his accessories. He wore a red undershirt that topped off the outfit. The man had style. We continued to recover, and the lingering vomit taste started to dilute.

To counter the taste, Geoffrey lifted a small cigar and lighter from his suit pocket. As the crisp tobacco burned, the smell wafted to my vicinity, and with it, my eyes closed to savor the aroma. Bates must've sensed that I liked his stogie because he held it out in offering after he took a few puffs. I savored the slow inhale, allowing it to cleanse my pallet. Bates was pleased, and he gave a friendly nod when I handed it back. We were like two old friends.

"Say, young man, what's your name?" he asked.

"Nick Jacobs," I responded, compromising myself. "And yours?"

"Geoffrey Bates," he said as smoke billowed from his puff.

It didn't matter much that he knew my name because, after the vomiting and the shared cigar, I no longer had the will or the heart to follow through with my plan. Still angry, though, I wanted to probe about the lawsuit.

"That name sounds familiar. Yeah, I think I recognize the name from a *New York Times* article I read."

He held the cigar to his mouth. An expressive eyebrow raised to acknowledge it was possible.

"What did you do to that woman? I read the trial was thrown out, but I also read her description of what you did. You're a pathetic coward. You must hate yourself." The brazen assault caught him by surprise. It didn't ease up.

"How weak does someone have to be to blackmail a woman with her son's future? I've never heard of a man so—"

"Don't insult me, boy." A snarl interrupted me. "I don't know who the hell you are or where the hell this is coming from, but I've never done anything of the sort."

My eyes shot back into my head. His blatant lie unsettled me. I leaned in for the first punch.

"The nerve of you to look me in the eye and tell me you didn't. I wouldn't see a more spineless, immoral piece of scum if I visited the isolation ward at Rikers. Since when did you become all right with forcing women to have sex with you to keep their jobs? When did you give your soul to Satan? And for what? So your limp dick might feel more powerful? I'm genuinely interested in what rationale you attach to this. I hope you go home tonight and count your lucky stars you got healthy kids, enrolled in some private school with a fast track to executive avenue because there are a lot of people that can't say that. She was a single mom trying to provide for her kid!" I caught my breath.

I expected some reaction, but during the entire rant, Bates remained solemnly silent. An unyielding stare matched mine as I beat him into verbal submission. When I finished, he took a long pause, sucking in a large batch of smoke and letting it exhale slowly. A sigh indicated he was ready to respond.

"Did Atina send you? Because then she's in trouble." I quickly shook my head "no," and he took a few more seconds.

"I don't know who the hell you are, but you know what? It doesn't matter. My lawyer will take care of it." His unfazed demeanor was befuddling. He repositioned himself to face me, giving the impression this was a verbal joust in which I had smacked goliath with a foam rock.

"You may think you're on some crusade for justice here, but let me get you a little more educated. I may have been young and naive at one point in my life, but I was never as stupid as you. What does yelling at someone in an alley for a charge they were acquitted for accomplish? And on the topic of accomplishments, look at that building there. You have been mooching off the world I have been building for you. In fact, your only accomplishment is sleeping with that drugged-out whore. That's the only way you would be here. Let me ask, how were my seconds?"

At the mention of his seconds, I was so enraged that I threw myself at him. He lunged, and I grazed him as we reversed positions in the alley. Bates began to back up to the point where he was only a few feet away from the relative safety of the street.

"I've built something with my life. Can you say the same? I have facilitated the development of apartments and homes that have improved the lives of thousands. My company has donated millions to charity." He paused, deflated from his rant.

He sighed. "But you don't care about that. Not when I 'used my position inappropriately.' Your searing naivety and jealousy deserve something more cynical, more pragmatic. You may say tenfold of good deeds can't wash away the bad, but that's where you're wrong, son." His tone turned agitated. "Every great advancement, every improvement in humanity and society in history, costs something. Many times, that cost is much more than dollars. That is the case whether you want to admit it or not. Now, I informed Atina that she would be let go because she couldn't handle the work. She practically threw herself on me, begged me with puppy dog eyes to keep her, saying she would do anything, including sleep with me, if I kept her on. Don't come here and tell me the responsibility lies on me. When do you put the responsibility on her, a drug addict single mom? Because nothing was forced! People will sue food companies for making them fat, doctors for saving their lives. People like you just expect that everyone should be the same. And that you can just prance around mindlessly living a great life while all the messy details and improvements are left to others. Others, who you seem to expect must be all right with slaving years away. Sacrificing family, friends, and happiness all for minimal compensation because they should share any extra money with those who didn't work as hard or achieve as much." His seething breaths were probably enough to ignite the stogie into a ball of flame. I stared into the ground absorbing the verbal blows.

"Listen," his voice relaxed. "Situations are tough, life gets hard, but I'm not going to baby those who can't understand. I've wasted my breath plenty on you." A look of disgustful disdain burrowed into me. He stared ahead, sucking his stogie down to half. "It was no coincidence we met today, was it"?

My face froze as I was sure he read me like a book. A sly smile formed on his face.

"One of us got lucky today." He was so casual. Taking another puff, he continued, "It won't take my friend long to find out who you are, where you live, and what family you have. I ever see you again… well, you have an imagination."

He strode off and disappeared into the sea of moving pedestrians. I grappled with what he said. I wasn't one to talk, but if everyone held his beliefs, the world would be a darker place. He really thought that since he had acquired money and power, it was his right to use that as leverage. He saw it as an ethical transaction, and if other people got hurt from it, it was their fault.

It was probably a good thing I hadn't gone through with the plan because it wouldn't have ended well. He had deserved every bit of it, but I had bitten off more than I could chew. He was right; I had been lucky. The drive home was a quiet one.

Chapter 9

Driving up to Rikers Island, my thoughts leapfrogged from one to another. My dialogue with Dupont needed to be witty, sharp, and confident but relaxed. I needed Alvin Dupont to trust me. I had acted in plays back in high school and played a mean Augustus Gloop in Willy Wonka. Although, the stakes were much higher now.

I drove over the bridge to Rikers, beginning what I'm sure inmates viewed as a descent into hell. I couldn't help but be intimidated by the place. It was massive, and with a facility that housed thousands of criminals, I was a bit nervous about my safety. Walking into the visitor facility was fairly unpleasant. The place was dark, uninviting, and decrepit. Rust painted the piping running along the ceiling, and the absence of any color besides white, grey, or black presented a bleak picture. I didn't expect rainbows and sunshine, but the atmosphere did nothing to settle my anxiety. Thankfully, I made it through security without issue. The zombie-like mechanics of the staff, along with the visible disdain for their job, only assured me that if someone wanted to get something through, they could.

I checked in at the visitors' counter and seated myself on one of the many luxurious plastic chairs. It was bolted to the ground, probably in case someone wanted to use it as a weapon.

I waited… and waited… *long* past my appointment time. There were quite a few others in the waiting area, many who sat down after me but were called up before. Either Alvin wasn't in the mood to talk, or there was no timeliness associated with the place. I continued to glance at the receptionist every few minutes with the hope she would suddenly realize how long I'd been waiting. Much to my chagrin, she had her head buried in a magazine.

Finally, the lady behind the counter yelled, "Nick!" and my head quickly shot up. I approached, finally relieved from the plastic chair. A guard ushered me into the visitation section—an open space with many other inmates conversing with relatives and friends. I presumed they were low-risk prisoners since no one appeared to be in shackles. I was escorted to an empty table and waited patiently as the guard brought in Alvin Dupont. He was dwarfed by the guard. No taller than 5'7", he wore orange overalls, had a scruffy beard, and presented an exhausted look. I couldn't tell if he wanted to see me or if it was more of a burden. Considering the way he shuffled towards me, I wasn't feeling too optimistic. He took a seat across from me, his face communicating unfriendliness, but I wouldn't let that deter me.

"Hi, Alvin, my name is Nick," I came off as peppy. "I work as an amateur journalist for a New Jersey weekly. Surely this must seem random, but I've been fixated on writing stories about career criminals." Unfazed disinterest met my greeting.

"So far, I've only tackled murderers. The pieces have been received so well, I decided to delve into other crimes."

Still, he looked at me without an expression. I hated not being able to read his face. I continued, "Anyway, I had a friend of mine run some background on thefts in the area I lived in, and your name popped up. I dug further and was impressed and intrigued by your work."

His face perked up. Once I threw out a couple of compliments, I had his attention. He may not have meant to since it was so subtle, but I could see some anticipation looming in his eyes. Acne scars marked his face, and he looked aged beyond his years.

"If you had the time, I would really appreciate hearing anything you'd like to share about theft, the thrills, the lows, any advice you might have. I'm really trying to put together a comprehensive piece." He shrugged and attempted to look disinterested, almost bothered. "I understand that you don't know—"

He put his hand up to stop my rambling, then waved it in a nonverbal scold. "You seem like one of those weird crime like'n people. I know the type. Little too goody, but really like livin' the thrill though someone else skin. I'm not here to judge, but you're asking a lot from me, mister. Nick, was it?" I couldn't decipher whether his habitual pauses and slow speech were deliberate or his natural pace.

"I could be working in the shop right now, so unless I'm getting compensated, I can't provide you much information." He sat back with a smirk and let me formulate a response. He was crafty; I'll give him that.

"Listen, Alvin, I can deposit $30 in your commissary. There are plenty of other inmates to interview, and I'm sure you're not getting more than pennies working here." It was the best I could do because it's all I had in my wallet. I hadn't even thought about bringing money for a bribe. In all honesty, I would've paid the guy $300 if that's what it took. He pondered the deal, then threw back a counteroffer.

"Say, there are a few books I've been dying to read. You promise to bring me those, throw in that commissary, and I'll give you any detail your heart desires."

I nodded, and Dupont rattled off five books which were surprisingly advanced reads. Then he got quieter. "Now that last book. I want you to cut out a section in the middle and slip a pack of cigarettes in there."

"*The Road to El Dorado?*"

"Fitting, I know." He was amused.

"I just…I mean…." I looked over at the guard like I'd already done it.

"Are cigarettes illegal?" Dupont swatted the air. "Even if they catch it, they would just bum 'em off for themselves. It ain't even worth a blink here."

It only took me a couple of seconds to consider the offer.

"Deal," Reaching over to cement the agreement in a handshake. *I could send it with a different name and address, no way it could be traced to me if anything did go wrong.*

"So that's how they barter in prison?" I chided. I was enthralled with our little back and forth and let the dorky comment slip.

"Stick to the burbs, man. All you got here to barter is that cute lil bum of yours. And that ain't last three weeks before you wish you didn't have it." A slight smirk showed on his face.

Point taken. At least I hadn't upset him. I began to pepper him with a few generic questions so he could relax and start talking. In the back of my mind, I shuddered at the thought of not being able to leave here. Was it really that bad, or was he trying to rattle me? I was anxious to get my real questions asked. Even as he responded to the first couple, my mind kept floating. So, I decided why dance around? He didn't skirt around the edges. It was early in the interview and a bit gutsy, but I had to get it answered. It was gnawing at me like a starving pup with a bone.

"So, would you say theft is a gateway crime? I mean, have you found it to lead you to more serious crimes? I saw you were investigated for murder a while back." The question was a reach.

"No," he shot back. "I never killed that guy." His tone was frustrated and assured.

"They thought I did back then, but they had it wrong. They had no proof. Yeah, I had robbed one of the neighbors, sure, but that was just a coincidence. They knew I was never even in the house. They searched my place for this watch that was stolen during the whole thing but never found it." I had him rolling. He continued, "The detective was a schlep. I knew it wasn't a robbery just by looking at it." My weight shifted forward. "The person only took his watch and some money. I was tellin' them, this place wasn't cased, they didn't even bother to steal the jewelry! I told 'em that, but they weren't about to listen to me. That dude was convinced it was a butchered break-in. Barely investigated jack before they dragged me in and started trying to pin it on me!" The irritation was evident in his voice.

I was completely fixated.

"You just knew it wasn't a robbery? Maybe the police had more evidence they didn't show you that pointed that way?"

He started getting defensive, "I mean, I'd be in jail then."

I shrugged, deciding to back off a little. After a moment, he took a breath.

"It was a long time ago, and I can't remember much from the whole thing. I do recall when they finally backed off. They had me in this room for hours, badgering, yellin', the whole schtick. That detective wanted to pin it on me bad. They showed me a picture of this dude murdered, and I told 'em I'd never seen the guy in my life. They didn't like that, and he shoved my face into it on the table. *'You're going to stare at it till you do remember!'*

"So I'm lookin' at this guy. He's a biggg dude. I asked 'em how I could kill this guy. They were like, 'Well, you got lucky.' I was like, no way someone kills that dude without a serious fight unless he is completely surprised. And I don't know any thief who just sneak kills someone twice their size and doesn't steal anything? You see any marks on me or him? That's the dumbest thing I've ever heard. That detective didn't have much to say after that."

I rocked back in my chair as his statement sank in.

Was the robbery just a cover-up for cold-blooded murder? My eyes wandered to the refracted sun shining on the floor. This could change everything, but I needed more. This Dupont guy wasn't the most trustworthy character, but his argument was compelling.

"You remember that crappy detective's name by chance?"

"Nah, I just know the type. I saw he got wrapped up in scandal years later. Can't remember what for, just saw his ugly mug in the paper and it made my day."

I was furiously recording every detail. *Chris was going to have his hands full.*

Despite the revelations, I needed to regroup and keep asking my BS questions to keep cover. I continued with the interview, but in the back of my mind, I kept going back to Dupont's thoughts on my father's murder.

During the interview, I developed a little fondness for the guy. He was a bit older than me and enjoyed baseball. He had quite a collection of stories and didn't seem all that bad of a guy, either. He was fairly educated and reasonable, just had trouble finding his footing with the law. We shared a few laughs, and before long, it felt like we had known each other for years. His father had fled the family when he was 10, and his mother did the best she could for his sister and him. Often times, though, he needed to steal to provide for himself and his family. After a while, stealing became essential to his life. It was more realistic than spending money to attend college and fall into debt. However, even when he had money, he felt the urge to steal. Sometimes it could be staved off for a while, but he knew he could never shake it. He said he wished he hadn't had to resort to thievery, but he couldn't let go of the past, and now it was running his life.

I felt for the man. He was obviously bright and driven, and it was just the vice of stealing that held him back. I began to lose focus on my main objective while learning more and more about Alvin's life. While we wrapped up, he asked when it was getting published. I told him I would try to run it in next month's issue, and he smiled and thanked me for visiting him. It was a change in his daily routine. He seemed genuinely grateful, and it surprised me, considering how closed and uninterested he appeared at first. As the interview came to a close, I thanked him, promising to bring him the books he bargained for. I was so satisfied with talking with the guy, I almost forgot that the whole conversation was a farce. All I needed was his saliva. The Nick charm was ready.

"One more thing. Listen, Alvin, one of my friends does research for the University of Pittsburgh, and he's trying to find a link between DNA and crimes people commit. Since you're a career criminal, I was wondering if you would like to participate in the study?" I held my breath waiting. Alvin looked at me, puzzled.

"What's DNA?" he asked.

Duh. DNA was new, and I'm sure someone in prison had little clue it existed. I began explaining what DNA was and how it was used. I told him it was sort of like fingerprints, except for bodily fluids. He listened to me and seemed intrigued, saying he would volunteer for the study.

"Well, I mean, I guess I have nothing to lose, and if it benefits someone, then I might as well, sure."

I thanked him profusely, but he shrugged the praise off. When I presented the cotton swab to him, he held it at a distance. The white cotton was apparently not harmless enough to be trusted.

"It doesn't bite," I encouraged.

It was amusing, watching him be so wary. To his credit, anyone at Rikers could probably turn that into a weapon. I made sure to keep that thought to myself this time. After building up the courage and returning the swab to a plastic bag, we parted ways. One last goodbye and a prison guard swooped in to escort Alvin back to his cell as I casually walked out the front doors. I was ecstatic. The meeting was a success. Alvin Dupont was definitely not what I had imagined, and I started to form doubts that he was the killer. He certainly didn't seem like he could escalate to such a crime, but then again, people are rather deceitful. At least this DNA test would prove it.

The drive toward Chris's house to drop off the DNA samples gave me more time to ponder scenarios. What would happen if Alvin Dupont did kill him? Could he be charged with the murder, or does the case have an expiration date? Would I even want a trial, or would I prefer to take measures into my own hands? There would be a lot of scenarios I could choose from if Alvin's DNA came back as a match, but based on my conversation with the guy, I hoped it didn't.

I pulled into Chris's neighborhood at about 7:30 p.m. East Village was a great area of New York City, and his duplex was a gem inside. It wasn't an exceptionally wealthy neighborhood, but it wasn't shabby either. I parked on the side of the street and made my way to the door of the cozy, historic house. Through the dark and up the step, I met the brass door knocker.

Before I could even rap the metal, it swung open.

"Nick, my man, how's it goin'?" Chris bellowed as he greeted me. I barely got through the door before I was bombarded. "So, how did it go? By that smile, I'm guessing well! You probably turned on the charm." His laughter was eruptive.

"Phaa, of course, I did, man, and don't mock the charm. It works!" A firm punch to the shoulder wouldn't deter the jokes, but he got one anyway. As I moved into the foyer, I was greeted by his wife Sandra and his two kids, or "little rascals," as Chris described them. My impression, however, was that they were pretty cute, well-behaved kids. Then again, I didn't live with them. We exchanged small talk as we migrated to the kitchen. Their house had a long foyer leading to an open layout kitchen, a dining room, and a living room. It was quite inviting, and the smell of dinner cooking was heavenly.

"Smells lovely in here," I said, the scent waking up my senses. "What's that cooking?" I took a deep inhale. "Something barbeque?"

"Nice nose, Nick," Sandra retorted. "It's cheese-stuffed meatloaf coated in a barbeque bacon glaze." My eyes lit up like a child's. The last time I had something edible that was home-cooked had been eons ago. I sometimes tried to cook, but I always resorted to a takeout menu after whatever I tried to make didn't turn out. I made burgers sometimes, but even I can only eat so many of those. "We expect you to stay for dinner, Nick," Sandra said.

"Oh no, I couldn't intrude. I was going to head back, sauté up some—"

"Ha, ha. Nick, stop! You and I both know that calling for takeout doesn't count as a real meal. You're staying for dinner, and that's final." Chris flashed a big smile my way before all three of us shared a laugh.

"So, mixing my sesame chicken with rice doesn't count as home cooking?" I smirked.

"Well, all that could be solved if you found yourself a girl. How's it going in that department? When do we get to meet a potential Mrs.?" Chris asked. He knew I didn't like him bringing it up. I mean, I was 33 with no potential prospects.

"I have one that has some potential. You two can meet her eventually if things pan out," I told them. "It's early." A complete lie, but it would at least drop the subject. I wasn't particularly searching for anyone, but I was available. If I was really serious about it, I would exert more effort into the search, but even if I found someone, I had reservations. Would they accept me? Could I share all aspects of myself?

We waited for the meatloaf to finish as we shared glasses of red wine and some cheese. We had quite a few laughs talking about old stories about Chris and me as well as his two kids. As we bellowed recalling the Tarzan story, Sandra felt left out of the loop and insisted she had never heard this story. A few drinks in and years behind us, we let our guard down and talked about our wild weekend in Vegas.

When Chris turned 23, we traveled to Vegas to celebrate his birthday in style. We had already spent many years being young and stupid and wanted a big bang before we focused on our careers. It was a reckless trip that we didn't have the money for, but when has that ever stopped anyone?

We booked a large suite for two nights at the Mirage for Chris, three college friends, and me. The five of us were like kids hopped up on too much sugar. We couldn't have imagined what was destined for us in Sin City. We landed, ready to conquer the city, and before even checking into the hotel, we hit the first casino we saw. Dazzling lights blinded our vision, cigar smoke choked our lungs, and the sound of chips deafened our ears. We had been wide-eyed rookies, eager to get into the mix.

Unfortunately, in just those first few hours, Vegas chewed us up and spat us back out. After losing $400 before mid-afternoon, we cut our losses, moping to the hotel. We had spent a third of our money in one fell swoop, so before losing more, we unpacked and grabbed a buffet dinner from the hotel. Man, they feed you for cheap there, but they took it back on the gambling floor. After nursing our food comas in the room, we were predictably a little deflated. The melancholic atmosphere had to change, so my roommate Rick gathered our group up, pouring a small glass of whisky for each.

"Listen, men." He stoically had one leg on a chair. "I know we lost earlier, but trust-fund Trev over here just has to milk his dad's nut sack one more time, and we're back in business." He grinned, holding up a finger. The man pulled no punches. "This is a place where your luck can change just like that. Now, I didn't come here with you riff-raff not to take chances, not to get crazy. We're in Vegas, and anything goes. We will party like brothers tonight…" he paused emphatically before continuing, "except for two-beer queer over there." He nodded at Chris. "I can tuck you in at eleven." We shared a laugh at Chris's expense as Rick moved toward the bottle.

"I'm known as the wild guy, the risk-taker, but you know why?" He again paused as if we had been begging for the answer all our lives. "Because you don't make memories with boring. You don't live with boring; you only *survive* with boring. I don't want to survive. I want to live. This trip is a bust if we leave Vegas and tell people, 'Oh, there was this crazy dude we saw.' No, I want us to be those crazy dudes and have other people spreading our story to the far reaches of this world!" He was looking up into the distance like he saw some glorious truth.

"Get off the stage!" Trev yelled from the back of the room. After a chuckle, Rick pulled himself out of the stratosphere.

"Now, here's what's going to happen." He looked everyone in the eye. "We're going to get hammered as fuck, gamble our asses off, hit the club, and then our night begins. Now, who's with me!" He raised his glass, a smirk spreading across his face as his eyes scanned the room. We looked at him intently in silence.

"And then does it end with you getting whisky dick again?" Mike pierced the rest of the confident façade Rick had left, and we lost it, falling over in laughter.

"You limp." I put a hand on his shoulder. In the middle of it all, I managed a "To Vegas!" and we let out a war cry, raising our glasses in compliance.

After the rally, we hit the ground running. We started the night off like any crazy one should—with tequila shots. Then we hit the gaming floor at about 8 p.m. It wasn't too bustling yet, and we spent a couple of hours at the poker and blackjack tables. We weren't losing as bad as earlier, but none of us were up except Mike. Around 10 p.m., we regrouped at the craps tables. We had all consumed a few more drinks and were getting buzzed. When we shamefully shared how much money was lost, Rick became agitated.

"Fuck, I'm putting an end to this!" he yelled as he stormed to a table. His impulsive nature, combined with being the most intoxicated at the time, was a dangerous combo. He barked at the dealer to fork over $500 worth of chips while placing Benjamins on the table.

The dealer barely raised an eyebrow. This was chump-change to him. He exchanged Rick's cash for chips with a smile and continued managing the table. Rick entered the middle spot at a two-dealer craps table. He slid right in, cool as a cucumber. The rest of us were a little unnerved.

He started off slow, winning a little money playing the pass line and winning $50 putting money down on 6. After about 15 minutes of smaller betting, it was Rick's chance to throw. Now up to $850, he looked back at us then threw all his chips into the hard ways.

Not being well versed in craps, I didn't understand the idiocy of the bet at first. Noticing how appalled the rest of our group was, however, clued me in. Mike started filling me in on what the hardways meant and what Rick needed to roll.

"Hardways, eight." Rick's confidence was little assurance with the absurdity of his bet. A frenzy ensued as we started screaming at him like he was crazy, but he was unfazed. He only anxiously tapped the rim of the table, waiting to be slid the dice. It was low odds, and the payout was ten to one. But he had a look in his eyes. There was no convincing him otherwise.

I held my breath as Rick tossed the green cubes of death. They tumbled in slow motion, each number flashing, and every time a four showed, I wished I could freeze it there. The future of our night lay in the outcome of the roll. Noise was canceled out as the dice settled. Our group eyed the two cubed devils, just daring them to turn up as aces.

They settled on the green felt. Two and a four.

A wave of relief overcame us. Live to die another day. The dealer made the appropriate payouts and took a few more bets. I paid little attention. My focus still lay on the marble twins. If

I stared hard enough, maybe they would be what I wanted. Two more nerve-racking rolls went by without a seven. The edge was taken off a little by the fourth throw, and I started to build a false sense of confidence. Like Rick couldn't throw a seven. Everyone was winning on the table, so they loved him.

"Take the bet down," Rick affirmed to the dealer, and he promptly received his chips back. His unshakable confidence must have been rattled as he second-guessed his play. I couldn't help feeling a sense of disappointment. The bet was so outrageous and daring that it was thrilling to be a part of it.

The guy next to us was betting large and had won handsomely off Rick's rolls, and he protested the move.

"Cold feet aren't for Vegas, pal."

He may have been trying to joke, but Rick took it as a challenge. Too late to throw it out there again for his next roll, he let them fly again. A three and a four popped up. A *hallelujah* was shared between our group, and we patted Rick on the shoulder as if he had just won a huge pot, but he just stood still. Rick put all the chips right back in.

More pleadings to stop came from Chris and Mike. I just silently watched the small pile being moved into the death square on the board. The casual comment from the neighbor reignited the unflinching, no-holds-barred attitude in Rick.

He turned his head slowly, like a menacing horror trope, towards his left, locking eyes with his new rival.

"Now roll, pal." The bet was about more than just the money now. Rick was in a pissing contest he couldn't win, and he invited our neighbor to open season. The menacing tone wasn't intimidating, seeing as we were about to lose all our money.

"Nice to see you brought your balls to the table, but it doesn't matter much when you put them on the chopping block," he sneered back. The condescending and casual demeanor made him easy to hate.

"Why don't you put your mouth where my balls are and put up some money on the table, you walking douche." Rick was savage.

We started going wild like a middle school roasting competition. It didn't matter that the insult didn't entirely make sense or that it was childish. The delivery and speed it was retorted at was a social knockout. Flustered and shaking his head, trying to diminish the impact of Rick's comment, the d-bag was ready to end this.

"I know how to shut you all up." He started reaching for the dice that were just pushed his way. He shook our prayers in his hand for a couple of seconds. With each shake, the laughter got quieter. The adrenaline surged stronger, and the table became more in focus as the two dimpled prisoners jumbled and clinked in their cage. The jail door opened, and they ricocheted to the end of the table. Scrambled numbers popped up in my line of sight.

Then, in one of the biggest rushes I had ever experienced, both dice settled on four. Immediately, screams erupted from the table. I didn't realize others had taken notice of our bet and little altercation. Even the tables around us stopped to eye the commotion for a second. Hugs, cheers, and high fives were exchanged between the group and the other players. The guy next to us was like a stunned statue. It was unbelievable the energy generated from the win. Rick just stood there, stone-faced, as the dealer pushed him $8,500. Before we had digested what had just happened, he did something that sucked all the air right out.

"Ten." The dealer's head shot up and the rival's shot left, but Rick didn't even flinch. The rest of us watched in disbelief. Our euphoria turned to terror as he bet everything again.

"I'm going to make this hurt." He stared forward, but it was directed to the gentlemen next to us.

"Listen, man, don't be stupid. I mean, that was incredible; I was just giving you a hard time," he pleaded.

"Ahh, let me check on that bet," the dealer stuttered, then called over the floor manager. He whispered in his ear, and the manager nodded then strolled over to the table. Looming over it, he eyed Rick with suspicion. During this time, we begged and pleaded with Rick to reconsider, to take the money and run. He bet the house and won, and now he was about to risk it again. But Rick stood there expressionless. I wasn't sure if it was the alcohol, pride, or what, but I motioned Chris to do something about it. He was his roommate, after all. Chris made a feeble attempt, but there was no negotiation. Rick's mind was set. The floor manager eyed us with amusement.

"Well, sir, good luck," the manager sneered.

By this time, a larger group had gathered at the spectacle. I was nervous. No, I was scared enough to piss myself, but at the same time, I felt like an utter badass for being part of this bet. The intensity turned the space under my shirt into a sauna. All eyes were on us, and our eyes were on the dice. The odds were two to five, and the payout was five to nine. We needed a four and six or two fives from the dice. The rival, who had spurred Rick on before, had now become an ally, engaging with our small entourage like he was one of the group. Even he was pulling for the roll! He tentatively reached for the die.

As our new friend readied, I was losing my mind. The entire table was. My heart pumped violently, about to pop out of my chest. The roll rebounded off the end.

A four and two lay face up. Sighs were heard from around the table, with everyone relaxing for a minute while the dealers shuffled around the chips. The gauntlet came around a second time with even more anticipation than before. I was gasping for every breath. A brief pause, then the roll.

My breathing ceased. Fellow well-wishers huddled over and behind the table, feeding off the action. We stared at the dice hard enough to bend matter as they tumbled down the table. Everyone was silent, hoping our numbers popped up. The red cubes rebounded off the felt end and laid to rest near the opposite side. We couldn't see the results from where we stood. For a moment, nothing, and then cheers erupted from the end and surged immediately to us. A six and four appeared on the dice.

We went crazy. Arms flailed widely in the air accompanied by screams. I was pinballed around our circle of sweaty yellers, high-fiving any hand in my vicinity.

"I can't believe this," was all I could mouth while shaking my head and making eye contact with Mike. Hordes of people yelled with us and congratulated us on our payout. It was pure pandemonium from everyone but Rick, who stood arms extended against the table and head down.

Our ex-rival hugged and jumped his way right into our posse. Rick finally spun around, the biggest smile I've ever seen on one man's face.

"Well, boys, what did I say? Your luck can change just like that!" He bellowed something fierce as we let out our war cry and smothered him.

"You crazy bastard, Rick," Chris yelled. The dealer slid over almost $15,000 worth of chips and Rick paused.

"Snake—"

"No!" we screamed.

Rick wheeled back around. "Gotcha! Ha, ha, ha!" He let out a long string of laughter. "Relax, I'm not quite that crazy." He laughed excessively in what I could only guess was a spillover of emotion that finally rushed in.

We started taking turns pounding on him for almost losing it all. Our complimentary drinks soon arrived, and we polished them off while parading around the casino with our newfound wealth. We were drunk with power and felt like we ran the place. Intoxicated and overconfident, we lost $2,000 over the next hour. Finally stopping the bleeding around midnight, we celebrated our historic night with a bottle of champagne while getting rowdy in the lobby.

Drinks were comped, tips were plentiful, and laughs were nonstop. We could hardly have dreamed something so lucky, and we were going to make the most of it.

Eventually, we overstayed our welcome in the bar. The staff suggested we move our entourage to the nightclubs. By then, we had picked up a few ladies eager to mooch off our small fortune, but we didn't mind. We could do anything we wanted. We owned Vegas.

Hogging the sidewalk, we moved to a nightclub down the strip, where we were stopped by a bouncer. He pointed to a line of partygoers stretching down a ways. It wasn't the college bar bouncer that we were used to—a guy that lifted a dumbbell occasionally. This guy was a hulk. Muscles bulged out of his shirt sleeves, neck stiffer than a college mixer, his calves nearly the diameter of my torso. Our loud bunch was silenced by his towering presence, but then Slick Rick went into action.

"Listen, I'm going to make this easy," he said, slurring the "s."

"Rick, don't try to befriend him. This isn't amateur hour." I was cringing.

"We have a few newbies here, and I'm trying to show 'em a good time. How 'bout a table and a couple of midgrade bottles to start?" His appeal was sweetened by the pile of chips he placed into the behemoth's hand.

The bouncer looked down at the chips, his gaze then moving to the girls and finally, to me. I felt like a college freshman trying to get into a party as he stared into my soul. Was I going to get us rejected with my uncool? His stone face settled finally on Rick. If I thought he saw my soul, he was having a conversation with Rick's.

"Right this way." A smile broke way to a gesture inside.

We rushed in as another wave of excitement overtook us. The peasants waiting in line must have been jealous. The bouncer, whose name was Gus, barked at what must have been another worker.

"Put these newbies on the main floor," he barked at someone inside.

Chris took a sip of wine and tried to set the scene for Sandra. I was shaking my head, hoping he omitted some details.

"This gentleman escorted us in. The lights were overwhelming, the music overpowering. I was as dazed as I was mesmerized, and felt as in slow motion. Everyone in the place was in their own world.

"Anyway, we were brought to a large table where we took a second to allow the atmosphere to sink in. But once the first bottle arrived, it was time to party like none of us ever had before. It was like a movie. Women, booze, and money flew around in a blur." Chris was really getting into the story.

"Ya know, one minute, I look over, Rick has two dancers on him. The next minute, I look over, and he's ripping a line of coke. Needless to say, we may have indulged in a little ourselves."

"Chris!" Sandra was agitated as she slapped him across the arm. "You told me you never did drugs!"

"It was a long time ago, honey. I wasn't even a cop back then," he said defensively, "I don't even think I participated really; I was just drunk," his voice jumping near an octave.

Chris and I exchanged a cheeky smile as we held back a laugh, but Sandra met Chris with a cold stare. She wasn't done with the subject.

It was funny how details from a story that were long forgotten or omitted come to the surface eventually. Now was a good time for a beer break, and once we settled back down, I took back the storytelling. Didn't need more heat on Chris.

"The energy in Vegas had been invigorating, and it was a crazy few hours. I understood how people got wrapped up in the lifestyle; it was addictive. The energy, the love, the laughing. The ceiling had no limit. We nearly closed the club and stumbled out on the streets at like 4 a.m. We were lit off our asses. Chris and Trev had already puked, and I probably wasn't far behind.

"We were having a hoot wandering around the main Vegas drag, which was still semi-lively, until out of nowhere, a guy grabbed Rick's chip bag and bolted. Now luckily, the bouncer had suggested we keep the high-value chips safe and only keep the tipping chips in the bag because theft was common. It was only a couple hundred in there, but it didn't matter to me, I was drunk, and I was irate. Almost instinctually, I took off after the guy.

"Unfortunately for him, I finished third in the 400m at state in high school and was under the illusion I still had the speed of my youth. Adrenaline had masked my intoxication as I sprinted down the Vegas strip in pursuit. The streets were sparse enough at that time, so I could keep my eyes on the thief. I bobbed and weaved through the remaining partiers, and the occasional shove was needed.

"As I caught up to him, I felt my heart pulsing, racing. It felt really good. I felt like I could've chased him forever." It was the weekend of September 21, so it held extra significance.

"Within grasp, I started to tackle him as he began to turn to avoid a fountain. Unfortunately, he was slightly bigger than me, and it took a bit of an effort to take him down. He scuffled in a jog for a few feet, fighting hard to regain his balance and leverage. Suddenly, we slammed into the fountain and flipped over the edge. The last thing I remembered from the night was splashing into the water.

"I woke up to white lights that scalded my retina and blurry vision that took minutes to adjust. Panicked, but quickly realizing I was in jail, I rushed to my door and frantically called for a guard. Finally, one grudgingly showed up. His impertinence was evident.

"I was asking him where I was and why I was there. He was completely disinterested until he took a glance at my chart hanging outside the cell.

"Instantly, a smile emerged from his face. He told me Las Vegas detention center, detox room six. When I asked him what was so amusing, he told me the boys were talking about some Tarzan character, and I was him.

"I was like, 'Tarzan? My name is Nick!'

"He started flipping through the chart and told me that my friends would fill me in. They had been waiting a couple hours and just had to make sure I was awake and orientated before release.

"I couldn't for the life of me figure out what the Tarzan reference could have meant. Luckily, Rick had paid my fines, and it didn't take long before I was released to the crew. I was greeted like a hero.

"They swarmed me and asked how the accommodations were.

"'Well, if you want to sleep like they did in the Stone Age, then I couldn't recommend anywhere better.'

"On the taxi ride back to the hotel, they filled me in on the details of what happened. Apparently, after I tackled the thief, he left the spilled chips and fled. Once people realized what had happened, there were some claps and cheers.

"I took it as an invitation for an encore and climbed halfway up the fountain, taking my shirt off and letting out the war cry.

"They were too intoxicated to get me down and, instead, laughed their asses off along with the small crowd. Apparently, I got agitated when police tried to remove me from the fountain, and eventually, I was taken into custody. As I was being taken, my insensible screaming, including chest thumping like Tarzan, topped off the charade. Chris still claims to have never laughed harder in his life.

"All in all, I think Rick achieved his goal. Of the $15,000 he won, he left Vegas with $4,000. The nightclub had gouged out the majority, but it was well spent. I always wanted to go back, but I knew nothing could come close to that night. It exceeded any of our wildest imaginations, and we all took home some epic stories."

Just as the story was wrapping up, the timer went off, indicating the meatloaf was ready. Both kids came rushing in like race cars.

"Finally! Food, food, food. We're hungry, Mom!" they shouted. Damn, they were cute. So genuine and innocent. Their dimples concaved against their little cheeks.

"Boys, show some manners toward our guest. Calm down," Sandra said politely but sternly. As we settled into our seats and the feast was laid out before us, I began to feel like one of the rascals. "Just let me eat!" my mind was screaming.

Finally, after a short prayer, I was invited to dish up, and oh did I. Half my plate was occupied with meatloaf, the other with mashed potatoes topped with a generous amount of gravy. I saved a sliver of my plate for deep-broiled asparagus so I would be a good role model for the kids. That was about the only example I set. I wasted little time eyeing my meal before I gorged myself like a Mongol. Attila would have been proud.

The meatloaf melted in my mouth. Every chew brought out the sharp cheddar infused inside the juicy meat. My mouth dripped with greasy happiness. The kicker was the BBQ bacon glaze that was just unique enough to distinguish itself from the rest. It was a smoky BBQ, which was unexpected but complemented the sharp cheddar surprisingly well. A credit to Sandra's talent, the sauce wasn't too heavy as to pull too much flavor toward it. The bacon was peppered throughout the sauce, and every third bite or so, I was able to enjoy a piece. The bacon's sparing use allowed it to remain fresh and succulent. I ate myself into a food stupor; nothing but the greens remained on my plate. My satisfied look and belly pat communicated well enough that I enjoyed the meal, but I thanked Sandra profusely anyway.

"Well, that's why I married her!" Chris joked, causing another stare to shoot over from Sandra. He wasn't getting many brownie points tonight.

I asked for the recipe to change the subject, though I was sure I wouldn't be able to replicate the taste. We wrapped up the rest of the meal talking about the kids' days. Damion, the older one, had taken a field trip to see "Romeo and Juliet" at the theater. He complained it was boring, and I couldn't blame him. I was never one to enjoy theater. It wasn't usually so much the actors' abilities as I just couldn't get myself into the atmosphere of plays. Damion never stopped talking, but he was entertaining to listen to. He pinballed from one subject to another without even finishing his last thought. Interruptions from other family members were ignored or cut off as it only opened a new avenue for Damion to talk down.

Finally, Sandra cut him off and excused the two from the table. They rushed from their seats to whatever action figure or race car they were playing with before. I began helping put away dishes, but Sandra quickly shooed me away. So, Chris fetched us a couple more cold ones and we moved into the living room, relaxing into the cushions of the couch. It was fairly dark except for the light from a lamp illuminating Chris's face.

"Hey, Nick." His tone was relaxed. "Glad you got a sample from that guy. And I will look at the bloke who investigated the case, but doesn't sound like nothin' to me. Anything that can get you some closure I'm sure will feel… well… good? I mean, I know it's still painful for you, and I'll get this sample done as soon as possible. With that said, it might be a while before you get the results back. This DNA thing is pretty new, and the backup is substantial. It could take six to ten months for me to get the samples run." I had barely noticed he was leaning in close.

"Oh, no problem. Hey, at least it will get done." The words hung in the air, and I felt like I needed to add more.

"I don't want to get too sentimental here, but I really appreciate it. You're the closest friend I have. You're family, and knowing you… well, I owe you." My voice shook with adolescent awkwardness. I felt a hint of embarrassment being so emotional and took a sip of beer.

"You asked about my father, and you're right—it still hurts, I guess I've never dealt with it. I just continue to bury it," I confessed. "Sometimes…" A lump had started to form in my throat, and it was tough to talk. "Sometimes I deal with it in unhealthy ways." Chris inched closer from his side of the couch. He had a commanding demeanor, and it loomed over me; his presence was as a wise man and me a commoner. The weight of my sins was suddenly overpowering. I wanted to unload—I wanted to share the burden of the truth.

"Sometimes, I just want to hurt people that deserve it. The people that the law never got to. It feels so good, like a temporary release. That's okay, right? They deserve it." I hung my confessional out there in camouflage. I turned my tortuous eyes to Chris, hoping he could figure out what I was trying to tell him.

"I know, Nick, I know. I've watched it eating at you for years. I've never forgotten the pain I experienced from my father dying. It's something none of us can forget, but you gotta develop a way to move past it."

No, no, you missed it, Chris.

"I've told you this before, but I'm not going to dance any longer." I was about to tell him outright what kind of a vortex I put myself into each year.

Now he was the one who paused to take a drink. "How are you going to move past it, Nick?" Chris's voice startled me. I couldn't remember the last time I heard such aggression. "You walk around like the world owes you something, and it does, but it owes everyone. Being angry so long as to forget what it's like to be happy is embarrassing. You're better than that. It happened 17 years ago. You have to find a way to create happiness for yourself now. He's no longer here to create it for you." His words hung thick in the air, ringing through my ears. It gave me just enough time to come to my senses. I may have been about to give away too much if I shared my transgressions.

He exhaled, taking deep breaths. Beads of sweat formed on his forehead. His hand on my leg had become a squeeze, crushing my kneecap, which he released quickly once he looked down. I realized how stern and loudly he was talking to me when I noticed the kids staring at us from the other room. Chris merely had to take one look at them before they scrambled over each other to reach their sanctuary at the top of the stairs. I wanted to follow.

I stuttered something inaudible as I grasped for my thoughts. I felt frozen as they raced. Never had he been this stern with me. *I really do have a problem. Maybe Chris missed the bullseye, but he hit the target.* I looked into his eyes, looking for some escape, some hint of uncertainty in what he just said, but all that refracted was my own reflection. His face was stern. He had chosen his words carefully, and he had meant every one.

"Y-You're… r-right," I finally muttered.

Instantly, Chris's stern look broke and formed into a smile of a proud father. "I gotta change something," I fumbled out. Chris gave me a pat on the back. His momentary smile turned somber, and his voice became a comfort.

"Listen, I'm here for you, man, through anything. You know that as well as me. I don't want to beat you up, but you have to hear it. I've bit my tongue and danced around it too long. It's time for you to beat it, to beat the beast. Whenever you need an ear to listen, or better yet, a beautiful voice to listen to, don't hesitate." Chris's smile returned in full force. Even I managed one for a moment. It made the message all the more heartfelt that he tacked a shameless joke onto the end of it.

"Thanks, Chris. It means a lot." My mind was still recovering from the shock, racing for the right emotions to feel. "I have some thinking to do."

With that, I excused myself, thanked the two for the wonderful evening, and promised to call Chris later in the week. "I couldn't ask for anyone better," I said to Chris as I walked out the front door. Shuffling to my car, I sat down and stared ahead into the distance, into the steering wheel. *What just happened?* I asked myself. *I feel good but incomplete.* I knew that was as close as I could get to sharing with Chris the whole truth.

Once home, I opened up a bottle of rum and poured myself something strong. After a few sips of warmth, the alcohol turned sour. I left for the roof of the apartment complex with a chair. Plopping down, I gazed into the sky. *I need to change; I need something different.* I thought I was managing before the talk with Chris, but deep down, I knew I was lying to myself. I had lied to myself for a long time.

The stars were beautiful this time of night. The city lights blurred out many, but the darkest corners of the galaxy still shone brightly in the cloudless sky. The stars are nature's sketch board, and I experimented with them, forming my own constellations.

As I lay on the roof, one of my father's favorite sayings echoed in my mind, "The cheapest vacation is to close your eyes." I needed one, so I took a trip back to the days before his death when I was that energetic kid full of life. I was carefree, and the biggest choice I had during those days was whether to take a hot lunch or a cold one. I would joke and laugh spontaneously, never worrying about a thing. Shifting through memories of birthdays, holidays, and sports, I realized I had never been as happy as those early days. Why couldn't I be as happy now? There was no one to stop me but me.

I let the vivid images flow, eventually rising from my chair and drawing in a deep breath. Looking around the city, I let out a war cry, much like the one in Vegas. Shouting with all the air I had, I shattered the silence that shrouded me. I shattered myself. As the last whispers of my shout trailed off, I felt liberated, alive.

I began a long chuckle. That felt… fresh, but it was only the tip of the iceberg; there was plenty more in there. I grabbed my chair and walked to bed.

Chapter 10

Meeting my sister for lunch wasn't first on my to-do list, but she had asked, so I obliged. It wasn't that I didn't enjoy being with my sister; I did. We just didn't have that much in common. We weren't very close growing up, and that distance carried into adulthood. Despite that, when I saw her and the family for holidays, we always had a blast. Her husband wasn't in attendance much because of work, but her son Will and I always found some mischief to get into. I enjoyed being the cool uncle, and I didn't let that title go to waste. It became a Christmas tradition for us to plan a prank for someone at the party. We collaborated on who the victim would be and then drew up the battle plans. I usually provided most of the brain power, but Will carried out the deed.

Last year, we had our eyes on Aunt Edma. She was a humorous type, so I knew we could push the boundaries with the prank. After meeting to plan the target, Will and I had a little trouble brainstorming, probably since I was already a few drinks deep. So, I relied on Will; I mean, he was 10 years old by then and considered a "big boy." He could contribute.

While trying to conjure up ideas, I asked Will what he liked. It was a futile exercise until he said fireworks and the light bulb went off. *Fireworks!* We took the idea and ran with it. At first, he suggested using the party poppers lying on the kitchen counter—the ones that explode confetti. Now, though they were amusing, we needed something bigger, something crazier. Being a little intoxicated, I wanted to test the limits. While searching the basement, we found our answer: firecrackers.

At that point, the wheels really started turning as I became giddy with excitement. Will was a little surprised (and concerned) when I first showed him, but he quickly warmed up to the idea with some encouragement. The explosives were the small outlet type, not the caliber to shave off a finger. I recruited Will to steal the cake from the counter and Aunt Edma's present from under the tree. He went full spy stealth mode, peeking around corners. He was James Bond in the flesh. Ducking, diving, and crawling his way around, he retrieved the supplies I asked for, and I praised him like a proud general.

"Nice job, recruit! You've been promoted to captain," I told him. He beamed back at me and promised not to disappoint. I have always been jealous of children's imaginations. Why did that ever have to leave people? I studied my materials and began the construction of Operation Cake Bomb, or OCB for short. Will drew up the battle plans while I worked.

Carefully opening Aunt Edma's present, a slow cooker that I was going to gift to her, I replaced it with the cake Will so skillfully stole. Once the cake was in the box, I pushed the firecracker into the middle, making sure to cover all but the fuse and trying to smooth over the frosting. It was a smaller firecracker, so I hoped there was a low risk of injury. I closed the box, rewrapped the bomb, and then laughed something evil. I felt like a mad scientist, and Will was my assistant. We put the box back in its place under the tree and waited, the anticipation mounting as the minutes dragged on. I could hardly contain myself, and I could tell Will was just as excited as me. He kept tugging at his mom's blouse, asking when "present time" was. I knew I would get a little backlash for being such a bad influence on the kid, but it would all be worth it.

Finally, the time to open the presents came. No one had even noticed the missing cake, as there were more desserts than people. I waited patiently for Aunt Edma's turn. Of course, she was last, but it would be like a grand finale. Will eyed me with a grin as she unwrapped the box. Lifting the treat up, she looked puzzled.

"Thanks for the cake, Nick, but I'm fairly certain this was the cake Abigail brought for the party," she chuckled.

"Ha, ha, I know, but light the candle, close your eyes, and make a wish. It's all part of the present," I responded. I could barely keep from laughing. She shrugged again, looking confused, but asked someone to grab her a lighter from the kitchen drawer. Will enthusiastically volunteered and bolted to fetch it. Many a year, someone in the family conjured up an elaborate gag gift, so instead of garnering suspicion, everyone was probably curious. When he returned, Aunt Edma did as instructed; she lit the "candle" and closed her eyes. Will watched eagerly. I wondered what she wished for, but I was certain it wasn't what happened next. There were a couple of dead giveaways that, if she had looked closely, would've raised her suspicion that what she was lighting was not a candle. If she had kept her eyes open, she would've seen the wick disappear too quickly to be a candle.

The "candle" burned down quickly with a hiss, disappearing below the surface of the cake. It felt like an eternity, even though, in reality, it had only been a couple of seconds. For a split moment, I was worried it wouldn't go off, but then the firecracker exploded in what sounded like a muffled gunshot. Cake was blasted straight up into poor Aunt Edma's face. It hit her with force, and the splatter flew a few feet. Luckily, it was a tall box, so much of the cake was contained inside, but it went just how I imagined.

I looked at Will, mouth agape but smiling. That little rascal was about to get away with murder. It was dead silent as the cake settled on her face and the floor around her. Then I began to laugh, quickly joined by Will and a few other males at the party as they realized what had just happened. The women at the party quickly ran to console the cake-faced Edma, but she began laughing… *hysterically*. Her laughing reinforced our laughing, and soon, the whole room was in an uproar. As the chaos settled, Edma asked who did it, like she needed a hint, and I motioned for Will to take the glory. Had the reactions been negative, I would've stepped forward, but he deserved his moment in the spotlight. He wanted everyone to know that he was Captain Will. So, for the rest of the evening, he was referred to as the captain. While Aunt Edma got cleaned up, I came forth with her slow cooker as a peace offering. She said the cake bomb was gift enough.

"I haven't laughed like that in as long as I can remember. That was just so… needed." She held a beaming smile. The rest of the night was a hoot, and to this date, it was one of the best family gatherings I can remember.

I was still laughing to myself thinking about Operation Cake Bomb as I pulled up to the quaint café to meet with my sister. As I walked over to the building, I took a deep breath and prepared myself for the rich-housewife atmosphere. Opening the door, the bright colors bombarded my senses. My eyes adjusted and I scanned the tables, spotting my sis along the wall. Her eyes caught mine and we exchanged a quick smile. Making my way to the table, I noticed how well dressed she was. She wore a rose sundress with lace covering her knees. She had plenty of makeup, a designer purse, and too much jewelry for 1 p.m., but I guess she had to keep up appearances. She greeted me with a hug.

"Hey, sis." The embrace gave me a whiff of perfume. The smell was strong but lovely.

"It's been a while," I said as I sat down. "What's the occasion?"

"Oh, no occasion. We just never see each other." She hung her purse strap on the chair. "And I know this time can be hard for you," she said, looking at me, searching for some indication on what I thought about her bringing it up.

"Thanks, it usually is, but I think it's going to be getting a lot better. I've been working on it. Chris and I talked about it, among other things, and... well, I won't get into it, but I'm good."

Before she could respond, a waitress came by asking about drinks. Ann ordered a piña colada, and I ordered water. The waitress smiled and quickly started off to fill our orders.

She raised her eyebrows in surprise at my answer. I never said anything more than "fine" because I couldn't lie. It felt pretty good to be honest.

"So, hey! How's the family?" I asked.

"Nick, no rum and coke?" my sister asked, puzzled.

"Nope," I chuckled. "Not before 5 p.m. anymore. And you know it's Dr. Pepper. Though I see you're starting early."

She gave me another furrowed look. "What's gotten into you, huh? Where's Nick?" She was smiling suspiciously like I was an imposter or something.

"He's still here, sis. I'm just feeling great, that's all. You think it's bad?"

"Oh no, no. I think it's a good thing. You seem like... hmm, I can't put my finger on it, but it's a good thing." She smiled, and the conversation shifted back to her family.

"The family is busy. Between Nate's job, my job, Will's soccer, and school, I feel like I have no time. I wish Nate would cut back on work. It seems like he isn't there all the time to father Will. It's not his fault entirely, he's supporting the family." I sensed the heaviness in her voice.

"Like this Saturday with the amusement park. He was disappointed he couldn't make it. I genuinely could tell that, but if he truly wanted to, he would make time," she said, playing with her nails as she looked down. The acrylic chipped off her ring finger, and she adjusted in her seat.

"I'm really grateful you're coming. Will always has a blast with you, and I think you do, too. I'm not sure I've ever seen you laugh so much as when you two exploded cake in Aunt Edma's face last Christmas."

My sister continued on with stories about Will's soccer games and what he was doing in school. She had always been the talker in the family. She could go an entire meal having a one-sided conversation. I could remember some breakfasts where she would talk from the table to the door, barely letting my dad get in a word. This was a fortunate thing because I was the quiet type, which was also probably a blessing for my parents because otherwise, it would have driven them off a cliff. If our drinks hadn't arrived, I'm sure she would've talked for another hour straight. When it came time to order, I realized that I was lucky I ate beforehand because soups, salads, and skimpy sandwiches that were basically salads between bread crowded the menu. I ordered the meatiest item I could find: Caesar salad with extra chicken. How this overpriced salad bar managed decent business was beyond me.

Collecting our menus, the waitress complimented me on my choice and then disappeared into the kitchen. My sister began to fill me in on the details for Saturday.

"Nick... Nick, you listening?" Her voice brought my attention from some mom booty at the counter. I nodded my head *yes*. She treated me like a child sometimes. "Okay, so the plan is to arrive at Wild Springs amusement park at 10 a.m. sharp. Will is finally tall enough to ride the big coasters, so I'm sure he will want to hit those. Um, dress appropriately." I rolled my eyes.

"OK, OK, well I guess that's it. Meet us at our house at a reasonable time. And don't worry about bringing a present. Will doesn't need to be spoiled anymore," she finished, giving me a moment to clarify or ask questions. Anita the planner always needed everything organized and functioning smoothly.

"Sounds good, sis. I'll be there!" I assured her. She looked at me skeptically, so I poked back, "Oh, come on now, have some faith." Her expression remained unchanged.

"Ugh, fine. I won't drink Friday night, so I'll be sure to be there on time," I relented.

"Just what I wanted to hear," she beamed.

We then turned the conversation toward work. She was contemplating leaving her part-time job to free up more time for Will. It wasn't an issue of money, but she always liked being busy and productive. Turning into a housewife could drive her to insanity. I suggested that she take a week off and test it out. She at least owed herself that much. A level of interest in following through with my advice appeared to be there. She seemed to give it serious thought and was able to mull it over further as our food arrived.

Now, I'm never one for salads, but the foliage was a delicious surprise. The lettuce was crisp, the chicken was broiled and seasoned quite well. The dressing blended everything together, and I was actually quite satisfied with the meal. My sister stared at me.

"Who are you really?" she said, her eyes wide. I looked up, lettuce dribbling out of my mouth, dressing clinging to my lips.

We both laughed, with me choking on a leafy green that hurled down my esophagus like a wind tunnel as I bellowed. I told her sometimes trying something new can surprise you. She scoffed at that.

"Whatever you say, Nick." She shook her head.

As we ate, Ann asked about our mother. I told her I had visited her last month, and she encouraged me to visit again this week.

"She's lonely, Nick, and hurting. The least we can do is visit her once a week," she pleaded. Although I sighed, she was right. There was no excuse. I promised to see Mom tomorrow. Ann always got her way. As lunch lingered on, I started to feel worse about the fact I wasn't visiting her much. After heart surgery, she had trouble recovering and had spent the last few months in a nursing home. It had been difficult for her to suspend the freedom of living in her own home at such a young age. I mean, she was only 60 years old, though doctors were confident she could make a full recovery.

My mother was a docile person, though I had seen fits of anger, like the time she had hit my dad with a pan during an argument. I was so terrified that when she came to apologize later, I hid under my bed ready with a slingshot and grazed a polished rock against her cheek when she bent down to get me. But for the most part, she really held things together when times were tough. When my father passed, she was a rock. My sister was a drug addict, and my mom forced her into rehab, all while juggling the funeral and my delinquency. She never flinched, and I wasn't sure she even mourned. Perhaps she didn't have time. After my sister got out of rehab, my mother held down two jobs, still kept us in line, then shipped us off to college. Maybe the stress over those years contributed to her ailing heart. I loved her, even though there were very few bonding moments. She gave me every opportunity at a great life.

"Yeah, sis. I'm sorry I haven't seen Mom for a while. It's just hard for me to see her like that. But you're right. She was there for us; I should be there for her," I confessed sheepishly.

Ann grabbed my shoulder. "She'd love that." She looked down at her wrist.

"Say, wow, time went by faster than I thought. I gotta head out to pick up Will from soccer. I'll see you Saturday, right?" She started to rise from the table, scrambling through her purse for cash.

"Oh, c'mon! Yes, you will! Jeez, I'll see you Saturday. No hangover, promise," I chuckled back. Man, she was relentless.

We left a sizable tip on the table and departed—her in her minivan and me in my beauty. It turned heads even in this ritzy neighborhood, and I loved it.

When I got home, I immediately called my mom at the nursing home, informing her of my impromptu visit tomorrow. She sounded tired but perked up as the conversation continued. She asked if I could bring her some real food because the nursing home served food she claimed tasted like woolly mammoth anus. She still had her spunk. I conveyed my sympathy over the anus and told her I would stop by Burger King on the way over for a Triple Whopper with fries and a large Coke. I probably could've been charged with attempted murder for giving it to her, but showing up empty-handed wasn't an option. If she wanted the food, I sure wasn't going to stop her. She was a tough bird, and it would take more than heart surgery and a few Whoppers to take her down.

I decided to grab a couple of beers at the bar, then left for Cyrus Park. It was early evening, and the sun was beginning to settle in the sky. It cast a beautiful shadow across the fountain. The park was fairly busy, with a group of children and their moms enjoying the playground and quite a few couples walking their dogs. I really enjoyed dogs and loved their loyalty and their affection—they were always excited to see you regardless of who you were or what you did. I had always wanted to get a dog. A big husky would be ideal. I toyed with the idea in my head while playing with a loose splinter on the bench. Why couldn't I get a dog? No one was stopping me. Why was I restricting myself? So, right then and there, I decided I would pick one up the next day after lunch with Mom. The declaration brought a surge of excitement and anticipation.

Later, I was feeling anxious, so I decided to brainstorm a name for my soon-to-be companion. I scribbled out a list and pitted them against each other like a tournament bracket. After much deliberation and second-guessing, I settled on the name Buster. Picking a name cemented my decision. It was impossible to renege now as I imagined little Buster running around. It made for a difficult night's sleep. I tried everything: milk, a nightcap, counting sheep, but nothing was working. I spent hours, eyes alert behind the shade of my eyelids, until, mercifully, I dozed off in the morning.

The next morning started like any typical morning... except I couldn't get Buster off my mind. I wasn't sure what he even looked like, but I could picture us on walks and playing fetch. I skipped coffee as my excitement masked my sleep deprivation. I made a quick stop at the pet store on my way to my mom's and bought a few accessories—a collar, a leash, food, treats, and toys—further cementing my decision. I almost purchased an indoor dog bathroom but reeled myself in from the impulse buy. I didn't want any excuse for Buster not to adore me. Even without the indoor bathroom, I left the store feeling I was well-equipped and on my way to becoming the best dog owner this side of the Mississippi.

Heading to my mother's, I was expecting a little awkwardness. Meaning, I wasn't sure what we were going to talk about. We could converse about my soon-to-be best-bud Buster, but I was sure the conversation would turn stale pretty quick after that. The last thing I needed was an awkward silence, which would no doubt be accompanied by her asking if I had found a "keeper" yet. Either way I answered, I'd be bombarded with questions and advice like I was a wayward teen searching for his first relationship.

The nursing home she was recovering at was rather nice. My mother had money, and my sister pitched in. Insurance covered some, but not much. The place was named Eternal Residences. It's kind of a sick name if you think about it. At the front lobby, I was greeted by a receptionist and asked for Eloise Schlosser. My mom had taken back her maiden name after my dad died. She politely responded, "Room 223," and pointed me in the direction of the elevator. Thanking her, I scribbled on the sign-in sheet and strode through the lobby, catching a few stares from the elderly residents along the way. I'm sure they could smell the delicious food I carried with me. Before arriving at my mother's room, I was stopped by a staff member.

"You must be Nick! Hi, I'm Sue." Her nametag read CNA. "I look after your mom, and she told me you'd be stopping by." She eyed the Burger King in my hand like a bomb. "Ahh, I hope that food is for you. Your mom is on a restricted diet. You're not trying to kill her, right?" Her tone was serious, but she acted playful.

"No worries. It's for me. She won't get a bite," I responded with a smirk. Sue thanked me and then scurried off to deal with a patient in need of assistance. Nursing homes always have an odd smell. It was a scent of its own. The reverse of the new baby smell. The odor wasn't the only unsettling thing. I had never seen so many people sleeping during the middle of the day. The main dining area had a quarter of the residents being fed by staff, another quarter eating slowly, and about half in a purgatory stupor between groggy and passed out. I knew that would never be me. Walking into my mom's room, I received a fresh burst of nursing home as well as perfume. She was sitting in her living room on a recliner, enjoying daytime television. When she saw me, her face lit up.

"Nick, I'm so glad to see you. It's been so long!" We shared a long embrace. She looked tired, and although she was enthusiastic to see me, it was evident she needed more recovery time. "How are things going? Anything exciting to share?" She was eager to hear anything.

"Ah, well, I'm going to get a dog today." I decided to throw that out right away. "A Husky, to be exact. I'm going to name him Buster."

"Oh my, wow, that was unexpected." She was a little taken back, resting her hand on her chest. "What on earth compelled you to decide that?"

"Well, you've known I've always wanted one, and the apartment was getting a little lonely. Seemed like a perfect fit."

My explanation received a warm smile from her, "If it matters to you at all, I think it's a great choice. Whatever dog you pick will be lucky." Now she was exaggerating a bit, but it made me feel assured regardless.

"Thanks, Mom. I'll be sure to bring him by."

Her attention then turned to the contents in my hand. I handed over her favorite order. She was grateful for the delivery of "real" food. Like processed, genetically modified substances thrown together in a grease chamber counted as "real," but who am I to say otherwise? While she gobbled it down, she asked how I was doing since it was around the time dad died, and she knew it was hard for me.

"Surprisingly well," I answered. She looked at me like I had just told her that the moon landing was staged. "I'm not kidding. Chris and I talked, and I've done a little soul searching. I have a long way to go, but I believe I'm off to a good start."

Mom stared proudly at me, "You have no idea what joy it brings me hearing that from you. I tried forever to break through but couldn't. You needed to discover it yourself. And Chris, I'm not sure where you would be without him. Honestly, he's probably the best thing that's ever happened to you." I looked at her and nodded. She was right regarding that. My mom cleared her throat, leaning forward in her chair.

"Listen, Nick. I know you have the fondest memories of your father, but it wasn't all roses. You only remember the good, but there was plenty of shit."

"Mom, not right now," I interrupted, putting my hand up, "I don't really want to hear it. I know you two had problems sometimes." My feeble protest wouldn't stop her from saying what she wanted.

"Nick, stop ignoring the truth. He cheated on me, for Christ's sake. Don't be naive. He wasn't an angel. A great father, no doubt, but a great husband he was not…" her voice trailed off, and a silence encased the room. I found it difficult to look at my mom and difficult to find my breath.

"I know. I've heard it all before. Let's just drop the subject," I said. My mom's saddened expression looked down on me. I thought she regretted saying what she had, but she needn't be.

I broke up the conversation with a trip to the restroom, and upon returning, I focused on talking about the puppy. I also told her I was going to the amusement park with Will and Ann.

"Fun Uncle Nick," Eloise chuckled at herself.

"You two were something special when planning those pranks. You know he really looks up to you."

"Yeah, I know. Sometimes we get a little too carried away. Maybe I'll regulate myself this Christmas, make sure we don't go overboard."

We finished up an episode of *Jeopardy* with Alex Trebek. Man, the elderly loved him. I told her as entertaining as the silver fox was, I had to run to pick up my new companion. A hint of dejection ran across her face.

"Do stop by soon, Nick. I really enjoyed it," she pleaded.

"I was thinking sometime next week," I offered. "By then, I hope I'll have Buster a little under control." Mom seemed very receptive to the idea, agreeing with an eager nod.

We gave each other one last hug and kiss, then I slipped out into the hallway, walked by rows of zombified elderly, and left for an address outside Trenton that was selling Husky puppies.

I had brought along a small kennel for transport, but upon arrival, I decided there was no way Buster was going in a cage. The property was a small farm that I had to bob and weave through the backroads to find. The ad in the paper gave a lot of details; otherwise, it would've been some challenge. The dirt road I drove up was laced with potholes filled with muddy water from yesterday's rain. It pained me something fierce to watch the mud splatter against the pristine siding of my car. The waft of fresh manure leached through my windows. Buster was worth it.

I met the owner, a rather skinny and well-groomed fellow. He told me there were only a couple left and that they were going fast. He brought me to the back porch where he let the parents out, both of which were large and beautiful, their coats fluffy masterpieces.

Yep, there was the shedding. My hand was coated. Of the three that had yet to be sold, two were female and Buster was a male name, so my choice was easy. Picking up my pup melted my heart a little. His tail wagged fiercely against his backside. The little bud had a white face with black around the eyes. The rest of his fur was black, with white near his paws. The owner could sense my instant fondness.

"$1,000, and he's yours," He proposed. The offer struck me as odd. The ad in the paper asked for $700.

He stared me down, and it took me a second to come up with a counteroffer. $1,000 was quite a bit, but he had me. He told me that he got $750 for the others, and since there were only three left, he needed to raise the price. I wasn't going to leave without Buster, so we finally settled on $800, although I would have paid his $1,000 if he didn't budge. It sure felt like a lot when I shelled out the money, but I was confident Buster was worth it watching the dopey pup fumble around.

I walked to my muddied car with the new member of my household, his fluffy fur a soft pillow in my arms. I couldn't wait to get him home. The owner warned me that shedding would be rampant, but that wasn't of concern to me. Sliding into my car, I placed the little fella in the passenger seat. Already strands of hair whirled around the cabin and prominently showed against the dark interior. Almost as safe as a cage, the passenger seat was slanted at an angle that ensured Buster would stay put. He was only a month old and still finding his bearings walking.

We drove off, Buster by my side. I couldn't help but feel a sense of accomplishment. It was the first time I had responsibility for anyone but myself, and the feeling made me feel important, valued.

Arriving back home, I rushed the pup up to my apartment. I held the little fella cozily, giving him a tour of his new home. After the tour ceased, I rested him in his recently purchased dog bed, as I'm sure he was exhausted. I watched him nestle and nod his way to a comfortable position, finally settling into a slumber, his head cocked sideways while the rest of his body lay flat. How peaceful and cute he looked at that moment.

How could people abuse such an innocent and defenseless animal—or any animal in that case? I had seen animal abuse first-hand about five years ago while visiting a dog breeder with Chris to pick out a new puppy for his family. We hadn't understood the less-than-ideal conditions some of the dogs were living in until we showed up looking to buy a dog. We had been disgusted at the overcrowding, the filth, and what looked like malnourishment and disease.

There were clearly abused and neglected dogs among the older, unadopted dogs, while all the cute newborns were in front on display. They didn't try very hard to hide some of their abusive practices. I guess they didn't think their customers gave a damn as long as their pup was healthy and cute. It made Chris and me sick. We left disturbed and called a few numbers trying to highlight the abuse to those who had authority, but our pleas didn't make much headway. The only comfort was that they were "looking into it." A common excuse was they had few resources and too many places to investigate, which was probably true. Chris and

I fumed about the issue for a few weeks but realized there was nothing we could do.

Well, nothing that Chris could do.

I decided I couldn't idly stand by while someone abused these animals. September 21st was fast approaching. The breeders were going to get a taste of their own medicine.

Visiting the mill again, I gained information on the owner from the business cards they had on the front counter. I had learned from previous years that I needed to be thorough in my research. From the business card, I called the owner's number that night from a payphone. I took a deep breath and readied myself as my fingers punched in the buttons. It was three rings before a gruff voice answered the phone.

"Hello?" the voice answered.

"Good evening, Mr. Kubicek. Sorry to bother you at such a time, but I visited your kennel about a month ago and have been writing a research paper on animal breeding for The College of New Jersey. I was hoping I could ask you a few questions?" I rattled off the little spiel I prepared. I presented myself as confident and respectful, but I thought I rushed it a bit.

There was a pause then I quickly interjected.

"Oh, I apologize; I forgot to introduce myself. My name is Scott Simmons."

Why not heap on the lies.

"Ah yeah, sonny, listen." He sounded polite but disinterested. "I'd love to help you out, but I wouldn't know what to tell ya. I own a few businesses and only recently bought that business. I've pretty much left everything to my general manager. You're welcome to call him, though." Anything he could say to get me off the phone.

I told him I would take him up on that offer, and he rattled off the GM's number. Richard Sinclair was his name, and abusing animals appeared to be his game. I thanked the owner, and although I'm sure he wasn't completely absolved from guilt, the main culprit was no doubt the GM, Mr. Sinclair.

After I hung up the phone, I was relieved I did at least *some* digging before jumping to conclusions.

A few days off work were in order so I could sort out the details, and trailing his car from work gave me a start. At night, I sifted through his garbage and mail. It appeared he lived alone. No girlfriend or kids. It didn't surprise me much that Sinclair was a loner. It also made my job much, much easier.

My stomach churned when I discovered he owned a dog himself. I'm sure he didn't treat his dog any better—probably worse. The dog also complicated matters, and it took some time to figure out how I would deal with it. After stalking the house for a couple of nights, I observed that Sinclair let his dog outside before bed and would leave her there for the night. The mutt had to be neutralized, but I couldn't kill the dog. Other than being against my morals, it would be religious-level hypocrisy.

The following day, I headed to the local library. I spent most of the morning researching how tranquilizer is produced and how to make it. Four books in, I found a source with specific amounts, but I had to do some math to scale it to the dog's size. Hopefully, that was how it worked.

Since I couldn't let my purchase of tranquilizer darts and chemicals raise suspicion, I drove to upstate New York to make my purchases. The clerks helped me acquire the needed supplies, and I made certain to pay in cash. After stopping at a nearby hardware store to grab a few more necessities, I was geared up. This revenge would require quite a bit of finesse. I brought home the tranquilizer and practiced shooting it across the apartment. I actually wasn't a bad shot, and after a short bit, felt fairly proficient with it. I would wait till the dog laid down for the night then I would have a steady target. It helped that I would have five shots to hit him. I even worked the gun in the dark to make the situation more realistic.

September 21st came fast. It was a glorious fall day. Clear skies, sunny, with a stiff breeze.

I started with my usual morning routine and then coasted through work. I had brought my needed supplies in the trunk and made sure I didn't touch any of it without gloves.

Waiting till dusk, I killed time relaxing in Cyrus Park, taking in the beautiful day. The wind was just strong enough that a couple of families were flying kites. One father and son duo caught my attention. Their kite was homemade and shaped like a baseball. The two operators were having trouble getting the thing in the air. The kid, who was no older than 10, would bolt through the park holding the kite and enthusiastically toss it, hoping to catch the wind. Unfortunately, the breeze wouldn't catch, and time after time, the kite would fall back to the ground. Discouraged, he would mope back to his dad, kite in tow. His dad would kneel and whisper something. Instantly, the child would giggle, and the frown would change to a gleaming smile. With a little pat on the back, the kid would take off again across the park, giving the kite another chance to fly. On the fourth attempt, the kid sprinted right past the bench where I was sitting and chucked the baseball into the air. Momentarily, a strong gust gave him hope, but the momentum subsided and, yet again, the kite didn't take flight. I could tell the kid was pretty discouraged as he shuffled back toward his dad. I stopped him in front of my bench.

"Hey, kid." His head snapped toward my direction. "If you and your dad get that kite in the air on the next try, I'll give you a few bucks to buy an ice cream." I motioned to the stand across the park.

His eyes instantly lit up, "Really? Can my dad have an ice cream too?" I nodded *yes*, and the kid took off toward his partner.

I watched him bolt back. This time the kid whispered in his dad's ear, both glancing over at me. Now the biggest smile was on the dad's face. This was a challenge.

Then, to my surprise, they switched roles. Either the kid really wanted ice cream, or the dad wasn't about to lose a bet. I was still doubtful the kite would fly. A baseball wasn't exactly the most aerodynamic.

As the dad took off across the park, the kid yelled in anticipation and excitement. I found myself entertained by the sight of a grown man in a dead sprint across a crowded field. He was focused, sprinting like he was on a mission. Blowing past my bench, he launched the baseball into the air.

It hung for a split second, the white outside rippling under the force of the wind.

Then, miraculously, the kite caught, climbing quickly in the sky. The dad looked as surprised as I did, and the kid was shouting with joy.

Panting heavily, the man walked over to where I sat and took a seat. He looked back at his son.

"Looks like you owe us a couple of cones. I like mint chocolate chip," he chuckled, then turned toward me.

"I'm Marcus, but call me Mark. And that over there is my son Preston." He produced his hand for a firm shake.

"Nice to meet you two. I'm Nick. That was quite the show." Mark nodded along. "I saw you guys struggling, and I thought I'd make things interesting. I have to say, I was fairly surprised that thing got up."

"You aren't the only one," he said, and we both laughed at that.

Suddenly, a panicked shout pierced our ears, "Dad! Dad! Help!"

Our heads whirled around. It was Preston. He stood empty-handed, pointing toward the sky. Apparently, he didn't have the best grip, and the baseball kite was quickly gaining altitude. We watched as it slowly disappeared from sight. A distraught Preston made his way over to where we stood. He appeared to be on the verge of crying.

"Oh, bud, it's alright. I'm not mad." Mark brought him into an embrace. "We can make another one," he offered

"No! I liked that one," he asserted.

"Well, then we'll have to make a better one, son." He patted him gently on the back. Mark must have been charmed or amused by his son because he was smiling through the embrace.

"A better one?" Preston sniffled, and it appeared he was calming down. "You promise? And what about ice cream?"

Now, it was my turn.

"Well, seeing that the kite made it in the air, the offer still stands." A beaming smile emerged from the pouty frown. The lost kite was now an afterthought.

"Let's go right now!" he exclaimed. "C'mon, dad!" He tugged at his dad's sleeves. I started to pull out my wallet.

"OK, OK, hold up," Mark said. He turned in time for me to hand him a ten, holding up my end of the bargain. He took it reluctantly.

"You know you really didn't have to," he conceded.

I just shrugged.

"Well, why don't you at least grab some with us then?"

I hesitated, trying not to convey a weird level of eagerness.

"Yeah, sure. Why not?" I conceded. "I don't think I've ever turned down ice cream before, and it's not about to start today." I got a quick smile from Mark, and then we headed off to the stand. Both of us had to almost jog to keep up with the rascal.

"Where was this speed when you were running with the kite?" his dad joked.

At the stand, Mark bought his mint chocolate chip, and Preston picked vanilla. I decided to have mint chocolate chip also. I never had much of a taste for it, but I thought I'd give it another shot.

"Nice choice, Nick. You a big fan?" Mark asked.

"Oh yeah, I love it. Best flavor out there," I shot back.

We grabbed spots at a picnic table to enjoy the treat. Mark and I started talking as Preston's attention was torn between the other kites still in the air and his waffle cone. I found out that he lived with the kid and his mom in a suburb nearby. He and his son frequented the park, usually to play catch. Baseball was Preston's favorite sport, if it wasn't already evident from the kite. He himself was a Philly fan. I gave him a hard time about that, but he had some rebuttal once he found out I was a Mets diehard.

We continued the small talk. It was a while before I noticed that the air had gotten chillier and the sun lower. I had lost track of time, preoccupied with Mark's stories. He just had a way of making everything sound interesting. Dusk was setting in. My meticulous timetable was in jeopardy, and I rushed to wrap up the conversation, informing Mark that I had to run. I told him I hoped to run across them sometime again and regretted having to leave mid-story. He seemed to understand, saying it was nice meeting me, and he'd keep an eye open for me next time he was in the park. I parted with Mark and the kid and swiftly made my way to the car.

I sped down the interstate, letting the horses run wild. The radio blared, fueling my brazen law-breaking. The freeway was still crowded from rush hour, but I managed to weave my way through traffic. Cruella de Vil had nothing on me.

I wanted to get near Sinclair's house by dark, so I could find the place easily. Not doing so added an unnecessary variable. I cursed myself for losing track of time. I was an hour behind schedule, even with the speeding.

Squinting at the poorly lit streets and landmarks, I finally pulled up to the house at 8 p.m. Sunset was at 7 p.m., and by now, it was almost completely black. I parked off the curb across the street from his house to begin the waiting game. It didn't take more than 20 minutes for me to become a little paranoid with the number of cars driving by. It wasn't like my vehicle blended in, especially in this neighborhood.

I felt more comfortable parking a couple of blocks away, which meant I had to stake the place out on foot.

While pacing the surrounding blocks, new worries crept into my consciousness. The dilapidated area and eerie quietness didn't bode well for my nerves. Neighbors could be nosey or notice me as an oddity in the neighborhood. The more I blended in, the better.

If the neighborhood didn't give off a very welcoming vibe, neither did Richard Sinclair's house. It was small with a large yard, which sloped slightly down toward the road. A poorly fenced area accompanied the side of the house where the dog slept. The neighbors' houses weren't as close as I feared, but nothing like what would be ideal.

The lawn wasn't very well kept, as there was no landscaping except a sickly-looking pine off to the corner. I couldn't tell which area of the property was covered with grass and which was weed. Evidently, Sinclair had as much difficulty taking care of his lawn as he did taking care of dogs.

After a couple of hours, I witnessed Sinclair shoo his dog outside and, shortly after, turn the lights off. I still decided to give him a couple of hours in order to ensure he was asleep.

I moved back to my car again, parking closer, nestling it against the curb a couple of houses down. A tick after 1 a.m., I stepped out of the car and popped the trunk. Then I crept alongside his house, tranquilizer and darts in hand. I felt exposed by the moonlight as I scurried across the open lawn. It made it feel as if there had to be someone watching me, ready to call the police. Simply being out at this hour made me suspicious. Add to that the ski mask, black coat, and black sweats and I looked completely criminal.

I used the neighbor's foliage in the form of thick hedges alongside the house for cover as I navigated the space between the hedge and house until I finally reached a point with a direct line of sight to the dog. I was careful not to approach too close. The last thing I needed was the dog waking up.

I focused on my rifle and loaded her up, taking my time at every step. The gun's name was Betsy, I decided, and I was about to put my faith in her. Lifting her up, I whispered a few words of encouragement to Betsy and stabilized my aim.

Deep breath, I thought as I steadied myself, my hands sweating profusely inside my gloves. I held my breath as my finger tugged against the trigger.

The dart lasered into the fenced area. I lowered the gun and waited a moment. I couldn't tell if I hit my mark. No movement or sound. I had to have missed.

"Damn it," I had hit this shot a dozen times at the apartment. Wasting no time, I reloaded and brought Betsy against my shoulder. Not as patient anymore, I let another shot rip.

This time, I heard it click against the fence. I couldn't believe I was missing.

A moment of panic began to set in. The unfathomable was becoming a possibility. What if I missed all five shots?

Perhaps if I got just a little closer, then it would be a sure shot.

On this reload, I took my time and rallied myself for the shot. I stared down my target as I went through my aiming progression and raised Betsy once again. I was creeping just a few steps closer to make the shot easier when

"SNAP!" a large twig broke underneath my right foot.

"Shit, shit, shit." I froze in the moonlight. The mangled twig strained beneath my boot as I watched the dog for movement. A few breaths passed, and I thought I was in the clear. But at that moment, when I lifted my foot, letting the twig relax, the dog perked up and scanned the yard for the source of the sound. I made sure not to move a muscle. I posed frozen so long my muscles started to ache. Finally, he put his head back down, and I allowed myself to exhale.

I counted my lucky stars that he didn't bark, and I began to retreat slowly back to my original spot.

A second twig snapped under my foot. This time there was no scanning. The damn dog bolted toward the fence and let out one piercing and frightening bark.

In hindsight, he probably couldn't see me, but I panicked and bolted back to the neighbor's brush. Now he saw me. At my retreat, he started going crazy. Barking so loud that I was sure it could be heard all the way from the police station. They were probably sending the police that very second. I could physically feel the dog's bark as it echo-located me.

I laid crouched behind a large bush, hugging the neighbor's house. Quivering, I wanted to sink right into the ground and disappear. The damn dog wouldn't stop barking either. Was that thing even breathing? Flashes of me headed to jail danced across my eyes.

After what seemed like an hour, a light flickered on the side of the house, illuminating much of the yard. The dog just continued to bark right at the bush where I was hiding, and I was sure I was about to be discovered. I thought about getting up right there and then and making a dash to my car. I mean, there would be no way he could tell who I was. At least I could escape with my freedom.

"What the hell, Nicky!" It must've been Sinclair.

My heart stopped. He knew who I was! How?

My life was over.

I was just about to bolt before I glanced up to see him looking at the dog. "Stupid mutt. Useless piece of filth." He gave the dog a swift kick, instantly silencing her and forcing the dog back into submission. The dog whimpered and scurried away.

"I should just leave you out here in the winter, then I don't have to worry 'bout this bullshit." He mumbled a couple of other inaudible sentences, invariably insults, and then turned off the light, slamming the door behind him. I couldn't believe my fortune.

The dog's name was Nicky.

I chuckled to myself as euphoric relief washed over me. I folded and let myself sink into the cool grass. It felt like a needed embrace. I could've laid there for the whole night—and almost did, as I had to wait at least a good hour to make sure both Nicky and Sinclair were asleep.

I laid down, nestled against the side of the house and stared up at the stars. They were a sight with no city lights to dim their illumination—the sky was nature's drawing board, and I loved the picture. Amusement overcame me. I was content, as jovial as ever, yet in a couple of hours, I would have Sinclair strapped to a chair, gagged, and experiencing a beating few could imagine. I would make it very clear that his animal abuse was the reason for the affliction. When finished, I would leave with a warning. If he ever abused another dog, I would be back and wouldn't be as forgiving. I planned on calling the police from a phone booth a few miles away, anonymously reporting the crime because I doubted anyone would come and discover him until it was too late. The cringing and scrunch of my face as I went over the plan in my head told me something.

I no longer wanted to go through with that level of brutality. In fact, I shouldn't press my luck at all. I already had a close call. I should just consider myself lucky and head home. The decision overcame me in a wave.

I started to pull myself off the lawn, but a glimpse back at Nicky forced me to reconsider. I couldn't just leave her to suffer. Perhaps I could just transport her to a better home. The more the idea bounced around, the more assured I was that this was the correct course of action.

I rose from my spot with a newfound resolve. Taking aim with my third dart, my doubts seemed to melt. I inhaled deeply while my finger danced with the trigger.

I fired. Nicky let out a whimper and jumped up. Her head shot around the yard as she took a few steps but kept her yap shut. My guess was she didn't want another kick. After about a minute, she circled and slumped into the dirt. I waited five more minutes just to be certain, cautiously approaching with the expectation that she would jump to life and start wildly barking. To my relief, that didn't happen, and I managed to get inside the gate after a loud creak from the hinge that threatened to take the last of my nerve. Very carefully, I picked up Nicky and began carrying her to my car. She was surprisingly light for her size. I could feel the ribs that protruded from her thin fur. Her body felt warm and calm. It felt like she sensed what was happening. She understood I was trying to help her.

After lifting her into the passenger seat, I quickly scrambled to the driver's side and peeled off, heading to my apartment. I couldn't help but relish what Sinclair's face would look like when he saw his dog was gone. I would've paid money for that. Even though he hated his dog, I knew he would be pissed. That dog took the brunt of his anger, and now there was nothing to channel it into. Well, not entirely. My hands sank from the wheel, my high waned as I realized the animals at the mill would still be abused and Sinclair would just find new victims to endure his anguish. I vowed to continue to bombard animal control with complaint calls until they took action. Saving Nicky was the right decision, and at least some good came from the whole ordeal. I planned to drop her off at the Humane Society the next day.

By the time I reached home, Nicky was still subdued. Feeling her becoming chilled with a faint heartbeat, I laid a blanket over her next to my bed. Beside her, I left some water to drink and some sausage to devour. I closed my eyes to her calm breathing with a smile on my face.

The next day, I awoke, immediately rolling over to check on Nicky. The water remained in the bowl, and the food was untouched. She lay sideways in the same position. I removed the blanket, and sunlight from the exposed window bore down on her. She remained still. I reached down to nudge her shoulder. She was cold. Dark realization set in as I rested my hand on her chest and felt no expansion of her chest cavity.

Sinking back onto the sheets, a wave of nausea overtook me. I rushed to the bathroom, dry heaving over the toilet. I had calculated my tranquilizer measurements for 80lbs, I glanced back at her; she couldn't be more the 40lbs. As the heaving subsided, I rested, defeated and disgusted, against the porcelain.

I didn't shake the nightmares of Nicky's body or the chills when I saw a dog for a year after that.

Chapter 11

"Hello?" I answered. Crusty dry morning breath seeped forth. *It was a good thing you couldn't smell through a phone.*

"Nick! Don't forget to be here in half an hour!"

I could barely make out the voice from my stupor. I glanced at my clock. 9 a.m.

Shit.

"Oh yeah, don't worry, I'm about to leave," I mumbled.

"Nick, you soun—"

I hung up the phone and violently grabbed the alarm clock next to me. I had set the alarm for 8 p.m. *Son of a—!*

Springing out of bed, I threw on some deodorant, left some food for Buster, and ran out the door. I couldn't believe myself—I was actually excited about this. Halfway to my car, I realized I had forgotten to take Buster out. I guess the carpet would be his bathroom today.

Despite my jarring start, it couldn't have been more ideal weather. Sunny and 70 with a cool breeze. It was warm for this late in the year, but I sure wasn't complaining.

Cruising down the interstate, music blasting, life felt great, and I couldn't resist the smile that settled on my face.

Arriving just on time, thanks to my lead foot, I greeted my two passengers, hustling them toward the car.

"Wait, wait, Nick. Shouldn't we take mine? Yours only seats two."

I looked down at my silver stallion with disappointment.

"I guess I didn't really think about it." I turned ever so slightly back to the house, but Will caught my eye. He was still eyeing up the hot rod.

"How bout we take mine? Will can sit on your lap," I suggested. I stopped mid-turn and began back. Ann's facial reaction didn't approve, but I knew Will would.

"What do you say we take my car to the amusement park? It goes fast!" My silly tone sounded better suited for an infant.

"Yes! I like fast!" He beamed with excitement and bolted toward the car. I flashed a sly smile at my sis. She knew it was checkmate.

"Wow, this looks like a racecar!" He was practically screaming.

"Don't touch anything, or Uncle Nick won't take you," she warned.

As we packed into the car, I was prepared to put on quite the show. Ann would scold me afterward, but it would be worth it.

In a silent, stoic routine, I put down my aviators and turned the key. The engine roared to life, pistons firing a missile barrage, then idled as our eardrums adjusted from the burst. The settling purr of the engine persisted.

Will had been waiting long enough. I revved the throttle till the roar was deafening. The vibrating thunder from the RPMs could be felt in your core. I could sense Will's excitement. Then I let off, a preview for the open road. Will was giggling beside me.

"How'd you like that?" He just sat there wide-eyed, smiling and nodding. Oh yeah, he was hooked.

"You haven't seen anything yet." I smiled. We drove out of the suburb calm and cool, and I watched my sister tense up every time I accelerated. It wasn't long before we neared the freeway.

As if on cue, the song "Back in Black" began playing as we turned onto the ramp.

"Hold on," I said, turning up the radio to prepare to really let loose. Pedal to the floor and clutch out, we were rocketed back into the seat like a space shuttle. Even with the volume all the way up, you could barely hear the song over the roar of the engine. We merged onto the freeway, already screaming at 80 mph. At 100 mph, I could hear Ann yelling to slow down. Teetering on the cusp of pure recklessness, the silver bullet careened like a loose train down the road. I finally relented on the pedal at 115, being jolted from my euphoria by a slap on the arm. Perhaps I had gone a little far. Silence ensued as I cruised down to the speed limit.

"You okay, bud?" I was actually a little worried I had pushed it too far.

"C-c-cool." Lips pursed and eyes wide, a sly grin like he pulled off a heist on a cookie jar.

"Sis?" I asked, her face ashen.

"Yeah," she said, her expression unshaken. I'd probably hear about it later.

We drove the rest of the 20 minutes in relative silence until we caught a glimpse of the park, and then Will went bonkers. He had been scanning the horizon for miles. Ann finally seemed to relax, too, as the safety of a stationary parking spot awaited her.

Pulling into the parking lot, the little guy's face was glued to the window. "Wow, those are huge!" As soon as we were parked, he threw open his door and set out toward the entrance.

"Hold up, hun. I gotta grab some stuff." His mom tried to corral him back.

"Yeah, kid, hold your horses. The coasters aren't going anywhere," I chimed in. We hurriedly grabbed a few items and rushed to catch up. Will kept ushering us forward like we were late or something.

A decent amount of people were waiting at the entrance, as the park had already been open for half an hour. While we waited in line, we debated which ride would be conquered first. I told him that big boys were able to ride the Stratosphere, and his eyes lit up at its mention. He must've taken it as a challenge because once we were in, I was grabbed by the arm and dragged in the direction of the coaster. After a quick scolding from his mom, he let go but continued to lead. He would get about 30 feet ahead and then look back, motioning for us to hurry up. We were already in a swift powerwalk.

Now that Will was out of earshot, I was prepared for a lecture from Ann about my driving.

"Nick, back there in the car. That was beyond stupid. I don't want my son thinking that's alright." Her stern lashing probably was just beginning. "If you had lost control, we could have—"

"There was no chance we would've crashed."

"I don't want you to act like that didn't happen. I've experienced enough of that from you for two lifetimes."

I had my mouth open, ready with my next response, but I was so taken aback, the words hung in my throat.

"Wow," I said. It was all I could retort.

Her tone broke. "That was pretty exciting, just don't do it again."

"Okay, sis, noted. Now, where did that come from?" I stared her down with confusion. Before I got any reaction, Will beckoned us.

"Hurry up, guys! Everyone is beating us there!" Will's impatience was evident. Ann went quiet, but I knew the conversation wasn't over.

It hardly mattered how fast we got there since the line was still long. Waiting, I introduced some quirky games to pass the time. We started off with *buzz*, where a number is picked and every integer of that number, double numbers, and numbers with the picked number in them are replaced with "buzz." This continues in a circle, and every time "buzz" is said, the order reverses. It was pretty entertaining watching Will mess up and get frustrated. I was impressed, though. He was pretty sharp for his age and caught on quickly.

After dominating in *buzz*, we moved on to the *thumb game*. Each person puts their fists together, and one person says a number. Once the number is said, each person immediately puts up a random number of thumbs (or no thumbs) in the air. If the number of thumbs up is the same as the prediction, then the person removes a fist. First one with both fists out wins.

Apparently, this was Will's calling, and he took the first four games. I started getting irked because he was unbeatable. It seemed like he was in my mind. Things got competitive real quick, and it didn't help that the kid knew how to gloat and trash talk like the best of 'em. He gave me a run for my money. I had taught him too many of my tricks over the years, and it was backfiring on me. Though dominated at first, I made a rally and started to throw it back at him, but the comeback was cut short as our wait was over.

We had made our way through the metal maze and secured ourselves the first row for the ultimate experience. The small metal gates opened, and we rushed onto the platform. The attendants came by pressing firmly on our harnesses. That sure felt nice. I paid $40 bucks to wait in line for hours to get scared out of my wits and get my crotch crushed.

I didn't admit or show it, but I was terrified as we climbed the first drop. The suspense was killer. I hadn't been on a coaster since I was a child, and never one on this scale. Will looked nervous, too, but my sis was cool as a cucumber.

"What if the track breaks?" Will asked.

"Oh, that would never happen. They test and inspect these all the time," I reassured him, although there was no confidence in my voice. The thought of the disaster lingered and only added to my anxiety. Thanks, Will.

"Honey, don't worry. It's safer than riding a bike," his mom chimed in. The ludicrous statistic did nothing for me. Rationality had left my neural tissue. I wanted off this deathtrap.

There was a brief second when we reached the peak where I was able to overlook the entire park and the miles beyond it. It was a moment of calm before the storm, taking in the beautiful view. The people waiting in line, walking, riding, so many lives I was looking down upon.

Then came the edge, which overlooked our impending doom. Our front car crested as the others lagged behind. Then it happened. Nervous anxiety transitioned into a dangerous thrill; I felt so alive. I wanted to scream but felt my voice choked back against the wind. It was wild; the turns, the speed, the drops, the rush. My neck was tossed so violently and in such directions that I hoped they had chiropractors on-site. I let my arms elevate from their grip of the harness to flail like noodles in the air.

When we finally thundered into the unloading zone with a six-G stop, my heart was pounding. My face must've looked flushed because Ann asked if I was all right.

"Wow, that was sick!" I blurted.

"You feel that drop?" Will asked.

"We rode that drop, buddy!" I held out my hand for a high five.

Before our adrenaline wore off, we hustled back into line and rode that coaster three times in a row. Will and I could've ridden the behemoth all day, but his mom suggested we try something else.

We tried some of the smaller coasters, and they were a blast as well. The lines there were shorter, too, so we were able to get back on them a lot quicker.

"You guys are riding these things like they're crack," my sister commented. And if coasters were anything like crack, then I would be addicted. We rode until two, when my sister insisted we get something to eat before we passed out on a ride.

We indulged in some crispy golden funnel cakes slathered in powdered sugar and topped off with a generous helping of whipped cream. The dough meshed together into heart-clogging heaven.

After devouring the treat, Will turned his attention to a basketball game. It was a typical amusement park gimmick. Make one of three shots and get a prize. Except the rims were small, and the balls overinflated. There was no forgiveness for the shooter. Will begged us to let him try. He yearned for a stuffed turtle that hung on the prize rack. After pleas and promises, his mom relented and gave him the money. The attendant had barely handed over the ball before it was hulked back up.

"Will, wai—" I caught myself. Just let him do it, I told myself.

We watched the attempt fall way short, as did the second. I couldn't bite my tongue and advised him to throw it with an arc to make sure he got it there. My sis and I shared a look of doubt as he was handed the ball for his last try.

He let himself pause this time. His eyebrows furrowed, and his stare fixated on the rim. He stood off-center so he could put his weight into the throw, making sure to get it there. Winding up, he chucked the thing hard at the backboard. It was dead in line. Hitting the glass hard and low, it rattled between the backboard and the rim before dropping in. A shout of glee erupted, including a small celebration dance. A fury of high fives were exchanged as we congratulated him on the unlikely victory. I could feel the glow coming from Ann.

"I'll have that one!" Will pointed and asked for the stuffed turtle.

The attendant looked with awkward sheepishness at Ann and me. "Sorry, you have to make two of three for the top shelf. The one-shot prizes are here." He pointed at a sign detailing the reward possibilities, then presented some dollar store trinkets for Will to choose from. The disappointment was palpable. He picked out a sad-looking plastic toy, and his mom tried to cheer him up, but the heartbreak was too much. He asked for more money, but not wanting to shell out more for the gimmick, his mom told him she was out.

I couldn't bear to see the little man so sad and feeling cheated by the game. I marched up to the attendant and slammed down the money on the counter.

"I'm getting that turtle," I told him firmly. Worry about my state of mind met my gaze. He handed me the ball without so much as a word of good luck.

The first shot was dead on but bounced out thanks to inflation that turned the sphere into a massive bouncy ball. My second shot looked just off-center to the left. I was worried I had just embarrassed myself in Will's eyes, but it fell in off the backboard. I let out a sigh.

"If I hadn't made that," I mumbled to myself.

Now the pressure was on. I spun the rubber ball in my hands, finding my grip between the ribs of the grove. By now, I had a two-person cheering section, and the butterflies set in for the next shot. I took a deep breath and let the shot sail. It looked like it was on the perfect line.

The sound of a swish was glorious as I sunk the dagger. It felt like I had just sunk a game-seven winner. Outlandish celebration ensued. Yelling, jumping, and fist pumps were all part of the routine. I strode around chin as high as the sky. I proudly snatched my prize from the attendants and handed it to Will.

"Happy birthday, kid." I smiled.

"Really! Oh, cool! I'm going to name him Swish cause that's how I got him!" He squeezed the thing to the suffocation point. "Thanks, Uncle Nick." He wrapped around my midsection. "You're really good at basketball. I will have to tell my friends that I know someone who probably could be a pro."

"Ha, ha, oh man, not quite that good," I scoffed.

My sister flashed me a smile, relaying her appreciation.

"That was awesome, Nick."

I jabbed Ann in the side. "Did you hear that? I'm a pro."

We conquered every coaster the park offered, and although the lines were long, we found ways to amuse ourselves while waiting. Swish the turtle started becoming a nuisance to carry around as the responsibility mostly fell on me.

As the afternoon wore on into early evening, Will was becoming tired. But before leaving, we made sure to hit our favorite coaster, the Stratosphere, one last time. Riding it at dusk added an extra element.

On the way out, we picked up a few ice creams. I suggested mint chocolate chip to Will, and, to my delight, he loved it. We sat on the hood of my car, enjoying the treats as the sun began to set. It was a perfect end to a perfect day.

"How was the birthday, bud?" I asked.

"It was the best birthday. Can we go again next year?!" he pleaded. I gave him a firm nod, and then he reached out his hand. "Pinky promise?" he asked.

"Ha, ha, yes, kiddo, pinky promise," I said, chuckling as I made the pact.

Finishing up our dessert, we packed into the car and had an uneventful drive back. Will fell asleep almost immediately while Ann and I talked about my new dog. I dropped the two off at their house and promised to visit soon.

"Thank you for today, Nick," Ann said as she leaned over the passenger door.

I drove home, fighting the urge to sleep. Once back, my exhaustion only grew as I pounded a glass of milk in the kitchen. Buster was jumping off the wall, but I couldn't be bothered to take him for his walk. It could wait until tomorrow. I turned off the lights and headed to bed.

Chapter 12

I awoke to a gnarly stench. A search of my apartment revealed its origin; Buster had left a surprise for me. A couple of hot steaming turds lay on my decorative rug while Buster sat nearby staring at me with a dumb look of innocence.

"Dammit!" This was not how I wanted to start my day.

"Shoo! Go!" He scrambled to miss a soft kick coming his way. He was already trained, for Pete's sake. This wasn't supposed to happen anymore.

Mumbling obscenities, I got on my hands and knees to clean up the excrement. During the maneuver around the stain, my right knee had become damp, even though I was confident I hadn't cleaned that area yet. I stretched my knee up to my nose.

"Buster, you son of a—"

Then it dawned on me that I had been gone all yesterday. And when I came back, I forgot to let him out for the bathroom. With no one to blame but myself, I stopped my tirade and assured him it was okay. I was sorry about not getting him outside. He seemed to understand through my reaffirming tone and soon returned within arm's reach. I hoped for no stains, but after soaking for a night, I didn't hold my breath.

After I was satisfied with my cleanup, a walk was in order to make up for the neglect. My immediate area wasn't ideal for pets with its concentration of people and limited green space.

Therefore, I tried to hustle Buster along until we made it to Cyrus Park, where things were less chaotic.

I had brought a Frisbee along, hoping Buster could actually retrieve it. So far, he had about a 10 percent success rate. The problem was either he would get the Frisbee and lay down so he could chew on it, or he would bring it back but refuse to drop it. Grabbing for it made it worse because then it turned into a game of "keep away." I never won that battle without breaking a sweat.

Once exhausted and defeated, he would nuzzle up and grace me with the beat-up Frisbee. I was feeling hopeful for this session, though, and with the park relatively empty, I was really going to launch the saucer. A gorgeous day was upon us as we took the field.

"Buster, please just make this easy."

His tongue hung out the side of his mouth as he slobbered on himself. This was my stallion. I wound up and let the disk fly. Immediately, Buster bolted down the field, slowly gaining ground on the Frisbee. With a leap, he just missed grabbing it. So close. I anticipated that he wouldn't bring it back and began toward him, but to my surprise, he started trotting back, Frisbee in his mouth. Before he could reach me, however, he stopped. Something on the ground caught his attention. Without hesitation, he preceded to nip at the mystery substance.

"Buster, you dummy," I cursed under my breath.

I jogged up to him just in time to slap half a hot dog out of his mouth. He gobbled the other portion of the compacted pig before I could retrieve it.

"Oh, c'mon, get outta there," I scolded, shooing him away from the leftovers and moving us toward the middle of the park.

A second throw and Buster actually brought it back. I almost didn't grab it from his mouth I was so shocked.

"Atta, boy!" I exclaimed with a tousle of his fur.

"Good boy. Good boy." I took a treat out of my pocket and let him scarf it down. I was doubtful he could do it a second time, but he brought it back once again and once again was rewarded. Now we were in business.

The goal shifted to catching the saucer on the fly. I was belting throws, and although Buster had a couple of hiccups in the recovery process, he was becoming reliable. Maybe he wasn't as dull as he thought he was.

"I betcha can't catch up to this one, bud," I challenged.

I really put my force behind the throw and let it soar. My hand came over my forehead to watch it sail. Even with air under it, the Frisbee looked out of range. There was no way he could snag the thing. It was also headed toward the fountain, which had me worried. At the speed he was running, he just might get there. I almost yelled out as his strides brought him closer to a collision with the fountain.

C'mon, Buster, look ahead, pull up, jump, anything! He was a few feet from the fountain wall. I cringed for the brutal impact.

At the last second, in convergence with the Frisbee, he leaped for it right over the fountain.

His back legs slammed into the concrete, sending him flipping into the water. The birds perched on top of the fountain scattered. I bolted toward Buster, expecting the worst. I was already figuring out the quickest way to the animal hospital. People turned to see the commotion. Right before I got to him, he lifted his head above the concrete side.

At least he was alive.

My gaze quickly focused behind him. No blood in the water, no wincing or barking. Without hesitation, he hopped right out to my side and graced me with a shower as he shook the water from his coat. I squeezed his soaked legs. I couldn't believe he was unscathed. I circled him, looking for any abrasion or any other sign of injury.

"You're one lucky SOB, Buster!" He panted and just looked at me, clueless as ever. What an adorable thing.

"Well, let's get in a quick jog, then head back," I told him.

In part, the run was to see how he would do. We took a few laps around the park, then made it to the apartment where I made sure he was uninjured. We collapsed on the floor in front of my recliner, wrestling for a minute. Grabbing a juice from the fridge, I plunged down into my favorite chair. Flipping through the channels, some reruns of *Happy Days* piqued my interest. I pulled out a deck of cards, setting up a game of solitaire. I barely made it through one hand before calling it quits. I turned my attention back to the TV, but it didn't keep my attention, and I dozed off.

When I awoke, it was late afternoon. The sun was just starting to dim. It took me a few groggy minutes before I decided to hit the bars instead of bumming around. I always found it really difficult to wake up from those midday naps. The chair had me glued down, and my eyelids were magnets attracted to each other. Even when getting up, a cloudy mist clogged my brain, and its function was similar to a rusty gearbox. I finally peeled myself from the recliner and perked up after throwing some cold water in my face. I definitely wanted to catch some eyes tonight. For some reason, I was feeling really good, and when I began to blast some Motley Crue, my mood really picked up.

Everything was enjoyable—from showering to shaving, everything. As I was gearing up, Buster was trying to jump on me and join the excitement. I was galloping around the apartment with vigor, singing Pat Benatar hits with a combination of rock star and raspy soprano. It took me a while to transform myself, but I did a fine job. I'm not one to boast, either. *Definitely a classier bar tonight,* I thought. With one last glance in the mirror and a quick goodbye to Buster, I descended upon the scene, confidence through the roof.

I first stopped by Dillies, a large restaurant/bar off 9th and Chedister that usually had entertainment going on. I had seen a flyer for a speed-dating event. I was lukewarm about the prospect when I saw it, but I warmed to the idea while getting ready. I wanted in, especially once I saw the ladies that would be sitting across from me. I approached a busboy and asked about it. He pointed me in the direction of the host.

"Excuse me, sir," I said to the host, who met me with a perky smile. "This event, is it too late to sign up?"

"I'm sorry. You had to reserve a seat last week, but we will be doing another next month, so if you would like to reser—"

"No, no," I said, rather disappointed. "Thanks anyway."

I turned and headed back to the bar, wishing I had committed earlier. I had trouble finding an empty stool, so I looked aimlessly between pockets of people until I found a small table in the corner. Now at least I had a place to sit and wasn't as lost as it looked like I was. I grabbed the waitress's attention with a hand wave and ordered a drink.

I relaxed a bit, leaned back, and began to scan the crowd. It was amusing to watch the awkward scores of attempted flirtation and speculate on their success. As entertaining as it was to watch, I bet I wouldn't have fared much better. I mean, one awkward phrase or silence and you're dismissed, eliminated like another contestant. It's nearly impossible to drum up a conversation or introduce yourself. If the other person thought you were attractive, then you were deemed friendly and engaging. If not, then you were creepy and annoying. It was a game, and I envied those who were so good at it.

A lanky fellow in khakis caught my attention. He wasn't overly attractive but approached a gorgeous blonde sporting a tight green dress and a thick body. Guys were eyeing her up three dates away.

As khaki began to engage her in conversation, I could tell she was having none of it. Her eyes were wandering the room. She appeared to give short responses, and it was becoming painful to watch. I'm sure this guy had to really muster up some courage, or at least drank himself some. After a couple of minutes of negative progress, he leaned in to whisper something to her, put a 20 on the bar, and left for the other side. It was an odd exchange. One that got me curious. Evidently, I wasn't the only one, as the look on her face mirrored my puzzlement. She sat frozen and stumped for a few seconds, then whirled around to give him the attention she'd been withholding.

Khaki was already introducing himself to another woman halfway down the bar. This one appeared much fairer, though. The two barely made it through introductions before the blonde interrupted, 20 in tow. After a brief exchange, in which I couldn't get a read on the intrusion, she headed back for her original seat at the bar. What on earth? Khaki slid right back into conversation with a casual laugh.

Mr. Khaki and the new woman continued to talk for the next few minutes, and it was apparent they were enjoying each other's company. During that time, the blonde kept glancing toward his direction even when talking with her new suitors. She also polished off a couple of drinks.

Eventually, the khaki guy was alone, and I needed to know what that whole exchange between him and the woman at the bar was all about. It might be awkward and weird approaching him about it, but I wasn't going to let my speculation dwell. I rose from my seat.

"Finally built up enough liquid courage to talk to her?" A woman's voice froze me mid-squat.

"Ahh, no," I stuttered as I crouched back into my seat.

"You know, I think you should give it a shot. You might be one of the few guys here that will earn a second look from her." Was she attacking me? Hitting on me? The confusion wore on my face.

"Ahh, ha, ha. No, no, it's not like that. I mean, I wasn't going to go talk to her," I stammered. I was just beginning to recoup from the blindside.

"You've been staring at her for about 10 minutes," she chuckled and raised an eyebrow at me.

It was only then that I turned to grab a full look at her. She was tall with straight dark hair, a sporty type with a firm expression and a subtle smile. She was rather attractive for intimidating me so much. I quickly regained some semblance of myself.

"No, no, I was just watching her and this guy go back and forth, caught my attention. Grade A bar entertainment. It was really odd. I was trying to decipher what actually happened," I rattled off the explanation, relieved to finally set the record straight.

I flipped the surprise on her. Watching for a moment as a clever smile turned into terror and embarrassment painted her face, if only for a moment. That quickly broke into a facepalm.

"Well, I was people watching, too, and I was convinced I had you pegged, but man, was I off. It's weird how that works."

She came off as playful, but my expression probably didn't portray amusement.

"This is a little embarrassing," she chuckled. "Oh, I'm sorry. I'm Deniece." She extended a hand my way.

"Nick," I replied, and we quickly shook hands with awkward smiles. After a few more uncomfortable seconds that seemed more like minutes, she grabbed her purse.

"I'm sorry, Nick. I've really embarrassed myself, and I can only imagine how crazy I seem or sound, so I'm gonna head out to another bar with my friend."

"Oh, c'mon. Hold up a sec. You didn't come off crazy at all."

She paused and put her purse down, glancing at me sternly.

"Okay, maybe a little odd," I conceded. "Caught me a little off guard, but I admire the approach." I had her attention, but I knew I had to break the ice just a bit more. "I mean, we were both essentially doing the same thing. Some people call it people watching; some call it stalking."

Her face turned to a gleaming smile.

"Well, that makes me feel a little better. I guess I'm a terrible judge of people. Although, I do actually have to run to the bar down the street. My friend doesn't like staying in one place too long."

"Well, would you like some company? Can't offer much protection, but I *can* offer riveting conversation," I smirked.

She pondered, tapping her chin.

"You make quite the case for yourself. I guess you can tag along." She tried to conceal a grin.

We found her friend on the other side of the place and pried her away from a burly, bearded fellow that was crowding her. He definitely had too much to drink.

"Who's your friend?" She eyed me with a suspicious smile. "You know she never goes out?" She was slurring.

"Okay, Alexa, how bout only one drink at the next bar?" Deniece cut her off before she even got started.

She probably wasn't trying to be curt, but Alexa wrinkled her face at the interruption. I decided to change the subject before things escalated. "How do you two know each other?"

Deniece spoke up, saying they met at work. Alexa didn't add much, still sour about her hushing.

We continued to make small talk down the block. Alexa started opening up, and it became apparent to me that she was definitely the go-with-the-flow, sporadic type, while Deniece was stepping out of her comfort zone. Perhaps it was the liquor or the pressure from Alexa, but whatever the cause, I had the inkling she was enjoying it. At the street corner, we pushed past a black iron door under a neon sign that read "Cages Bar."

My pupils slowly dilated, adjusting to the light-quenched bar as we wedged past disgruntled pool players, ready to shove the ball where the sun didn't shine. Alexa charged through and even interrupted a shot without so much as an apology. The dive bar was for locals, and we weren't one of them. It was a weird feeling, and one not easily shaken before settling in.

We grabbed a table toward the center of the joint, and Alexa offered to grab us drinks from the bar. Deniece wanted a Long Island iced tea, and I responded with a rum and Coke.

"Well, that's boring," Alexa remarked.

I barely bit my tongue from scolding her for such lies. Instead, I held a cheesy smile in response.

"You know what? How 'bout you surprise me with a specialty drink? I'm feeling adventurous."

What I was actually starting to feel was the second rum and Coke starting to kick in. As Deniece and I settled in, we began to talk about ourselves, starting with the basics. Alexa arrived back with our drinks and then scuttled away to the bar, as there were plenty of bearded patrons ready to enjoy her flirtatious company. I didn't even get the chance to ask what she got me, but it had a pickle in it, and that was all I needed to know. Deniece eyed it with suspicion.

"That looks, um, different." She was holding back a laugh.

"I might have to down a couple of shots before I give this thing a try." She got a long chuckle out of that. She had this moment of high-pitched squealing in between breaths when she laughed hard, and I thought it was the cutest thing. I decided to call the drink the "snot shot" due to the green pickle and brown hue that contributed to its questionable look. I let it sit for a minute, but it was daring me to drink it. I knew Deniece wanted to see me try it, and, well, there wasn't much I wouldn't do for a cute girl. Mustering up some courage, I brought it to my lips. A sharp recoil followed my sip. The initial taste was repulsive. But as the bite mellowed, there came a pleasant aftertaste. The spices kept the drink lively while I detected hints of tequila and rum. There was a bittersweet aftertaste that must have been a fruit juice or syrup. It was a pretty good combination.

Deniece eyed my reaction with anticipation. "Well?"

"Not bad at all, actually," I said, immediately coughing as I put it down. She seemed doubtful. I handed her the glass for a taste. After a few sips, she concurred. "That's surprising!"

"Right? Alexa probably tried to order me the worst thing on the menu... joke's on her." Deniece rolled her eyes. "We are a bit opposite, but sometimes you need a little of that."

We began to talk at length about her life, her friends, and her goals, and the conversation quickly got personal. After voicing a couple of insecurities and concerns about her life, she told me that this was completely unlike her. She wasn't a very open person, and she didn't know if it was the liquor or if I was just easy to talk to. I thought she was really down to earth, and it was refreshing getting past the friendly-go-lucky stage with a woman. Many times, I only got the bright side when I went out, where I felt like it was a façade—the lying about being secure and pretending like there wasn't a single flaw in their life. It was nice to get the real side of someone, where it wasn't all roses and sunshine. I relayed my thoughts that her openness and bluntness were refreshing. She smiled and thanked me.

"Well, you've heard quite a bit about me. What about you, Nick? Any average guy would've been spooked, but not you. Why?" she prodded.

"Wow, well, ah... who says I'm not..." I kept a puzzled look. Her smile started to transition from a smile to uncertainty. "It helps you were one of the most attractive women there."

She rolled her eyes but was blushing. The smile was back.

"No, I mean, honestly, curiosity at the beginning, but the more we talk, I really like your personality. I know, I know, two cheesy lines in a row, but seriously, it's nice knowing I'm not alone in some aspects." The words felt odd as they came out. It was like I just released a little bit of myself, just slightly, like I lifted the face guard from my helmet. Waiting for the few seconds before her response yielded a moment of panic and regret. I didn't want her thinking I was soft.

"Well, Nick, your charm and candor are appreciated. And I would be lying if I said I didn't want to get together sometime soon." A warm smile formed on her face. Her cheeks were rosy from makeup and her eyeliner and lipstick didn't match up too well. It was sort of cute.

I was relaxed as I was reassured that she didn't judge me for my comments. "Of course, that would be lovely." *Lovely?! Who says lovely?*

She looked at her watch, "Oh, shit! I gotta run, Nick. The babysitter was only supposed to stay until midnight, and it's already half past." She glanced around frantically, looking for Alexa. The bar was much emptier now, but the patrons were rowdier than when we arrived.

"Babysitter?" I asked.

"Yeah, I have a five-year-old girl," she said sheepishly as she scanned the bar.

"Oh, that's cool," I blurted out awkwardly. The words hung in the air uncomfortably long. She seemed flustered and must have been a little embarrassed for not mentioning that earlier, especially for how much she shared about her life.

"Yeah, I'm sorry if that… well, I don't know," she said.

"Oh no, that's really cool. I have a kid, too," I fumbled out. "Well, he isn't actually my son, but he practically is. He's my sister's boy, but you know?" I could barely believe what a reach that was. My son? I just didn't want Deniece to feel awkward or embarrassed that she had a kid.

She smiled. "Thanks, Nick. That means a lot." She began to pick up her purse and put her coat on as Alexa appeared from the bathroom. Deniece saw right through my lame attempt but appreciated my effort.

"I'll see you another time, Nick. My number is on the napkin. It was a great time. Thanks."

With that, she gave me a peck on the cheek and walked out.

I sat there for a few minutes after she left. I could still feel the kiss against my cheek. It felt rosy and… warm. I looked around the bar with a grin like I had just got laid, and that's how it felt. Just a kiss on the cheek had me feeling like that. I mulled my drink over, the grin cemented on my face. I laughed to myself quite a bit, and anyone watching must've thought I was mad. I started thinking about Will and how we really could get a lot closer. A baseball bat on the bar wall caught my attention, and the idea of a Mets game popped into my head. *What a perfect thought. There's no better bonding time than an ole ball game.* Lord knows it had been too long since I'd seen a game in person. If I was quick, I could snag tickets for the last game of the season.

I left a hefty tip on the table and strolled out of the bar. I took a glance around. Moonlight reflected off the cars, and muddled streetlights danced around the shadows like a game of cat and mouse. A few rowdy gentlemen down the street bellowed something fierce, but all sounded peaceful and quaint. As I moved farther from the bars and toward my car, the clamor of voices and music faded into silence, only broken by my echoing footsteps against the pavement. It was a chilly night, and although it raised goosebumps on my arms, I wasn't cold. I felt refreshed as the air chilled my lungs into constriction. I paused at my car to stare at the stars and then climbed on the hood to really take in the view. The chilly metal sent a shiver that reverberated in my toes while I looked up. I took in the magnitude of the scene. It brought me into an introverted moment of self-awareness of how small I really was, of how small everyone was. How the memory of so many is completely lost in time. I lay there for a couple of minutes, my mind folding into my subconscious.

Suddenly, headlights flashed directly on me. It stunned me for a second and ripped me from my trance. The cold simultaneously penetrated my false sense of warmth, and instantly, the chill set in. The hood of the car became uncomfortable since it didn't conform to my body. I probably looked really silly and rolled off the hood into my car and drove back home.

Chapter 13

The next couple of days went off without much of a hitch. They were mostly passed with training Buster, which was coming along well. I was pretty forceful, and I felt bad at times, but he learned quickly. In my mind, the end justified the means.

I called my sister to ask about the Mets game, and she voiced her excitement about the proposition. I told her it would have to be tomorrow since the season was drawing to a close.

"Ah, shoot, Nate won't be able to get off work, and I have a therapy meeting tomorrow. I canceled last time. It's probably best I don't again…" her voice trailed off.

Therapist?

"But please take Will! Besides, I'm not the biggest baseball fan, and I'm sure he would like it more if it was just you and him."

"Yeah, just the two of us will be fun." I paused. "I didn't know you had a therapist."

"Yeah, for a while."

"I mean, I don't want to make it seem like that's a bad thing. You know I've seen one or two in my day. But—" I bit my tongue.

"Yes? Go ahead, Nick, say it. I won't jump down your throat." Her tone was encouraging.

"Well… ah, what are you going to therapy for?"

Silence greeted my question.

"That sounded bad. I didn't quite mean—"

"Yeah, I'd like to hear what you mean," she interrupted. Now there was an edge to her voice. I needed to tiptoe around my answer.

"Well, what I meant was that… on the outside at least, I don't know about the inside because I mean… there could be—"

"Nick! Get to the point."

"You have a great life. Money, a wonderful son, no obligation to work. Granted, your husband works a lot, but others would kill for your family and what you have, so what problems could you be discussing?"

She asked for the point, and I could almost hear her gasp on the other side of the phone.

"Wow. It finally comes out."

Then she started laughing. Not an uncomfortable, "I can't believe your ignorance" laugh, but a genuine and spontaneous laugh. I could sense real enjoyment from it. Speechless, I waited for it to taper off but felt more inflamed the longer the laughter went on.

"Is this amusing to you? You know, Anita, I was just trying to be serious." I tried to keep my tone restrained. I was gritting my teeth as I spoke.

"Nick." The laughing finally subsided. "I know you've thought that forever. I've felt that resentment from you any time I've complained about something. Why that is so, I'm not sure. You'll need to ask yourself. It was rude of me to laugh, but I just couldn't help it. That, and I just can't believe what you just said."

"Oh…"

"Yeah," she started, her tone dialed back to casual. "As far as the therapist, I just meet with her every now and again. It's not like I desperately need one, but it's nice talking to someone else about stuff. A lot of times, it clears things up. Imaginary things, you're probably thinking." *Hmm, there's the sarcasm.*

"It's not an easy thing having Nate gone so much, but even when he's here, we just don't talk. Like we can hardly get past, 'How's your day going?' or only talk about some chore or errand. I haven't really talked to him for months. We never get past the superficial anymore. And I have brought it up a couple of times, but he's wrapped up in his business world, which, yes, provides for the family, but it just feels like he has formed his own world, and I've been edged out over the years.

"Plus, Will has been a handful. I just want him to turn out alright. I feel so much pressure and anxiety and think every little mistake he makes is going to derail him. I just mill around at home, driving myself crazy. I don't have anything I feel like I'm a part of. Jeez, Nick, sometimes I have the urge to go back to using again. That way, I can just blissfully fall into my own world. I don't have to serve others. The only thing that stops me is getting this stuff off my chest. It's kind of like a reset button. I just have to step back and appreciate and enjoy where I am in life. That, and after our father died, I vowed that I would never touch that shit again. It made me who I wasn't. The things I sacrificed for my world brought down so many others."

And here I thought she had everything figured out.

"Well, you don't have to say anything, Nick. I don't know how I would respond to that. It just kind of came out. But thanks for listening, and I'm overjoyed you're taking Will to the game. See you then!" She hung up the phone without another word.

I clung onto the phone. Processing what transpired kept the receiver glued to my face. I felt like a complete ass. How did I just assume things were great with everyone else around me? Do I just ignore the signs, or are people that clever at hiding it? I decided that I needed to talk more with my sister.

Feeling sentimental and guilty, I dialed my mom's number to chat for a few minutes.

"Nice to see you haven't forgotten about me, Nick, or are you just calling to see if I'm still alive and kicking?" she joked.

"No, no, just checking how that food is tasting." She laughed hard at that.

We had a pretty nice conversation. She shared some gossip about a few of the residents around the building, and, man, could she spin a tall tale. Hearing her liveliness was warming, and I told her I'd swing by soon.

I hung up the phone and played some tug of war with Buster, but I couldn't stop my mind from drifting back to my sister and drugs. Maybe I wasn't old enough, or I was too naïve, or maybe I really didn't care at the time to fully wrap my head around what was going on. She really struggled.

The next day, I awoke to Buster licking my face. His tongue was rough, but its warm tickle was a nice wake-up call.

"Who's a good boy? You crazy dog!"

I threw him around on the bed, wrestling and manhandling the runt. He was a rambunctious one, as I'm sure most puppies his age are. He just couldn't get enough roughhousing. I thought I was gonna break him as I tossed him around the bed. Even after I moved from the bedroom, he jumped at my leg like a hungry piranha. The only way to shift his attention was to rattle the treat bag.

Buster eyed it intently. "Okay, bud, you can have one. Just don't let it spoil breakfast."

Throwing the treat across the room, he clumsily lunged and missed, leaving it to skid across the floor. His floor-scratching scramble was like nails on a chalkboard, but it was so cute. I prepared a breakfast of toast and a banana while I checked my answering machine. There was one new message, and as I listened, I couldn't tell whose voice it was until about halfway through, at which they blurted, "Oh, and this is Deniece."

Deniece! Jeez, I had forgotten to call her about a date. I hope she didn't get the wrong impression, though she sounded cheery in the message. I flew back into my room, where I retrieved the napkin from the bedside drawer. Reading the number off the napkin, I quickly dialed the number. While the dial tone rang, I wondered how she had gotten my number. I had never given it to her, or had I? After a few suspenseful rings, it went to voicemail. Phew.

"Oh hey, Deniece. It's Nick." I chuckled to keep it light.

"I'm sorry I didn't get back to you, I never took the napkin out of my pocket, and it went through the laundry. I would love to get together soon. Later this week, like Tuesday would be perfect because tomorrow I'm taking my nephew to the Mets game."

That napkin excuse I had come up with was gold. I was sure I would be hearing back from her.

The workday was pretty typical. I was bored out of my mind, counting down the minutes to leave. Lunch was from a sandwich shop down the street that made a mean pastrami wrap. Slumping back into my office chair, I worked on some billing numbers for our recent victory in the Tompkins case. A contractor had cut corners on a new housing development, and the faulty cement foundations were beginning to fall apart. The suit made us a decent chunk of change and largely paid for all the repairs in the damaged homes. Unfortunately, or perhaps, fortunately, the contracting company was forced to fold. It was a shame for those within the business, but at the end of the day, they did it to themselves.

As I munched on my wrap, I got a ring from Chris. He wanted to see how I was doing, and I filled him in on the details. I told him that I was handling things pretty well and that it was a welcome feeling getting some of my resentment off my chest, but there was a long way to go. I also brought him up to speed on Buster, to which he was pretty surprised.

"Nick, the last pet you had was that goldfish, and that lasted less than a day!" He was chuckling.

"Well, Buster ain't a goldfish, Chris. You should see how well I've trained him." That got a scoff out of him.

"If that got you to laugh, then you'll get a real kick out of this. Guess who's got a dinner date Tuesday?"

"No way!" Chris could hardly control himself. "Where did you find this girl, Nick? She's not one of those mail-order brides or anything, is she?" He was really cracking himself up.

"Calm down, you loon." He needed to hear me. "Believe it or not, she actually came up and hit on me. It was a great night, and she was a really down-to-earth person… and cute."

"Well, listen, bud, I'm happy for you, and I can hear the excitement in your voice. You know I like to joke, but it's great to hear you're doing well. Hope you keep this new Nick up. I gotta run to another precinct now to deal with some report problems. I'll catch you later."

"Sounds good. Thanks, Chris."

I hung up the phone, finished up my lunch, crunched some numbers, and took off to walk Buster. It was too nice of a day not to get him outside, and there was nothing better to do at the office. I had a pretty set route when we went out, and people in my complex were starting to recognize us. They usually shot us a quick "hi," but sometimes, someone would stop and pet him for a minute. There was a video game programmer on the floor below me who always seemed to be out when I was. He was a pretty engaging guy being that most of his day was spent with a computer. There was a receptionist who was also friendly and usually chatted for a few minutes. She was going to night school to become a teacher.

After getting back, Buster and I settled in for a movie and some leftover pasta for the remainder of the night. After much debate and second-guessing, I selected *Grease*, and though it wasn't my normal type of movie, it just jumped out at me.

Before dozing off, I made sure to double-check the alarm clock. Tomorrow was the Mets game with Will, and there was no way I was cutting it close like the amusement park. The game was at noon, but one can never be too careful.

I picked Will up the next morning, and he was all smiles. He stood in the driveway with his mom, holding a brown sack lunch. He was wearing a Mets jersey, though I couldn't make out the number at first. Today was going to be a good one. I could feel it. Will gave his mom a hug and then jogged toward the car. Enthusiastically, he hopped in the car.

His mom approached the passenger door and leaned in. "Now, you two have fun today, but no pulling any pranks." She smiled and winked, then stared right into my soul. "Also, Nick, take it easy with him in the car. The last thing I need is for you guys to get in an accident."

I rolled my eyes. "Relax, sis; there won't be speeding… much," I bellowed as I revved the engine.

"Nick!" She sounded pissed. "I'm serious."

"I know, I know. Don't worry," I relented.

She leaned in for one last kiss from Will then sniffed the air.

"Nick, are you wearing patchouli!?" Ann's furrowed brow met my confusion.

"Uh, yeah, I think so. What, you like it?"

Ann shuddered as she shook her head, "I hate it." She closed her eyes as if thrust into a flashback. "I… I just can't stand the scent."

"Okayyy?" I wasn't sure what to do with the information.

She leaned over to give Will a kiss and a quick "Have fun, guys." And with that, we were on our way.

Once we got out of the neighborhood and onto the main roads, Will was getting antsy, "Uncle Nick, can we go fast again? That was like the coolest thing ever, and I won't even tell Mom!"

I should've never given the kid a taste.

"Maybe on the way back, okay?" I raised an eyebrow, and the false hope seemed to settle him. "Besides, you remember what your mom said. I would get in some serious trouble if we went fast." Hopefully, he'd forget about it by the time we were headed back, but I kind of doubted it.

"Say," I nodded toward the brown bag, "what's with the lunch, kid?"

"My mom said that you already paid for the tickets and—"

"Listen, this ain't a field trip, son. Lose the bag," I interrupted.

He looked shocked but then saw my grimace and gladly threw it under the seat. "Your mom may have said something about driving, but she didn't have any restrictions on eating." His clever smile mirrored mine.

The rest of the drive, I educated the youngster with '70s rock on the radio and bantered back and forth about who was gonna have a big day for the Mets. His favorite player Rico Brogna had been slumping lately, but Will was convinced he would break out this game. We were both iffy on the pitching. It was always hit or miss. The starters were serviceable, but the bullpen had seen better years.

Entering the stadium was always magical. Anticipation would build during the speed walk to your section, only to finally reach your corridor and emerge from the shadows of the concrete and lay eyes on the immaculate field below. A field engulfed by stands, grass patterned in perfect diamonds. Yes, entering a baseball diamond was like a separate world, a bubble of paradise.

That day, it was still a "whoa" moment for me. The spectacle of the stadium never got old, and the thought of how it must feel to play on one always sent shivers down my spine. A quick tug on the sleeve brought me out of my stupor.

"This way," Will pleaded, pulling on my arm, trying to herd me to our spots.

"There's no rush. The seats aren't going anywhere," I countered, but his boyish charm was too much. We hustled up the stairs to our seats. They weren't too bad, upper level and a halfway down the third base line. They felt familiar. Before we even settled in, Will was already making food demands.

"Hey, Uncle Nick, I'm hungry already." He flashed a set of pleading eyes.

"The game hasn't even started yet! Ahhh, alright, how 'bout some peanuts to tide you over?" I offered.

"I don't like peanuts," Will fired back.

I pretended to be shot. "Don't like peanuts! What kind of mongrels were you raised by? Have you even tried them?"

"No," he responded sheepishly.

"Well, then, this is a day of firsts!" I said gleefully. "Let's go."

"You won't be disappointed," I reassured him as we made our way down to the concessions.

There was no line, and I let the concession worker know it was his first bag of peanuts, gloating like it was his first beer or something. The worker was completely uninterested in my jubilation, and Will wasn't sharing my enthusiasm either.

"Just wait till you try them. Don't worry. It's just food," I promised. He looked at me with a puzzled look. "You're gonna love 'em."

I eagerly watched as he munched on a few. It took him a bit to figure out the shell, but once he cracked the secret, he was a natural. I let him sink into a couple on the way back before asking for the verdict.

"They're pretty good!" Will said. I nudged him with my elbow. "And you were right, I guess."

"You guess? Will, you're gonna learn quickly that I'm never wrong." He smiled reluctantly.

We settled in and enjoyed the pregame ceremonies. A beautiful rendition of the national anthem sung by a local college choir and a rather abysmal first pitch topped it off. The first innings flew by and found Will and me talking more than we watched the game. When we heard the pop of a bat or saw a foul ball, our attention would swing to the game, but for the most part, we discussed his school and sports. He talked with such enthusiasm about his baseball team and friends. I had forgotten how problems were at that age. They felt like life or death. His account of a disagreement at recess was exaggerated so much, it sounded like a gang war. There were a couple of times I held back a laugh because I could tell he was completely serious, but he caught me smiling once.

"I got put in the timeout circle for 15 minutes because Mitch told on me!" I was smiling. "That's not funny!" he complained.

"No, no, it wasn't that. I just saw someone spill their drink," I lied.

He bought the fib and continued about how Mitch was the biggest tattler in school and ate boogers. I then asked him if he liked any girls, and that quieted him up. There's nothing more embarrassing for a young boy than talking about girls.

His face blushed instantly. "No, girls are stupid," he responded swiftly. I was getting a kick out of making him uncomfortable, so I continued to press him for answers, "C'mon, it's Uncle Nick. You can trust me. We do pranks together. Your secret is safe," I prodded.

He looked around like one of his classmates was nearby, then leaned in to whisper, "Okay, but you can't tell Mom. She doesn't know, and I don't want to get in trouble." He looked at me for confirmation, and I nodded. "I like this girl Maya, and we hugged last week, but no one knows." He looked as though he just shared a national secret with the enemy, and I played right along.

"Wow! Don't worry, I won't tell anyone. My lips are sealed. Very smooth, Will," I gave him a wink.

By then, the fifth inning was wrapping up, and with the peanuts gone, it was time to get some food of substance. We hustled down to the concessions before the other lards and prepared to gorge ourselves on the questionable but delicious food. Will wanted a hamburger, but I convinced him to give the hot dog a shot. Lathering up his in brown mustard, I was only disheartened to find they didn't serve Dr. Pepper. What on earth happened to this place? A minor hiccup, but no matter.

We hustled back up to our seats, laden with hot dogs, sodas, and this new Dippin' Dots ice cream. I let him throw a wrinkle in the traditional ballpark food, though I was suspect. I couldn't understand what was wrong with normal ice cream. Why did it have to be in small dots? It seemed like an unnecessary marketing gimmick. Will trusted me before, and now it was my turn; I hope he didn't let me down. Right as we came out of the atrium, we heard a loud crack of a bat, and our heads shot up as we caught the ball sailing over the left-field fence. Quickly making sure it was the Mets, we joined the crowd in the uproar. High fives for us and the people around ensued, with plenty of screaming and hollering. The batter rounded the bases with ease and gave a quick wave to the crowd. Everyone loves a home run.

Once we settled back into our seats, Will told me that was the first home run he had ever seen. "Well, kid, cheers to that," I nodded, holding out a spoonful of Dippin' Dots.

They felt exactly as they looked—like little frozen balls. It was neat letting them melt in my mouth, but then I waited and waited and waited for the flavor to come, but unfortunately, it never did. I eventually came to the conclusion that fancy dessert went all for glam and missed out on tasting anything like real ice cream. What happened to the rich, creamy flavor and thickness of a cold cone? No, instead, people were clamoring for these liquid nitrogen milk pellets that got your mouth so cold, it tricked your taste buds into thinking there's any real taste. I couldn't let Will sense my disdain, so I told him they were pretty good and quickly scarfed down the rest so as not to drag out my dissatisfaction. The more I shoveled into my mouth, the more my taste buds became paralyzed, and I became worried I wouldn't be able to taste my other food. Finally rid of those frozen lactose bombs, I was able to experience the real food.

To my delight, the hot dog tasted even better than I imagined, which was pretty surprising considering my lofty expectations. Will didn't seem to like it quite as much, though.

"Don't like that brown mustard, huh, bud?" I asked him. He looked at me with panic in his eyes. "Don't worry," I chuckled. "Just scrape it off onto the ground." He gingerly removed the mustard from the dog. I couldn't fault him for not enjoying it. Maybe he would come to like it one day.

The rest of the game finished up rather slowly, and toward the later innings, I just wanted it to end. The Mets were losing by five runs going into the top of the ninth, and I could tell the game wasn't keeping Will's attention.

"Hey, how 'bout we leave a little early? I think the game's over," I offered. If they came back, then shame on me, but any later and New York's rush hour traffic would have us home the next day. He nodded enthusiastically, and as we left the stadium, Will looked back for one last glimpse.

"Thanks for the game, Uncle Nick. It was really cool."

"Well, you're welcome, Will. It wouldn't have been much fun without you," I said.

"Yeah, all my friends have talked about how their dad took them to a game and how big the stadiums are, and they're right," he continued. "And they hit the ball so far. Do you think I will ever hit it that far?" A smile crept onto my face.

"I bet even farther," I responded.

Will fell asleep on the way home, and I was pretty jealous. There is no sleep like that you find in a car, and it had been so long since I had the opportunity. Luckily, driving didn't make me drowsy. The plus side was there were no complaints about which radio station was playing. We pulled into the driveway just before suppertime, and Will rubbed his eyes as he lifted his head up. Kids always know the moment you enter their neighborhood when asleep. It's like a sixth sense. He thanked me again for the game and bolted out the door.

"Don't forget your lunch." He quickly trotted back and snagged it.

Right as I was about to back out, my sister came running out and flagged me down.

"Wait, Nick!" She came up to my window. "How 'bout you stay for dinner? I made plenty, and Nate's working late." It was a tempting invitation.

"You know I can't turn down an offer like that," I remarked and shut off the car.

"Great! I hope you like beef stroganoff."

It had been years since I had been inside her house, and walking into the place stunned me. It was even cleaner than my apartment. The front hallway led to an open living room with a second-story balcony overlooking it. Their kitchen was connected by an open layout and looked fit for a master chef. The aroma played a role in the allure, too, as the seared meat tickled my nostrils and invited me in.

I hunkered down at the granite breakfast bar, the cheese spread in front of me calling my name. Will ran off upstairs, probably to play his new PlayStation. Ann explained it was all the rage now and that Will's friends were constantly over at their house playing it. I had seen the systems displayed in stores, and just couldn't quite see the appeal. What happened to playing some catch or tag? It seemed as though the new generation was going soft and lazy.

"Nick, that was an awesome idea to take Will to the game. I'm sure he had a blast. He was so excited; he couldn't stop talking about it the last couple of days," she said as she set the table.

"Yeah, it was no problem. I had a ton of fun, too," I mumbled, trying to talk with a mouthful of cracker. "You have a really good kid there. Plus, someone has to teach him about baseball," I retorted. Ann grimaced as she removed a pan from the oven.

"Dinner's ready!" she shouted, hoping Will heard. After a few seconds, she asked if I could go grab him.

"No problem," I said.

Towards the top of the stairs, I caught my first glimpse of his room. The walls were a generic white with a sports wallpaper banner running horizontally around the middle. A wood twin bed with racecar sheets was tucked away in one corner. Opposite the bed sat a breathtaking dresser, which appeared completely out of place. As I approached it, the craftsmanship began to show. I wasn't too enthusiastic about furniture, but my father was a carpenter, and I had developed an eye for quality pieces.

By all measures, I bet the dresser was a least 100 years old. The frame was probably maple, from my guess, and it had redwood inlays running the length of the top and bottom. Far too nice for such a young kid. The drawers slid out like they were oiled, and the joints and edges were perfectly flush. I became so enthralled with the dresser that I forgot my purpose for the venture. I turned toward Will, who hadn't even noticed I waltzed in. His eyes were fixed on the screen, his hands mashing the controller vigorously. No wonder these systems cost so much. The controllers must've been made out of steel. He was playing a fighting game, and it was rather violent. Before realizing it, I had almost watched a whole match, but then Ann yelled dinner again, and I was snapped out of the trance.

"Hey, Will, time for dinner," I said rather loudly. His head snapped around and met my gaze.

"Just let me finish this fight," he pleaded. I obliged, and after a few more kicks and punches, the match looked all but done.

"This is pretty cool," I said, almost breathing a sigh of relief. And then Will's character ripped the other person's spine out. I watched, puzzled, as Will casually got up and acted as if it was all normal.

"Let's go then," he motioned to me. I was still a little confused

"Uh, you know you just ripped his spine out, right? That's not alright. What kind of game is this?" I said, not even attempting to disguise my concern.

"It's just a fighting game. It's all make-believe," he assured me. *Because, of course, if it's make-believe, it couldn't possibly be harmful.* Still dumbfounded and suddenly judging my sister's parenting style, we made our way downstairs to a gorgeous spread.

Beef stroganoff over noodles with sides of mashed sweet potatoes and corn on the cob was a perfect counter to the greasy ballpark food earlier. Barely a word was said before we began digging in. I helped myself to a heaping pile of everything and let the cinnamon waft into my nostrils as I lifted a spoonful of potatoes to my lips. The creamy texture of the potatoes blanketed my mouth with the sweet flavor blending alongside the undertones of vanilla, all culminating in taste bud bliss. I must've looked rather silly because my sister asked if I was alright.

"Never better," I responded. The meal continued in relative silence until Will, who inhaled his food, asked to be excused. His mother argued that there was company, and he settled back into his chair, but Will sensed he could win the argument. Within a couple of minutes, he was granted his freedom. He shot upstairs to reunite with his video games. So, I turned my attention to my sister and asked her when she got so good at cooking.

"Well, when you do it every day for years, you're kinda forced to," she responded rather bluntly. She didn't seem all too perky at the moment. She rose to start cleaning the table, and I followed suit.

"Hey, I was thinking 'bout our conversation earlier this week. How 'bout I take Will out more often, and you can get some time for yourself? How's that sound?" I offered.

"That would be great, Nick. It was a relief to get some 'me time' today, and my session went wonderful." The relief in her voice was overwhelming. You could hear the exhaustion released.

"That's great! And... well... if you don't mind me asking, what did you discuss? I don't wanna pry, but I'm here for you."

She smiled at my sincerity.

"I just have patterns, and I gotta do my best to avoid them because although they're easy and comfortable, I know they're not the best for me. You know, I may not have touched drugs in a long time, but I still have my vices. They aren't as bad, but I can't use that as an excuse to use them as a substitute." She paused. "You know, Nick, sometimes I feel like I'm climbing a ladder, and it takes so much of me to get to the next rung. I look around and everyone is higher than me, so I climb faster an' faster, and then I stop and realize I'm at the bottom. I was sliding down the whole time."

Her eyes welled up, and agitation entered her voice. "Sometimes, I want to know where I could be in life. I love Will, but after I got clean, I was grasping for a stable life, and I found that in Nate. It was great at the time. I was able to run from my problems and fears by building a life everyone strives for. Deep down, though, I know now it isn't me. I'm not a rich housewife. When I go to a spa or 'mid-morning brunch,' I feel a ton of anxiety because I'm nothing like the other moms. They get flustered if their kid doesn't get an A or excel in everything all the time, and I just have to pretend I care as much as them, or I would feel like less of a parent. Will can do anything and make me happy, but that isn't enough here. This isn't the real world."

Her eyes told the whole story. She was breathing harder, too. I was locked on her, mesmerized by the candor. She continued, "I'm not meant for this, Nick. I'm meant to be crazy, spontaneous, rude, carefree. My dream is to travel, meet people all over the world, and finally settle with a man who doesn't care about money. We could scrape by, making just enough to send us on our next adventure." She stopped, pausing over the sink before letting out a long sigh.

"You know... that wouldn't make me happier. The grass always seems greener, but in my heart, I know that with Nate and Will is where I belong. I live an amazing life that most people would be jealous of. I'm just not living *my* life." Ann's voice drifted, and the room became encased in silence.

I didn't know what to say. I had never had anyone confess something so deep, so honest. All I mustered was a shoulder hug as she washed dishes.

We continued clearing the table. Silence still encompassed the room, and my mind was still recovering. Washing dishes, I finally broke the calm.

"I never knew those things, Ann. Thank you. Sometimes I can get so wrapped up in myself, really everyone can." She was scrubbing a dish furiously. I grabbed her arm to stop.

"Ann, you can make *this* your life." I made a gesture around the room, letting the words sink in. I wasn't sure what she thought about that. I continued, "You can still do some things for yourself. The only one stopping you is you. Nate is a good man. If you talk to him, he will understand. What's stopping you but the belief you can't?"

Her hands froze while she put a glass in the dishwasher. A throaty acknowledgment was all she mustered. But it was all she needed to say. I just needed to know that she heard me. We finished cleaning up, taking a few jabs at our lives, Will, Nate, and work. It really lightened the mood. Thirty-plus years and I was only just now really starting to know her. It wasn't long after the kitchen was clean before I headed out. I made sure to thank her one last time for the meal and then started for home.

.

Chapter 14

Sure enough, the next day, Deniece called back, and we planned on a dinner for Saturday night. I knew I could impress her with my ride and insisted on picking her up. I was getting butterflies just thinking about it! She was working at a non-profit group home till six, so we settled on seven and made small talk for a minute before I let her go.

Deniece working for a non-profit reminded me of my first job. It was a year or two after I had started my revenge tradition, and I was still bubbling with blinding hatred. It was my first year out of college, and I had trouble finding an accounting job, so I worked at a non-profit agency for a short stint that specialized in providing logistical services for churches and charities.

On my very first day on the job, Steve, the director of the organization, came into my tiny desk area and gave me a few pointers. He was slim and most likely in his mid-30s, but his face carried weight and he looked exhausted. I guess it was difficult to run an NPO. He started with a welcome, introducing me to the organization. He sensed I must've been nervous about my first job out of college, and I admitted it was actually my first job ever.

"Ever!?" He chuckled. "How did you get past the interview?" He was being playful.

"I do what I'm told." I shot back, grinning slightly.

I watched his face process the heavy tone, but once he caught my grin, he returned a wide smile, like a proud father. He took me by the shoulder, "Well, listen," he started, "your job is pretty easy here. You'll be managing a couple of accounts. Now, before your eyes bug out, there isn't much to them. You'll receive funds from some of our affiliates, donors, and the government. All you're responsible for is wiring and transferring the money to keep things balanced. Now, although we are non-profit, the government still breathes down our neck, so it's important to be thorough, you know"? I nodded but couldn't keep the puzzled look off my face, so he elaborated.

"Say you need to take money out of our main account. Make sure you indicate it as a specific expense like a janitorial service, even if it's not. At the end of the day, on paper, every dollar must be spent on something the government deems as necessary, but the real world isn't as black and white as those textbooks you just finished up with. You know what I'm saying?" He looked for my approval.

"Oh yeah, I gotcha now. Yeah, no problem," I replied nonchalantly as I leaned back in my office chair.

"Perfect! I have a good feeling about you. Any questions or concerns, come to me immediately. You'll do great, son." With that, he extended his arm for one last firm handshake, then strode back to the office. He seemed like a decent guy.

The first few weeks of the job had me scrambling from different ledgers, bills, and checkbooks working on getting everything in order. He made it sound so simple, but it was a mess trying to keep track of the few accounts I was in charge of. I frequently asked Steve about the accounts. The main account was active constantly. That one gave me the most trouble as there were multiple people with access, and anytime someone withdrew money, they usually sent me a receipt to prove they were allocating the funds appropriately. The problem with this was people got lazy or would forget, and I had to hunt them down.

At first, I tried email but quickly found this was useless and soon was going door-to-door like a medieval tax collector. It took time, but within a month, I had the system down pretty well. I even began getting somewhat acquainted with the coworkers. There was a cute secretary who was hired around the same time as me. The guys in the office drooled over her, and she knew it. I tried to flirt a little whenever I was near, but they were mediocre attempts. I was sure she had already been asked on a date by a few guys in the office, and I found it hard to muster up the confidence to get rejected. Unfortunately, by the time she began coming over to my desk to flirt, the place had begun to unravel.

It started when I stayed late once and caught the light on in Steve's office. On my way out, I stopped in to see if he wanted to get a drink, but he had beat me. There was a full glass next to a bottle of bourbon. That didn't give me pause, though—instead, it was his blank stare, with eyes glazed over.

This wasn't just one after-work drink.

"Nick!?" A slightly slurred but giddy yell echoed from behind the desk. Steve waved me in, his office dimly lit. I approached with a hesitant smile.

"You've been doing great work, kid. I was just talking to Katie yesterday, and she mentioned how well you were doing, how you could be relied upon." He see-sawed back in his chair.

"Just doing what I'm told, sir," I retorted with a sly smile.

"Indeed, you do." He chuckled softly and started swirling his drink, bringing his attention to the window like he was thinking.

"I got a dilemma here, and I'm thinking now you might be the man to help me out." He lingered on the sentence and raised his eyebrow, gauging my receptiveness.

"Of course, anything I can do!" I shot back enthusiastically. *Hopefully, the eagerness convinced him I was the right fit.*

"Well Nick, I leave for Europe next week for the company. Long story short, I need to send funds to an account I establish there with a new partner. Obviously, I can't send it myself as I'll be abroad, so I would need you to take on that account while I'm over there." I nodded in understanding.

"As a director, I also have a separate account that I need managed while over there. It includes part of my pay, but also a stipend to be spent on clients."

He had already finished his drink and began to pour another. The liquor sloshed violently with his unsteady pour.

"Now, Nick, I'm trusting you with this. This is… uh… director stuff, and I shouldn't be delegating this out, much less to a new hire. But… I like ya, and you are reliable. There is a lot to be said for that. But let's just keep this between you and me because I don't want to start creating office drama playing favorites. You know." He gave me a wink as he pulled back a drawer.

I obliged with a firm nod.

"What do you say we drink to it!?"

"Just one drink, though," I interjected. "I have dinner with the girlfriend and the parents tonight." I gritted my teeth like I was dreading it in order to sell the lie. I did not want to get caught up finishing the bottle or seem rude after he had just given me such an important job.

His eyes lit up instantly.

"Oh, I see, and here I thought you were going to take a stab at Maya one of these days. She likes to linger around your desk." He beamed at me. "You dog."

I dismissed his comment with a hand wave, and he began to pour a generous serving into a nice crystal whisky glass.

"You know, I could give you some advice about that situation."

"Now you're starting to sound like my father," I responded back.

Steve puckered before relaxing. "You know… it must be the glasses. They were my father's before he gave them to me. Swear he's there every time I bring them out." He laughed at himself, but there was a somber undertone to his casualness. I picked it up quickly.

"Sounds like my watch." I pulled up my sleeve. "Just like his. Like father like son."

Steve released a subtle but approving smile and half raised his glass.

"To our fathers…" he chuckled.

"To our fathers," I repeated, holding my drink in the air a few seconds before knocking it back.

Everything went okay for a while. When Steve got back, he kept me on the accounts. It continued like that until a nagging feeling started to come up every time I did transfers.

The account was based overseas, and I thought it was odd that a non-profit had an account overseas, especially since I didn't know any affiliates over there. I thought maybe after some time it would be revealed to everyone we were working with new entities in Europe or something, but nothing. It seemed fishy to me, and I decided to put a hold on the transfer until I could ask Steve about it in person since he had been out of the office that week. That mistake got me my first and only earful at the job. The next day Steve came in not just stressed like his normal self but blisteringly mad. The dreaded feeling of regret set in as he approached; I knew I was going to be chewed out.

"Nick, did you transfer money into all the accounts?" The tone of his voice told me he already knew the answer.

"Not all," I said sheepishly, making sure not to look him in the eye.

"Can you step into my office, please?" He was doing all he could to keep a lid on it, and the "please" at the end stung.

I followed him into his office, where he locked the door, pulled the shades, and made his way to his desk.

"Have a seat, Nick." I obliged.

"Do you know what your job is?"

"Yes."

"Do you know that the only essential part of your job is fucking easy?"

"Yes."

"Do you know you didn't complete your job?"

"Yes."

"Now, am I asking too much of you? 'Cause if I am, then, by all means, tell me and I will head to the school down the street, pull an eighth-grader out of class, give him your job, and he would have the finances in order next month!"

"Sir, I—"

"No, I don't want a fucking excuse. Did I not tell you to come to me with any questions or concerns? 'Cause I think that's a fucking big one!" He sat back in his chair and took a breath. "Why didn't you transfer the money into the Swiss account?" His steely eyes cut right through me.

"The account was foreign," I mumbled.

"What?"

"I said the account was foreign. I'm not an idiot, sir. Why would a non-profit with no affiliations have an offshore account for which I need to make up expense statements to cover the money unless it was to siphon off funds? An account that can only be accessed by two people. Since I didn't set up the account or truly know where the money is going, that led me to only one conclusion." I was nearly yelling when I finished.

"So, you're accusing me of embezzlement?" he responded calmly.

"Well, no. I mean, that is sure what it looks like." He caught me off guard with his calm reaction.

"Ahh, Nick, I should've anticipated this and just been transparent to begin with. The reason we have that overseas account is because we're trying to establish a small charity there." He could tell I was skeptical. "My sister Lauren—who is still employed here and is still on the payroll—is running it. Check for yourself. She left six months ago on a simple vacation to see some sites in Europe." He took a sip of coffee.

"I'm sure you're aware of the Bosnia conflict, right? Well, she was so moved by the refugees and survivors that she begged me to establish a charity. She's the only person I have in my life. Both our parents died a few years ago in a car accident, and her husband developed a freak heart condition and passed away. I knew it would be difficult, but I couldn't say no. It was the right thing to do.

"That account is for the money she needs to live over there and begin the charity. She needs to make connections, find places for people to stay, food, clothes, you name it. These people have nothing, and Lauren gives them a little hope. Granted, I wish we could be doing more, but it already skirts legality. I'm working with lawyers trying to get everything straightened out, but when you don't transfer money into that account, people and my sister are suffering.

"*That* is why I'm upset, but in the end, it's mostly my fault for not informing you. So, I'm sorry, Nick, and I understand if you feel uncomfortable handling the account. You don't have to anymore. I just got a real sense of trustworthiness from you." He pulled out a bottle of Scotch and a glass from under the table.

"I had no idea. I'm so sorry about this," I began. "Now that I know, I understand. There won't be a problem from here on out. Thanks and sorry again. Give my apologies to your sister. I'll take care of it right away." I began to scurry out toward the door.

"Nick, care for a drink?" Steve asked as he poured himself one.

"No, I'll pass. Another time though." He shrugged, and I almost second-guessed myself. That drink looked heavenly.

I immediately transferred the money into the account once back at my desk. Steve asked me to keep it around $20,000 at the end of the month and replenish it slowly the following month. I felt so stupid and disrespectful for questioning him. He seemed like a standup, sincere guy.

A couple of months went by without me second-guessing the account, and things were going alright. I moved into a relatively nice apartment complex and had begun paying back my student loans. I told my mom how the job was going and how dumb I felt about managing the accounts.

"Don't be so naïve, Nick. You're just learning about finances and know even less about people. Don't buy into what he tells you so easily. Don't tell me you're not suspicious at all anymore?

I hesitated. "Well, I mean not really, but it makes sense. He's a good guy, and he didn't appear to be hiding anything when I brought it up. I'm sure things are on the up and up; plus, it doesn't adversely affect the finances in any way," I assured her.

"Think about why he might have given you, a new grad, this account. Because it stinks, and he could never pull the wool over the eyes of someone with experience. Just be smart, Nick," she warned.

"I will," I said and shrugged it off.

Although I brushed it aside at the time, the next time a transfer rolled around, I couldn't shake my mom's words, and the uncertainty began to mount. It ate at me for a few weeks before I determined I had to find out if what he was saying was legitimate.

The first stop was his sister. She did, in fact, show up on the payroll and was on the employee list. Discreetly asking around, the office consensus was that she went on vacation a while ago and then never came back. Steve said she was over in Europe helping with the Bosnia crisis, and that checked out okay. I then found her address from payroll and decided to pass by her house on my way home from work. There were no lights on, and it appeared empty. I checked back during the day on a weekend, and there were still no signs of life. However, I took it a step further.

I stopped at her neighbors' house across the street, posing as a lawn care service provider. I went to great lengths to play the part, and it was a thrill. I asked the neighbors if anyone around the area needed any lawn care service that they knew about. I pointed to Lauren's house across the street as it looked like it had been neglected most of the summer.

"I'm not sure. Sure looks like she needs it, but we haven't seen her in months. Rumor is she moved to Europe, so unless you plan on going all the way there, I don't think she'll need it," he chuckled. I thanked him and found myself back at square one. I was truly doubtful anything was askew, but knew I had to be thorough.

One thing that wasn't going anywhere was the account. There was a large sum of money withdrawn every month, usually in cash. It made sense. She was helping people who just came out of a warzone; credit wouldn't go very far. Steve's story was, again, checking out. I finally took a closer look at Steve's account since it was the last avenue I could think of. Perhaps there was something linking him to an expensive house, car, or boat. He was spending a lot, but the charges puzzled me.

Most of what I found were extensive hospital billings about a year ago. He was spending tens of thousands a month, then his activity switched to cash withdrawals six months later. Steve's finances were nothing to write home about. He was virtually broke, so where was all his money going?

This really aroused my suspicion, and I spent hours poring over as much as I could to see if there was anything I could've missed. Looking over the overseas account again, I remembered it was in Switzerland. Some gut feeling got me curious, and I stopped at the library on the way home to check out a map. The minute I looked at Europe a bit closer, my stomach dropped. I froze, making sure to double-check before I let the feeling sink in.

"Son of a bitch!"

I had never been one for geography, and with all the countries in Europe, it's easy to think all the small countries border each other. That was evident because the first time I saw it was a Swiss bank, I assumed they were neighbors with Bosnia, and the charity was getting started in a stable country, far from the threat of violence. "Far" was really what Lauren had in mind because the two countries were separated by Italy and a couple of others. I put the map down. How stupid and gullible could I be? This whole time, it was right there. Everything else checked out, but they couldn't hide it all.

The wheels continued to turn in my head. His sister was probably over there getting rich from embezzlement. Steve was taking most of his money and Lauren's paycheck out in cash and sending some over with every letter. I probably wasn't the only one in the office depositing money into a Swiss account, either. Then, after a few years, they would have enough for life, he would flee to Europe, and it would be months before the whole scheme was figured out. It wouldn't matter by then, though, because there would be nothing to be done.

I began to stew with anger. Steve was unbelievable. He had lied straight to my face without flinching. No wonder he was so on edge. I trusted him, and he betrayed that. He was a slime, and I felt shame for participating in his little scheme. But that wouldn't happen any longer. I continued to vent my disgust, not quite believing what I had just discovered.

Pacing that night, drink in hand, I contemplated how to deal with the situation. I obviously couldn't go to Steve, and I couldn't go directly to the cops because I had helped embezzle for months—granted unknowingly. I also didn't have concrete proof. I didn't want to put my future in the hands of the local police. Plus, what could they even do about it? It was approaching late

September, but I wasn't sure how I could avenge the wrong. I wasn't a financial wiz that could trick Steve at his own game. He was much smarter than I was.

I called in sick to work the next day. I couldn't face that thief without resorting to something physical, and I couldn't muster the self-restraint needed to act as if I didn't know anything. I brainstormed the entire day but kept coming up empty. Every idea I had was either out of my capability or had a strong possibility of backfiring. The only viable option was to take what I knew to the proper authorities. It pained me to think of not handling the matter on my own, but I was ill-equipped to deal with a multi-national embezzlement scam. I resolved that on September 21st, I would turn all the evidence I could gather to the F.B.I., as I was sure the local authority would probably end up contacting them anyway.

I spent the next week gathering all the evidence and records I could that were associated with the two accounts. I made copies discretely and did my best to keep my shit together around the office. I put on my happy face for Steve, and I kept my emotions in check enough to avoid suspicion. Keeping myself completely focused on collecting the evidence was effective in avoiding my anger toward the bastard. By the fifth day, I thought I had gathered most everything I had access to and built a pretty solid case. I worried that word would get back to Steve if I asked around the office about other accounts people were managing, but the F.B.I. probably had the capability of figuring that out with discretion.

September 21st finally rolled around, and the time had come to put an end to Steve's charade. I decided to come into work for a half-day and then duck out just to save face. I didn't want Steve to suspect anything. I was terrified of the notion of him discovering I ratted him out before the F.B.I. stepped in. Who knew what he was capable of? There was a lot of money at stake, and the man was so on edge. Anxiety and anticipation ran rampant as I toiled away most of the day. Of course, it was blistering hot that day in the office, and I could only sit so long in my chair. Every 15 minutes or so, I would have to air out my pants by pretending to need a cup of water from the bubbler, or I would develop sweat stains on my ass.

I was taking a deep breath, holding down the nozzle, when I heard him.

"Hey, Nick! How's it going today?" Steve's voice startled me so bad I threw my arms up, tossing the water against the wall beside me. The splatter partially caught Steve in the face, and he wiped it away with his sleeve.

"Whoa, jeez, Nick, I didn't mean to startle ya." He rested his hand on my shoulder. "You don't have to act so guilty if I catch you taking a break," he said with a smile.

His laughing at his joke finally broke my surprise.

"I don't know why I got so startled there, but I need the breaks with how hot it is in here." Thankfully, his laugh had helped me relax.

"I should transfer some of that money from the account and put it toward air conditioning." I elbowed him and winked.

He didn't share my amusement.

"Excuse me?" The steel in his voice cut my smile.

"Steve, I was just joking, man. I—"

He started laughing, "I know, I know. You should've seen how worried you looked. Probably PTSD from the last time we talked about it." He was roaring now.

"Yeah, that was fun."

I just wanted the conversation to end. I wiped the sweat from my forehead and told him I should get back to work, then scurried to my desk. I felt like he knew.

Finally, the clock crept to 11 a.m., and I was relieved of my cubicle prison. I bolted out of the place, navigating the back corners to avoid any interaction. Surely, I thought my face was screaming, "I'm going to the F.B.I."

The rush of fresh air felt like freedom outside the building, and a stiff breeze cooled the sweat that perspired on my butt. As I made my way toward the nearest F.B.I. field office in Philadelphia, I couldn't help but think of all the possibilities. What if I had this whole thing wrong? It was a long shot, but anything was possible. I hoped to God that wasn't the case. If it was, then I was pretty certain the authorities would realize that before a forceful intervention, outing me as the leak.

The hulking building was imposing. The small rectangle windows looked like a prison of sorts. Security was a nuisance, and it took a couple of wrong turns to get where I needed to. Finally, I approached a receptionist with my briefcase. She was busy typing away at the keyboard in front of her.

"Hi."

"Welcome to the F.B.I. How may I help you?" She barely slowed her typing and didn't even shoot a glance my way.

"I would like to report a crime." Her hands still didn't stop. I continued, "A multi-national embezzlement crime." She finally raised her head and paused her fingers. I had a feeling she got her fair share of nut cases or petty crimes. She looked disinterested and skeptical.

"I'll get an agent for you. Just have a seat over there." There was just a bit of pep in her voice. Before I even got settled, an agent shot out of the side door and strode to the front desk. The receptionist pointed my way, and he wasted no time getting there.

"Good afternoon, Mister…?"

"Jacobs."

"Mr. Jacobs!" He produced a handshake. "Shaun Johnson, junior field agent. Nice to make your acquaintance!" He was sprightly. "I hear you have some information you would like to share?"

"Yes, I have a bit," I said, lifting my briefcase. I felt incredibly empowered walking into the back offices. It really felt heroic. He led me down a hall past dozens of offices where, presumably, other agents were working busting crimes. He turned into a small cubicle office toward the end of the hall. He was a younger agent, perhaps even younger than I was. I could sense his excitement as he ushered me into his office chair. He flipped through a couple of drawers and emerged with a pad, pen, and tape recorder.

"You don't mind, do you?"

"Ah, maybe see if you even think I have credible stuff. I don't want to get too far ahead," I told him.

"Of course, of course, good point. Well, what would you like to share?" He finally took a moment to relax.

I rested the briefcase on his desk, pulling out several documents as I began to explain. I disclosed information about my account management, who I worked for, and exactly what I did. He listened intently, not offering or asking much, but appeared to understand my situation.

I then went on and brought up the offshore account I managed in Switzerland. His eyebrows furrowed at the mention, and he began making notes on his paper.

"Does your organization have ties to others that may warrant a multi-national reach?"

"Nope, not one. Granted, I didn't dig the hardest there, but what company would go to lengths to conceal that?"

He seemed to agree.

I mentioned my boss's uneasiness and his frustration when I didn't put money into the account the first month and the fact that I probably wasn't the only one. When relaying the explanation about his sister, I couldn't help but feel stupid for my gullibility. I almost felt like I was indicting myself for my naivety. It sounded pretty farcical.

"So, this is when you got suspicious?"

"Well… no," I hesitated. "I was just so taken back and new to the job, I really didn't even question it." My voice trembled a bit.

He nodded as if he understood.

"See, I first thought it was fishy when my mom showed concern after I told her. Then I just couldn't get the thought out of the back of my mind when the next transfer came around." I paused, shooting Shaun a quick glance. He was still attentive.

"I wanted to just be sure I wasn't in on something illegal, so I checked out all the avenues I could. The sister was definitely gone, as none of her neighbors or people at the office had seen her in months. The overseas account made sense at first, and the cash withdrawals from the account didn't appear suspicious. Then I checked out my boss's account."

I was wondering if he was impressed by my investigative skills thus far. I mean, I was proud to have gotten to the bottom of the whole ordeal. I just wondered, why me? With all the others in the office, why was I stuck with the illegal one? Or was I the only one to find a problem with it?

I began to detail how Steve was almost broke, the constant cash withdrawals, and the fact that Switzerland was a lot farther away from Bosnia than I had previously thought. The agent asked a few specific questions that I couldn't answer or had simply not even thought of myself. After he appeared satisfied with the statement, it had been close to 45 minutes in the office. He had gathered all my documents and everything I knew.

"Well, Nick, I'm going to dig around a little more before I forward what I have to my superior. There are just a few facts I need to check out first. Hey, but listen, good catch here. I think you might have something. If we do decide to move forward, I will let you know. Until then, continue to work and make the transfers as usual. If this guy is on edge as much as you say he is, you never know how he will react if he thinks something's off. Don't mean to scare ya, but you just never know with people. I'm also going to need a sworn statement corroborating what you just told me." He leaned back and began rummaging through some papers, finally emerging with a blank document he handed over to me. "Just write down everything you told me, the accounts, the transfers, the sister. Be specific on dates if possible."

I froze with the paper in my hand, trying to process everything I was just told.

"Wait, I still have to work with this guy? How long is it going to take? What happens if he does suspect something? This is my safety here." Agitation crept into my voice.

"Slow down, relax. He's not going to know anything. The digging I'm doing won't alert him, and as long as you stick to your normal routine, it will all be fine. Besides, that's not how this stuff works. It takes time. Innocent until proven guilty, you hear of that?" He was stern and rather gruff; not the comforting response I was looking for.

"Let's just say what if, by some means, he finds out. Do I need witness protection?" I probably sounded like a scared bitch, but it was my neck on the line, not his.

"Don't get ahead of yourself, Nick. You will be fine."

"They really teach reassurance techniques here at the F.B.I., don't they?" I scoffed.

"You did the right thing. Not everyone has the guts. Thanks." He stuck out a firm handshake as he rose from the seat. "We'll be in touch."

And that was all I was left with when leaving the field office—that and a business card I slipped into my wallet. Shaun sure didn't leave me with a lot of confidence that my safety was a priority. Perhaps it had been a mistake to turn it into the F.B.I. in the first place. The ride home exacerbated my already racing thoughts. Not many of the situations I envisioned had a promising outcome.

The days following the interview had me in a constant state of unease. I kept cool, but every time I made eye contact or talked to Steve, I was convinced he knew. For the most part though, it was business as usual at the office, and within a week, I had begun to forget about the ordeal. Of course, it was impossible to completely forget about it, but it floated out of my conscious thought most of the time. Around the fifth week, I began to wonder if they were even going to take action or if their investigation had stalled.

A typical Wednesday was in the making, and I had my face buried in some paperwork that I had fallen behind on.

"Hey, Nick, got a sec?"

My head shot up. "Jeez! You startled me, Steve."

"Didn't mean to scare ya, but at least I know you're hard at work," he chuckled.

I managed a smile back.

"Can I borrow a dollar? I need a coffee from the cappuccino machine, and I left my wallet at home."

"Yeah, I guess I can spare a buck. Might have to charge interest, though," I quipped. It was a lame, cheesy attempt at comedy with the boss, but he seemed to get a kick out of it.

I began pulling out my wallet, "You know, you would think being the director, you would get some coffee perks or—"

Just then, the F.B.I. business card slipped out. It fluttered in the air briefly, almost in slow motion. I extended my arm to snatch it, but the laminated pulp eluded my grasp, skimming my wrist and then floating down on the other side of my desk. I stared at the card like it was a smoldering bomb.

"No worries, I got it!" He enthusiastically bent down to grab it.

"No, no, that's quite alright!" I blurted out in a panic.

The F.B.I. emblem was boldly printed on the front of the card. *Shit.* He looked at it, puzzled for a second.

"Why do you have an F.B.I. business card?"

Had I been quicker on my feet, I could've casually said it was my cousin or an agent involved in my sister's drug case or any number of possible reasons, but instead, I did the worst thing possible and stared directly at him blank face, panicked eyes, and guilt written on my forehead.

My petrified gaze continued, though I tried to wrack my brain for some response. "I don't know."

I sealed my fate with that response. I could've said I took my younger sister to a job fair, and it was from one of the agents who was there. Unfortunately, that quick wit eluded me in that moment of need, and I was left with jack squat.

"This… this isn't about the foreign account, is it?"

I couldn't tell if he was more puzzled or accusing. Again, I couldn't muster a response to deter him from knowing my betrayal. I simply pleaded with my eyes that he wouldn't connect the dots, although, by this point, a second-grader probably could have.

"Nick, why?" His voice trailed off. Steve stood in a petrified gaze. His eyes were sad, lost.

"I didn't mean to betray your trust. It's just the account was ill—"

Suddenly, it was like a brick collided with my cheek, and it sent me reeling. Caught off guard, I staggered back, tripping over my chair and falling to the floor.

Shocked, I looked up, mouth agape.

"Fuck you! I told you…. I told… Fuck! She was progressing so well," he yelled. His voice held more rage than I had heard in a long time, and it left me retreating slowly away from him. By this point, a couple of people had noticed the commotion. Steve must've sensed it because he seemed to relax and slithered back into his office.

Pain began to emerge from my previously numb face, and I felt around to assess the damage. I touched my lip to find it was definitely swollen. Pulling my hand away let me realize that it was quite bloody, too. I scrambled up to my desk in order to stem the bleeding with a box of tissues. My coworkers looked on like I was a circus freak.

"I'm alright, guys. Just a disagreement, nothing to worry about." I tried to assure the onlookers. I doubt that petty attempt quelled their concerns, but nonetheless, they began to herd themselves back to their workstations. The whole ordeal left a very bloody mouth and a cut on the cheek, but I was thankful it wasn't worse. Taking the tissue box to go, I rushed out of the building and took no time getting to my car. I only hesitated to look over my shoulder. It felt like I was on the run from some murderer.

I sped back to my apartment to make a call to Shaun. I wasn't sure how safe I was there, though, as Steve definitely had everyone's addresses in his office. What if the punch was just a preview, and he decided to come back in order to finish the job? My face was swollen by this time, and after a look in the mirror, I was shocked. It looked like I had gone 10 rounds with Rocky.

I concluded I only had time to stay for a quick phone call to the bureau. Since I no longer had the business card, I was forced to call the office.

"Hello, Philadelphia F.B.I. field office. How may I help you?"

"Is Shaun Johnson there? This is an emergency!" I'm sure I sounded like a maniac; my breathing was at a feverish pace. What if Steve were on his way here? I had to get out now.

"I'm sorry, he's out on lunch."

"Screw me!"

"Sir?"

"Damnit, well, just give him this message from Nick as soon as possible. He knows about the investigation, attacked me, I need help. Reach me at 609-182-8811." I wanted to scream into the phone, but I had already been rude to the lady.

"Alright, I'll pass th—"

I slammed the phone down and flew toward my bedroom. No use grabbing too much. I didn't want to risk it. That always happens in movies; you go back to grab one last item, and the intruder pops up right then. I only grabbed what I could carry and rushed out to my car. I'm sure I looked every bit as crazed as I felt. Adrenaline soared, and an unfamiliar fear limited my breathing to short gasps. I was barely able to find the air needed to keep from passing out. Sweat coated the steering wheel, and rubber coated the road as I burned the vintage roadster on the way to my mother's.

Once I reached her house, I was like a helpless child. I'd never been so terrified. The concern, along with the condition of my face, alarmed her immediately. Just like when I took a grounder to the eye as a kid, she iced my head and reassured me I was safe and alright. The nurturing began to bring me back under control. A call from Shaun got my mom even more worked up.

"Let me talk to that filthy pig. There's no reason this should've happened!" She lunged for the phone, but I jerked it back.

"It wasn't his fault." Well, in an indirect way, it was, but I put the blame game behind me.

"Nick, you alright?" He sounded quite panicked, which was a relief. At least he was concerned.

"Yeah, a little rattled and picked up a few beauty marks, but nothing a little foundation can't cover up." I laughed. I sounded so casual, but just minutes earlier, I had been a blubbering coward.

"Good to hear, good to hear. Where are you? I'm going to send a local unit to keep you safe and your mind at ease."

"Wow, well, I could've used one of those the last couple of weeks. I think I'm fine, just at my mom's house."

"Well, it might make you feel a little better to know it wasn't all for nothing. You were definitely right about the embezzlement scheme, and the sister was in Europe. We were just about to spring the trap on the whole thing in a couple of days, but I guess that has to be accelerated. But that's my job, bud. You just worry about resting up and relax; we got it from here. You've done all you could. Did you want to press charges for assault?"

"No. Besides, I probably deserved it."

"Well, to be honest, it might not be up to you. And you know, you might change your mind later. Be in touch real soon. Say hi to your mom for me."

"Oh, she's got a few choice words for you."

"I've heard it all."

I spent the rest of the day kicking back with daytime television before Mom left for card night with the neighborhood's sprightly elders. Many had their kids already shipped off into the real world, so they would sit and brag about whose child was doing what. I sure gave my mom some clout tonight. No doubt she would leave them speechless with the F.B.I. story. It brought me comfort knowing I provided my mother with some ammo.

Just before I headed to bed, I got a call from Shaun saying they caught Steve in the airport. He was attempting to leave on a plane to Europe, but they froze his passport just in time. He informed me that they would need me to testify in court against him. A hint of panic struck my chest. This wasn't over? I completely forgot that testifying was a possibility. I didn't want to face him again. Did he want to kill me? How angry was he? I asked if not testifying was an option.

"Not unless he pleads out."

I kept my fingers crossed, and a couple of weeks later, I got a call from Shaun informing me of just that.

"So, you need anything else from me?"

"Nope, we got all we need."

"Can I ask exactly what was going on?"

"Well, obviously, I can't share too many details, but you were right about the embezzlement, and there were two others at the office involved, but they were similar to you in their obliviousness."

"Oh, thanks." His disrespect was back.

"Yeah, no problem. Anyway, the reason money was flying out of his account and the reason for all the hospital bills last year were because of his sister. She had cancer, and her treatment was very expensive. When she went overseas, it was for experimental treatment. That's why the money was going over there—to pay for it."

And I thought I was going to feel better after an explanation.

"Yeah, sometimes these people break the law with good intentions, but they break it nonetheless. Take care, Nick. Don't beat yourself up. You did the right thing."

It sure hadn't felt that way at the time, and to some extent, it still didn't.

Chapter 15

It had been a little while since I had visited my mom, and I decided it was about time. After a long day at work, I just wanted to get a nap in, but I grudgingly swung by the nursing home. This time I switched things up and brought Wendy's instead of Burger King. Once again, I was greeted by an enthusiastic Sue.

"Oh, your mother is in the dining hall just finishing up dinner. I'm sure she will be delighted you're here!"

The dining hall was largely empty except for a few residents being fed by staffers. My mother was the youngest patient in the room by quite a few years. It was unfortunate she had so many health problems so young, but I was sure she would be home soon.

"Hey, Mom. How's it going?" I said rather cheerfully as I walked up.

She jumped in her wheelchair.

"Oh, Nick, you startled me. I didn't know you were stopping by." Her face was an expression of elated surprise.

"But since you asked, just horrible. I can't eat this stuff!" She pointed to the globular mass on her plate. "See that brown stuff? That's supposedly lemon-seasoned pork roast." I eyed the suspicious goo and shivered thinking about having to put that down my gullet. I think I'd rather die than be forced to eat that stuff. But hell, maybe it wasn't as bad as it appeared. I reached down and grabbed a small spoonful.

"Nick, no," my mom pleaded.

"Relax, it can't hurt."

As soon as my body comprehended the taste of the pork mush, it forced my tongue to curdle. There was no enjoyment to be found in that food. I tried to keep a straight face, but it was fairly obvious I hated the concoction.

"Let's head back to your room, Mom," I said. The taste still resonated in my mouth.

Back in the room, my mom was utterly delighted to see the fast food resting comfortably on her recliner.

"Oh, Nick, you're the best! You have no idea how much I needed this!" She coddled the bag like a newborn child.

"What's up with the food?" I asked.

"A couple of days ago, I was choking on a piece of chicken, and they had to give me the Heimlich. Now, they've switched me to that mush I can barely eat. It wasn't even my fault! That chicken was so dry, it was criminal. The cook should be charged with attempted murder!" I started rolling my eyes, but she kept on. "Hell, fat people need to go on that diet because it's a guaranteed way to lose weight." She began gorging herself on the hamburger.

"Hey, how 'bout a bite? I need to get that taste out of my mouth."

She hesitated and pulled back slightly but reluctantly gave me one—along with a stern look. It was like a little kid not wanting to share a toy with a parent who had just bought it. I guess I couldn't blame her. She had barely eaten the last couple of days.

"How 'bout I talk to them and demand you get off that diet? It's just inhumane," I offered.

She grinned. "By all means, please do."

Mom continued to devour the meal, only pausing periodically to gasp for breath. If she scarfed down the chicken like this, it was no wonder she choked. I took the time to catch her up to speed on my life, the date with Deniece, the game with Will, and Buster. I was wondering if she even processed what I was telling her; she was so engrossed with her food, but when I finished, she asked if I was serious with this girl. I got flustered like a middle school teen.

"Well, I mean, I don't know, Mom. We only meet once. It wasn't even a date. She's really nice and pretty, but I have no clue." She shrugged and smiled, knowing she got me a little rattled.

"Hey, I got a question for you." I shifted back to watch her expression. "You talk with Ann much?" She gave me a puzzled look, shoveling in another fry.

"Yeah, of course. We're pretty close, always have been. She goes out of her way for me, spoiled me rotten for years, and even gave me the grandchild I always wanted. Why do you ask?"

"Just curious, I guess. I was just talking with her the other day, and it just popped into my mind." Mom sat quietly as more fries entered past the point of no return.

"I guess." I paused, shifting my weight in the chair. I was trying to find the right phrasing. "You know," I half-chuckled, "I guess I always thought of her as the spoiled child. We both had rough years, but she kind of always got what she wanted. She was popular. She has a nice life, husband, and kid. I don't know, just maybe I had some animosity toward that. It was misplaced and childish, but do you think Ann felt that?"

Mom stopped eating for a minute, weighing her response. Her tone grew soft. "You treated Ann fine, Nick, and no, I don't think she did. I think Ann wanted you to look out for her as a sister more, if anything. Me and her haven't talked about this in a long time, but Ann felt you were very much in your dad's camp, which was tough for me because it was the truth. So, in some ways, she associated you with that. She moved past it, but like you, regretted those feelings."

We held silence for a while as I thought. "See, I guess I didn't see that. Like, remember how Ann would always get the most and best Christmas and birthday gifts? She got to go on that one gymnastics trip to Los Angeles. I remember that clearly because it was a big argument between you and Dad. I remember you saying she deserved it and that Dad said I deserved to go to baseball camp. You told him that Ann deserved it more and he knew it, and then when he said no, you hit him with the pan. I was standing in the hallway thinking, 'Why did she deserve that stuff and not me?'"

"Did you hear the whole argument?" There was a heaviness in her voice.

"No," I replied, "I left my room after you two were yelling for a bit and then ran back after the pan." My eyes were glued to the ground.

Mom raised herself from the chair, and I watched her feet shuffle toward, then behind me. A warm embrace followed as her arms squeezed my chest from behind the chair, and I leaned into her.

"Oh, Nick," Her tone was sad. She kissed my head, "Of course you deserved it. Me and your father loved you the same. Being married and having kids is complicated—I can't explain it." She lifted her arm and sniffled. "I'm sorry I hurt you, Nick. I'm not proud of some things, and I regret a lot, but nothing as much as hurting you. You'll never know how much I mean that. Just know I love you, and that I'm sorry." She squeezed even harder. I wrapped her arm in a tight embrace against my head.

"I know, Mom, I love you, too." We held tight for a minute and spent a few in a peaceful silence staring blankly at the television.

"You know, I took Will to a baseball game the other day. Cute kid, isn't he?" I asked, shifting topics.

"Oh my god! That kid is just an angel, except when he's with you planning pranks. Those pudgy round cheeks he has are just heart-melters. Hopefully, Ann brings him by soon." She yawned. "I'm sorry. I'm exhausted, and I have physical therapy yet today, so I should grab a quick nap. It was great seeing you, Nick. Promise to visit when I head home? I'm supposed to go next week. That is, if I don't die from starvation before then." She laughed at herself.

The exit request caught me a little off guard.

"Well, that was quick. But, of course, Mom. Behave yourself in the meantime." We briefly exchanged a hug then I slid out. As I left, I stopped Sue in the hallway and asked her to put my mom back on the regular diet. She said she didn't have the authority and was sorry, so I continued asking the staff until I finally got the head nurse. By that point, I was irritated and demanded she be taken off her current diet. He reluctantly obliged. As he looked over and changed some forms, I thanked him and swiftly left.

The week shuffled on until Saturday and my date with Deniece.

I stared at myself in the mirror for a full hour before I had to leave to pick her up. *Am I dressed too fancy? Maybe being a little more casual will keep it cool for a first date.* I felt a cold sweat sticking my undershirt to my back. We seemed to click so well the first time, but what if we had nothing more to talk about? Should I avoid talking about her kid or seem interested? Contradictions and thoughts racked my brain as I made final preparations to head out. A fancy Rolex nearly identical to my father's except for different initials inscribed at the bottom of the face, along with a silver cross, completed the outfit.

I examined myself in the mirror, turning ever so slowly. Freshly pressed black pants complemented by a dark collared shirt with gold accents. I looked damn good. It didn't matter if I was overdressed, I knew she would be impressed. I did have one razor nick on the side of my neck, but it was barely visible.

I still had just over 50 minutes until I had to leave, and the anxiety was eating at me. Plopping down in my recliner, I instantly shot back up. What if sitting wrinkled my clothes or the recliner was dirty? I quickly walked to the bathroom to reassure myself that I had not tampered with my outfit.

"All good, all good," I said to myself. Then I spotted it. My ass was covered in dog hair. Buster must've been sitting in the chair earlier.

"Buster!" He came bounding in, all gleeful and innocent. "Look what you did!" I said, pointing to the clump on my butt. "You know you're not allowed on the furniture, you dummy. Dammit, I should send you to the pound!" I acted as though he could understand me, but he just sat there, panting, completely clueless of his transgression. I couldn't get mad at that face.

"You're lucky I have extra time." I grabbed a roll of masking tape and thoroughly cleaned the pants. It was impossible to get every hair, but there was little chance anyone would notice.

Once satisfied, I spent the remainder of my time pacing the kitchen, sipping on a glass of Merlot and glancing at the clock every few minutes. Finally, an acceptable time came to leave. Twenty minutes early, just to make sure I had enough time for traffic. One last goodbye for Buster, and I was gone.

It turned out that leaving early was a smart idea because, even though I studied the route, one of the roads was under construction, and I was forced to take a detour.

As I pulled up to her house, the butterflies were in full effect, I felt my chest tighten, and when she stepped out of her house, my mouth went drier than the Sahara. My hands felt clammier than what should be possible, and my heart raced like a tweaked-out speed addict. I felt a head rush that threw me into a momentary third-person perspective. I thought she was cute before, but now she was just stunning. I could barely muster anything but staring for a few seconds. A full-length sweeping dark blue dress with a diagonal silver strip, blue eyeliner, and subtle but prominent red lipstick enhanced everything. She looked like a woman in charge, and she sure was welcome to take care of me. I scrambled out of the car to greet her.

"Hi… wow… y-you look amazing," I fumbled out.

"Thank you. I hope I'm not overdressed."

"Oh no, no. You look perfect." I quickly scurried around the car to open the door for her. "Watch your head," I warned as I guided her in.

"Wow, what a gentleman you are. You take a course between the bar and now?"

"I think maybe your memory was just a little fuzzy after so many drinks."

"Probably was. Makes sense then why I agreed to this date." She winked at me. "Quite the car, though. I feel like a badass in this thing." She looked around the cabin like she had just entered space camp as a nerdy teen. She was cute.

"Well, let's see what she can do." I threw the throttle in reverse and hit the gas.

"Nick, car!" Deniece shouted, and I slammed on the brakes, lurching us violently backward.

"I saw them," I assured her, but my face sure painted a different story.

I somberly backed out the rest of the way. She didn't seem frazzled, so I still had the green light to open up the throttle. I screeched the tires once I threw it in first. Her face as she gasped after the maneuver was all the more reason to keep showing off the next few miles. She was getting a real kick out of it.

"This is probably the coolest car I've ever been in."

It was a good thing it was dark, or she might have caught me blushing.

"Well, you see, that was all part of my plan."

"Oh, really? Please share."

"You'll see, Deniece. A magician never reveals his tricks."

"Now you're a magician? First, a gentleman, then a motorhead, and now a magician. Who are you really?" she chuckled.

"Just a guy pretty nervous for the first date."

"Barely even feels like one. Feels like I've known you much longer." Right then, she cranked up the radio.

"Standing in the rain, with his head hung low…"

"Yes!"

"He heard one guitar… bauwm…"

She started getting into it, head banging, air guitar singing, and I didn't hold back joining in.

"Bought a beat-up six-string in the secondhand store, didn't know how to play, but he knew for sure…"

We settled down after the second chorus, laughing as she turned the volume back down.

"If you didn't sing along there, you wouldn't have gotten a second date." She flashed a sly smile toward me, one where it was impossible to tell if she was kidding or completely serious. I loved it.

We began a conversation about our favorite bands and songs. She was a big Foreigner fan, as I had guessed, but we had barely gotten started before arriving at the restaurant. Gallardo's was a fairly expensive place with a reputation for some of the best seafood around.

"I probably should've asked if you were a fan of seafood, but well… I didn't."

"Well, you're in luck once again, seeing as I was here last week and loved it."

What are the odds? I thought.

"You ate here last week?"

"Yup."

"On a date?" I inquired. The question just kind of shot out.

"Oooh, someone's a little jealous." She elbowed me in the side. "Naw, it was my mother's birthday."

Thanks to my reservations, we were quickly seated by a tall, lanky waiter named Austino. He was the kind of overzealous waiter whose enthusiasm and interest in drumming up conversation can be a little awkward and overbearing, but his efforts made the experience a lot better. He served as a sort of icebreaker after Deniece and I got settled. When it came time to order drinks, I saw my opportunity to have a little fun with him. I asked him for a wine recommendation, and apparently, *that* was his niche.

"Well, sir, do you have a preference for a red or white wine?" he asked.

"Ahh, I think a red wine tonight, something with a full body." I had no clue what I was talking about. I simply remembered some wine connoisseur lingo from my childhood since my parents used to be enthusiasts.

"In that case, I would recommend this Pinot from a little vineyard in the Carolinas. It's a hidden gem and recently won a couple of tasting awards. See, although it's a little on the dryer side, it doesn't hold that taste long before the sweet undertones kick in. It also pairs wonderfully with our salmon. Definitely would be my choice, but then again, I prefer a bitter element to my wine. If you were looking for something sweeter, then our house Merlot would be a great fit. It also pairs well with basically any entrée, so you don't have to worry about a conflict there."

This guy really knew his stuff, and Deniece seemed surprised at my interest in wine. I gave her a wink before addressing the waiter.

"I'll have a Sprite, please," I said, and handed him the wine menu.

I didn't bother looking up, and I tried my best to withhold my grin. The 180 must have caught him off guard because he claimed he didn't hear me. This time, I turned to look at him, his face a rigid mix between confused and frustrated.

"I'll have a Sprite, please," I repeated.

I could feel the steeliness of his gaze on the side of his face. I waited for a few moments after he took Deniece's order to relent on the joke. "Hey, Austino!" He turned around with a less than enthusiastic look.

"Would you like more wine suggestions, sir?" The subtle jest was enough to know that I had gotten under his skin.

"Yeah, about that. I was just messing with ya. I'll take that first glass you suggested." I smiled, hoping he enjoyed my sense of humor.

"Funny." And with that, he briskly turned and scurried to the kitchen, but not before I caught a glimpse of a smile. Turning my attention back to Deniece, I couldn't tell whether she enjoyed the small stunt or not.

"Nick, that was so—"

"Yeah, I know. It was kind of a dick move."

"—funny."

"Really? You didn't laugh."

"Well, that's cause it was so tense. I thought he was gonna sock you. Better check your drink when it gets here," she chuckled.

"It was tense, but you know, I was expecting a little more reaction from him once I told him it was a joke. I mean, he's been pretty lively, but I saw a smile before he left, so I think I'm okay."

"You're something else, Nick."

"A good or a bad something?"

"I'm not sure yet."

"Means I still have a chance!"

We continued to converse as we waited for the drinks, mostly about our jobs and hobbies. I told her I enjoyed Cyrus Park and my new pup, Buster. She insisted she had to see the little fella because she loved dogs and had a lot on the farm where she grew up. That shifted the subject to her childhood, what it was like living on the farm, her parents, and siblings. She had a brother and a sister, both older, but they stayed near home in West Virginia. She got out to see them a couple of times a year. It was tough since she had her kid Lizzie, but she still made the effort.

It was really interesting listening to her, and although she did most of the talking, it never felt like she was dominating the conversation. As she shared bits and pieces about her past, I interjected a couple of facts about myself, and the conversation flowed so smoothly, we barely noticed when our waiter set our drinks down.

"Have you two had a glance at the menu, or should I give it a few more minutes?" His question pulled us out of our trance.

"Ahh, yeah, just a couple more minutes," I chimed. A cross necklace around his neck caught my attention, and after he left, I segued that into a conversation about religion. I wasn't too religious myself, but it was always something I kicked around. I believed that God exists, but I wasn't sure about everything else, mainly structured religion.

"You want to get into a religious debate?" Deniece asked. "You haven't been on many first dates, have you?" She smiled cunningly. It didn't deter me from the subject. I felt like I could talk about anything with her.

"Well, not really a debate. Just curious about your viewpoint, I guess." I shrugged.

"Well, I was raised Catholic, so when I moved east, I became more… exposed. I scrutinized my faith a little more. There are times when I have doubted it, but there was one time that I just knew something or someone was with me when I was alone and depressed. It was at a time when I really needed it. I'll go into detail another time, but that moment cast many of my doubts away. I don't necessarily agree with a lot of Catholic practices, but I believe there is a God."

I let a few moments of silence pass, letting what she said sink in. She was pretty compelling. It was something to think about. I told her I had somewhat of a similar viewpoint, although I wasn't raised in a religious household, and I lacked a firm belief. We floated ideas and viewpoints on other religions, discussing a little further before the conversation died down.

"See, that wasn't so bad, was it?" I pointed out. She simply smiled back. "Now, we should probably order something since I'm already on thin ice with this waiter."

Looking at the menu was daunting. There were so many options that I was a bit overwhelmed. I enjoyed fish and lobster as well as most seafood, but I wasn't knowledgeable enough to really have a grasp on what I wanted to order. I panned through the pages, flipping back and forth erratically. I probably looked engrossed and deep in thought, but I was lost.

After a few minutes of no progress, I remembered the waiter said my wine paired excellently with salmon, so I focused my attention there. All of it sounded delicious as the description below each entrée made it seem like the fish was plucked from the streams of Eden and cooked by the hand of God. I finally settled on the "salmon amore." Looking up from the menu, I saw Deniece had already chosen.

"You find something in there? You were buried!" She chuckled at herself.

The waiter came shortly thereafter, and we placed our orders. We continued our conversation, talking about sports and my nephew and all the pranks we pulled.

The way she looked and me and smiled while I was talking made me feel a deep warmth. I couldn't tell where it was coming from, but for a fleeting moment, it felt like complete bliss. The feeling erupted out of me in the form of a chuckle and a beaming smile.

"What is it?" she asked, her face glowing.

"Oh, nothing." All I could do was smile and stare back at her for a second.

I continued with the story. "Anyway, so she lit the wick, and it disappeared. I was worried that it wasn't gonna go off, but then *blam*! The explosion ripped the cake apart and sent it flying into her face! If you're wondering, no, she wasn't hurt. She was a good sport about it. I just wish we would've thought to film it."

Deniece rolled her eyes while covering up her laugh. "Oh my god, Nick. How hasn't your family killed you already?"

"Your guess is as good as mine," I shrugged, reaching for the bread on the table.

After she shared a little about her daughter, our food arrived. I had forgotten how hungry I had become until I feasted my eyes on the platter. It looked immaculate, and I didn't hesitate a second before digging in. I grabbed a fork and reached down for my first bite, but hesitated. I needed to remind myself not to scarf down food like my normal madman self. But even the conscious effort only slowed me slightly.

There wasn't much conversation after our food arrived, apart from comments about the food or a quick taste of what the other had. I was able to focus on the delight of the meal instead of the distraction of entertaining my date.

The waiter was dead on, as the wine did complement the salmon perfectly. I couldn't pinpoint how or why, but I was tasting two separate palates, each enhancing the other. I made sure to pass the compliment on to him when he came to check up on us, and it seemed like he knew I was going to love it. I noticed that

Deniece kept up with my pace. Normally at this point, I would be finished with an entrée, and my date would still have three-fourths of hers, and I would spend the remainder of the meal tortured while she ate. To my delight, we both finished at relatively the same time and went straight back into conversation. It was like we just had a short food break to recharge and were back at it. As dinner began to wrap up, we declined dessert, and I paid the bill. It was pretty steep for two people, but money wasn't much of a concern. With no girlfriend or kids and relatively low living expenses, I had a lot saved.

"Nick, you're not paying for me next time," she warned.

"Oh wow, so you decided I am kind of a catch?"

She just shook her head, smiling.

We left Gallardo's, and despite the date going so well, I decided it was best to drop her off. I didn't want to rush things. It was a rather silent ride back, listening to some old tunes on the radio, but it wasn't awkward.

When it came time to drop her off, she hesitated opening the door. It was that uncomfortable moment where you aren't quite sure what is racing through the other person's head. Desperately wanting to make a move, but at the same time, not wanting to look like a buffoon if you overstepped your boundaries. The moment lingered, and the tension rose with every second. I yearned to lean over or at least say something, but the moment was escaping me. I nearly let out a gasping sigh when I heard her voice.

"Nick, I had an awesome time tonight. It didn't even feel like a date. It was just… It was…" She fumbled over her words. "I would like to see you again."

With that, she started opening the door but then hesitated once again.

"You know, you left me with just a peck on the cheek last time?"

And with that, she closed the door and leaned over. It felt clumsy as we fumbled over the stick shift and center console, trying to reach each other, but we made it work.

The warmth of her lips was intoxicating, blanketing my mouth with a thin coat of lipstick. Their supple nature fit like a jigsaw, and mine engulfed hers. I caressed her lips with my teeth, gently pulling them. I found my sense of time fade away as I surrendered more and more of myself. Our bodies started getting into it as I moved my hand up her body onto her cheek, softly stroking it with my thumb. I sensed she could feel the emotion. The whole night, all the laughs, the jokes, the sincerity were being shared in those brief minutes. When we finally separated, we stared at each other. Then without a word, she exited the car, and I managed a brief goodbye before it was over. I felt a euphoric numbness as I drove home.

Chapter 16

It was a cold Friday afternoon in Cyrus Park. It was chilly weather but manageable for the annual Ice Burrrg competition. Every fall, when the temperature dipped, the town hosted a super soaker competition for kids. It pitted two teams against each other in a chaotic frenzy of water. The goal is to hold the fountain in the middle of Cyrus Park, where the water supply was. It always got heated, but in the end, everyone was treated to ice cream and hot chocolate. I wasn't sure why they gave out ice cream when it was chilly, but who was I to judge? The kids loved it.

This year's intensity was no exception, and Will was in the thick of it. Mom and I watched from a sideline bench. Maybe a little close to the action, we sometimes cringed in anticipation of an errant shot. Will's team was pinned down between the forest and the playground, getting assaulted from all angles. It was getting lopsided and probably wouldn't be too long before they called it.

Mom didn't like her grandson getting ganged up on. "Doesn't this all seem a little cruel? And unfair? Look at Will's team." She was a little hard to hear over all the giddy screams coming from nearby.

"Mom, c'mon. Someone has to win." I set down my newspaper. "Besides, the biggest danger in this competition is catching a cold."

All seemed lost for Will's team until a small group emerged from the center of the onslaught, charging full force into the opposition, breaking the stranglehold. The charge included Will, of course, and it looked like he was just having a blast. He was barking at some kids, giving commands like a general.

"Oh, look, look, Nick. Will is doing so well! I always knew he was a leader." She looked as invested in the war as the participants.

"Not so unfair anymore, huh?"

"They are getting what they deserve!"

It was like she didn't even hear me.

"I have to say, I've never seen this side of Will. He's quite the warrior. It's almost a little scary," my mom said with a mix of pride and worry.

"Yeah, I haven't either. Maybe he's gotten it from the video games he plays."

"Wait! Will plays those things!" It sounded like she didn't approve. "I'm gonna have to talk with Ann about that. I've seen some bad things about those video games. They turn kids into delinquents."

I just rolled my eyes.

"Does Ann even know he plays those things?" She made it seem like he was handling nuclear bombs.

"Mom, it's not as bad as you think. Those reports aren't even based on any data, just opinion. And you can't tell her how to parent. I mean, you can, but she knows what she's doing."

"Well, some advice can't hurt, especially from her mother. I mean, I basically raised you two by myself, so I know a thing or two," she said, sounding like the all-knowing parent she liked to think she was.

"Yeah, look how we turned out," I scoffed.

"Perfect, I'd say. I did what I had to," she shot back quickly. I looked over at her, amused by her answer. She seemed serious, though, and just stared out at all the little munchkins surrounding the fountain.

The tide of the fight had turned. Will's team had become the aggressors, overrunning the opposition within minutes. The field was turning into all-out chaos. The team lines disappeared and turned into small pockets of close-quarter bouts. The water didn't even seem to affect them any longer. It wasn't too much longer before the fight began to drop off, starting at first with a few stragglers, then hordes, as kids began to migrate to the snack stand that was being set up. Will didn't seem too excited that the battle had ended. He continued to skirmish with the few that avoided the temptation of the snack cart until it became futile to continue the crusade since he was basically the last one.

Reluctantly, he made his way over to the stand. I followed his yellow cap for a moment, but lost him in the cluster. He finally reemerged, a huge grin on his face and an ice cream in his hand. He looked lost as he tried to find where his entourage was. With a quick wave, I caught his eye. He sprinted toward us.

"Grandma, you came!" He was ecstatic as he embraced her tightly.

"Careful, boy, I'm not as tough as I used to be. That hip still ain't 100%." He giggled through the embrace.

"Did you see the comeback?"

"Oh yeah, kid, that was pretty awesome," I chimed in.

"Yeah, my team said I did good," he boasted.

"What flavor you got there?" I motioned to his cone.

"Mint chocolate chip! Your favorite, can't you see?" He held the cone in front of my face. The green-hued frozen mixture peppered with specks of creamy chocolate morsels was enough to get me salivating. The irresistible double-mounded idol had me contemplating heading to the stand and trying to con my way into a cone.

"You've got some good taste." I gave him a wink, then ushered him along toward the car. "Let's go see your mom and Buster back at the apartment."

Ann had taken my car to go drop off her husband at the airport since he had a business meeting in Texas this weekend, so I had been left with a not-too-shabby Chevy Tahoe. I helped my mom walk gingerly toward the SUV. She could walk pretty well with just a cane but seemed a bit unstable. She would take a step, and then the side of her body where she had the surgery would dip down like a bobber. I was concerned that side would give, and she would collapse. After a long stint at the nursing home, she was scheduled to be discharged next week, although I'm sure she would be back there again. Her left knee was all but gone and would need replacement within the year, but they wanted to hold off until as late as possible.

I enjoyed my sister's SUV on the drive back to the apartment. It had some kick in the engine and maintained a rather nice interior, similar to that of a car. But what I really liked was feeling in charge of the road being higher off the ground. The fleeting thought of getting a truck passed through my mind as we made our way toward my place.

Will changed out of his wet clothes in the back only after we promised not to look, and Grandma held up a towel so others couldn't see. Even then, he huddled near the floor, changing as far out of the view of the windows as possible. A sly grin spreading across my face, I backed my seat up slightly.

"Oww! You're squishing me. Stop!" Will didn't like that too much.

"Guess you better change. People can see you! I need some room for my legs," I laughed as he retreated onto the backseat.

"Grandma!"

"Grandma can't help you here, bud." I sped up until we were next to another SUV.

"Say hi, Will!" I waved to the family in the SUV next to us. They didn't even look, but he immediately went prone and threw his clothes on top to cover himself.

I couldn't contain my laughter.

I eventually relented and moved us into an open lane, and Will scrambled to put his clothes on. I felt a swift punch into my shoulder.

"That was mean!"

Looking in the rear-view mirror, Will was sitting with his arms crossed, trying to look as menacing and mad as possible. With his face scrunched and his lips pursed, I couldn't help but chuckle, mocking his pose. Grandma couldn't help but take his side.

"Yes, Nick, you're a bully. You should apologize."

"Oh, c'mon. That was harmless." I made eye contact with Will. "I watched; that other family didn't even look." He just turned away from me and looked out the window.

I let out a sigh. "Fine, I'm sorry." I reached back to pat his knee, but he was still turned away.

He would get over it by the time we got back. He wasn't really upset, probably just embarrassed. It was best to leave him alone for now.

"Did you get some good pictures?" I asked Mom, changing the subject. She had brought a digital camera specifically for Will.

"I got a couple of decent ones. There were too many kids in the way most of the time, but that lady next to us took one that was really nice. I will probably get that framed."

"Mind if I get a copy?" I hardly had any family pictures around the apartment.

"Of course! Would you mind getting them printed? It's just too difficult for me to get out right now."

"No problem. Sounds like a fair trade."

Ann had said she planned to have burgers ready by the time we got back, so my stomach contributed to how quickly we got home. Will wasn't too upset anymore, but while making our way up the stairs, he pulled away when I tried to put my arm around him.

Walking down the hallway, we were met with an odd sight.

There was a lady sitting against my door. When she noticed us, she stood up and immediately straightened her clothes. She was short but cute, wearing a dress with daisies dotted all over it. Her hair was shorter than last time, only down to her shoulders. She was still as gorgeous as I remembered.

"Celia," I almost whispered in disbelief. I couldn't believe my eyes. I must have looked completely mystified.

"Uh, hey, Nick. I know you must think you're dreaming or something. This is kinda surreal for me too."

I tried to process why or how she was here, but I was coming up empty. I'm sure Will and Mom had no idea what was going on. Silence hung for a few more seconds until I asked them to go ahead inside and get settled, saying I would be there shortly.

I didn't take my eyes off her. They silently obliged and hustled in, leaving Celia and me standing in the hallway.

"So, I'm sure you have a lot of questions," she began.

"Just a few," I scoffed. My eyes were still wide, bulging from their sockets. I shuffled toward the wall, leaning against the drywall.

She smiled and grazed her hand over her head, glossing through her dark hair almost as if she were in slow motion.

"You know, you're looking good, Nick," she offered.

Butterflies bubbled below the surface. I pushed them down. She wasn't going to manipulate me this time.

"You didn't come here just to tell me that, did you? Although that would certainly be flattering."

"No, no, of course not." The smile disappeared. She looked down at her feet, pivoting on her left. Her eyes popped up just for a second to catch my expression then jumped back to the floor.

"Ahh, okay. I've gone over what I wanted to say a million times, but actually seeing you, well, I don't know where to begin."

"How 'bout why you drugged me then robbed me?" I wasn't giving her any slack.

"I mean, I guess I could ask you the same question," she snapped back. I simply sighed, giving her the hint that if she wanted to get anywhere in this conversation, hardball was not the way to do it.

"Okay, Nick, listen, I had an amazing time that night. That was one of the best and most unexpected dates I've had, but I had a problem, and I couldn't control myself no matter how much I tried to resist. I've had a lot of shit happen in my life, and I never planned or wanted to do stuff like that. It just kinda happened."

Her eyes were locked on me. They didn't hold that same confident spark in the bar; they were vulnerable.

"I woke up one day, and it had become a part of me. When you stole from me, it was the wake-up call I needed. That feeling of violation, humiliation, and helplessness finally helped me see what I had become. I saw the other side. I've gotten help since then, and that part of my past is behind me. It took me a few years, and my life has gotten so much better. Recently, I started to think about what spurred this whole thing on, and about you. I wanted to find you and apologize profusely. It took a little bit, but I guess… here I am now."

"How did you find me?"

"They have cameras in the parking lot. I obviously didn't call the cops, and I didn't even think about checking the cameras until I hired a private investigator. I recognized your car immediately. After that, it didn't take long for the investigator to locate you."

I hadn't even thought about that. It was so simple.

"But, seeing you feels like it has officially ended that chapter of my life, and… well… maybe… no, just… I'm sorry, Nick. You don't have to forgive me. I just needed to see you. To let you know."

I was frozen against the wall, my expression unfazed. I stared at her, not thinking but feeling. I felt heavy. My knees wanted to buckle. I felt hollow. Her words passed through me, and I felt guilt. My chest was painfully tight. I felt power. I stood high above her.

"Well, hey, I don't want to keep you from your family, and dinner is ready. I could smell it from the hallway. I really did think you were amazing, Nick, and you never deserved what I did. I wish you the best and, well, thanks for not just freaking out when you saw me." She began to walk past me toward the elevator.

"Celia!" She turned around. "Wait."

I was smiling. "How 'bout you stay for dinner?"

She seemed at a loss.

"I mean, this is so weird, but you spent all this time hunting me down. Plus, at least I got my stuff back. Yours got donated. I at least owe you this." Her eyebrows dipped.

"This isn't out of pity, either. I need time to process this. You can't spring this on me then just vanish." It didn't feel right to have her just up and leave right away.

"Uh, you sure, Nick? I mean, your family is in there. How would you introduce me? Here's the woman who drugged and robbed me?"

I mean, she had a good point.

"I knocked on the door earlier and a woman answered. Was that your girlfriend? I don't want to cause any drama. I told her I was a new neighbor."

"No, she's my sister." That got a smile out of her. Don't worry, I'll tell them you're a friend who I haven't seen in a few years, and that you're going to join us for the evening." It sounded like a pretty satisfactory introduction. "It might be awkward for a few minutes, but the best times are some of the most awkward." It was something my dad would tell me.

She swayed, weighing the explanation. "I guess I'll go along with that Swiss cheese of a story. You know, this could be fun. Just like old times." She smiled as she made her way toward the door.

"Old times," I laughed, swinging open the oak blockade. She flashed me a smile with a hint of disapproval.

We entered my apartment to a fresh blast of dinner. The aroma of meat grilling was infatuating, and the sizzle coming from the kitchen sounded delicious. We made our way to where everyone was gathered. They held their judgmental and puzzled stares while I made introductions. Celia sure did look terrific, and Ann gave me a look when I introduced her as a "friend."

Apparently, Mom was thinking along those lines as well because she asked how we knew each other and why she was waiting at my door. She always liked to be direct. I had already begun to sip my drink and choked violently once she asked. Mom was never afraid to make things awkward, but Celia had it covered.

"We met in a bar a few years ago, met up a couple more times but kinda lost contact for a while. I was only at the door… well…" She laughed and collected herself. "We've been trying to get together for a couple of weeks, and he told me about tonight but forgot to tell me the time. I leave for a trip tomorrow, so I decided to camp out." Smiling at her wit, I almost choked on my drink a second time while chuckling to myself.

"Nick!" my mom was scolding. "How could you stand this beautiful girl up?" She came to Celia's side almost as if to console her after a breakup.

"Mom, really?" She always had to embarrass me.

At least she believed the story. I finished serving everyone drinks and got myself a second while we milled around the kitchen till supper was ready. Celia had a comfortable glow to her and helped Ann with some of the cooking while Grandma shared her rendition of the events at the park. We were pretty lively, and the conversation was rather roaring for just us four.

They really got riled up when they asked me to dice up some vegetables. I had no problem helping out, but they had a hoot making fun of my "giant-sized dicing." Their glasses barely contained their contents with the sweeping motions and reenactments. They were all too eager to show me the "proper" way, and I threw my hands up.

"Fine! I give up! I try to help a little, and this is what I get."

More giggles from the peanut gallery.

Surprisingly, it didn't feel weird for Celia to be there at all.

It took longer than it should've to get the table set on account that we were distracting ourselves, but Will spurred us on with the constant refrain, "When can we eat?" He could only be preoccupied with Buster for so long.

While I didn't have much in the way of furniture or tableware for a family meal, Ann had made do. A bottle of wine was passed and poured generously around the table. After a quick grace, we assaulted the food before us. Plates flew around like Frisbees, getting passed sideways and across. I was lucky to have long arms. Poor Will was desperate to grab the hashbrowns, but he was too slow. Celia saw his distress and came to his aid, quickly filling up his plate and placing the ketchup in front of him. It was endearing to watch her help Will. I was so distracted watching; I almost missed a plate of burgers in front of my face.

"Just a friend, huh?" Ann scoffed as she handed the plate over. She obviously wasn't buying the charade.

I held the plate in front of me with a difficult decision at hand. Choose the burger with mozzarella seasoned with a little garlic or a cheddar burger with cheese just melting off the side. The mozzarella looked appetizing, something different. I couldn't risk it, though, so I guided the sizzling cheddar treat onto my Kaiser bun before quickly covering the patty with lettuce and tomato.

I turned my attention to the bun, layering on a thin coat of mayo then generously applying ketchup and brown mustard. In my mind, I felt like I was running an infomercial. "And that's not all" ringing out as I layered on a hearty helping of caramelized onions and two strips of crispy maple bacon to complete the masterpiece. I wasn't the only one admiring my burger. Celia was staring right at me with quite the grin on her face. I readied myself for the deliciousness that was about to greet me.

The first bite saw streams of grease cascade down my chin, and flavor rushed into my mouth as the soft burger gave way to crunchy bacon and lettuce. The condiments oozed from the bun onto my fingers as it was squeezed. I could taste each layer of the burger, and the bun presented a dull wheat flavor that complemented the bold tastes of the rest. I couldn't have bought a much better burger in a restaurant, and between bites, I thanked my sister for dinner.

"You did it again, sis. This is really good. Perhaps there's a chance you can come over and do this more often?" I sounded like I was joking, but in all actuality, I was kind of serious.

"Well, I think that it should be your turn next time, though I'm not sure. I prefer edible food."

With a mouth full of burger, she tried to quell her laughter, but it was too much, and chunks of meat began to spew out onto the table.

"Mom! Eww!" Will quickly recoiled with his plate.

Ann recovered and covered her mouth as her laughter turned into a cough, and the amusement to embarrassment. If it hadn't been for Celia's presence, she might not have been, but then again, she was. Once she regained composure, she apologized.

"I need a new burger. Mom spit on it." Will's mood turned sour.

"Will Han Mischker, come on now, it wasn't that bad." Ann pleaded, hoping that this didn't turn into a fit.

"I won't eat it. It's gross." He crossed his arms in protest.

"It's not that bad, bud. It's just like if your mom gave your food a kiss," I offered.

Ann leaned in close to Will's ear. "Honey, we have company," she reminded him.

He stopped complaining but remained perturbed with his arms crossed for a few minutes, still refusing to touch his meal. It turned the dinner conversation a little awkward as we tried to drum up something to talk about and ignore Will's behavior. Eventually, Ann gave him the hard approach with the ultimatum that he eat his food or leave the table. He reluctantly chose the latter and scurried from the table in shame. At least he had Buster to keep him company. The mood began to liven up again with his absence.

Ann poured another round of drinks and deemed the moment fit to bring up stories of my tantrums. I felt ganged up on as Mom added to the tales, and soon, they had Celia laughing hysterically, which only spurred their ambush. They shared how I wet my bed till I was 12 and how whenever I was angry, I would sit in silence like a little hermit. They had fun with that.

"Aww, little hermit Nick!" Celia said, using baby talk.

"No, remember when he used to get sick? It was like he was dying every time. He was such a drama queen," my mother said.

"Oh my gosh, I forgot about that!" Ann looked at Celia. "Loudest puker ever, I swear. He would drag himself around like he had the plague. I was surprised he didn't have us wipe his butt!" Another bout of laughter.

By this point, I had my fair share and wanted to turn the tables.

"You know, you weren't always a peach either, Ann. There are plenty of stories about you." I gave her an eyebrow, and there was a moment of silence.

"Nope! Ann was an angel, an absolutely perfect child!" Mother never saw any fault with her.

There was no winning.

"Sounds like you're a little salty, Nick," my mom chimed in, offering no support whatsoever.

Celia couldn't hold her tongue any longer and looked at me. "Wow, had I known all this, we might have never become 'friends.'" Her unexpected jest put the others into an uproar. I was sure the booze wasn't quelling the laughter. After a few grumpy seconds, I joined in a little. I couldn't be like Will in the car. After all, jokes were harmless. Once I reminded myself of that, I was able to enjoy the roasting. Watching everyone having a great time together was a real joy. It had been a long time since that had happened, and the first time in my apartment. We must've sat with our food finished for half an hour before we started cleaning up. We became preoccupied with Celia's stories about her travels. Ann was especially interested since it had always been her passion.

Celia went on about an experience she had while overseas in Europe.

"So, this time in Italy, it was our departure day, and just before heading to the airport, we stopped for lunch at an outdoor diner. You know, 'cause the airports just gouge you with food prices." Ann nodded, and we were all roped in.

"We leave, and not even a minute later, I realize I left my purse. I rushed back, not even thinking it could be gone, but it was. I just started crying. I had everything in there—keys, money, passport. My friend was running around to the wait staff, management, fellow customers, asking if anyone had seen the purse or who had taken it. It must have been quite the scene for everyone watching. My friend was shouting questions as I sat on an empty chair in tears."

"Eventually, we were guided by locals to the police, but they were no help. It was like finding a needle in a haystack. The culprit was long gone, and I had no identity." Celia took another swig of wine. "By this time, I had calmed down and wasn't panicked anymore. The crying really helped. My friend had to catch her plane, so I told her to leave me with her cash and let my parents know what happened. I would go to the embassy and get a new passport, and it would all be fine. Reluctantly, my friend Nicole agreed that it was the only feasible action. We said goodbye, and for a brief moment, I thought, *What if I don't see her again*?" But that was just the fear getting the best of me. So I was stranded with 110 bucks, which I spent 30 bucks of on a crappy hotel room and another 5 on a meal. I called the U.S. consulate in Florence but wasn't able to secure an appointment till the day after.

"When I called my parents later that night, since it was their morning, they were hysterical. I mean, I could barely understand them. They were shouting over each other and were firing off questions before I could even answer. It was a little funny because I felt perfectly fine. They canceled my card and wanted to look into wiring money to me somehow if I could hold out another day or two. They insisted I stay in the room until they called next, as if I was suddenly in certain danger if alone."

"Oh my god! If that was Will, I would die." Ann was bewildered.

"That is probably what they felt like, and in the beginning, the whole ordeal was scary, but at the same time, it felt invigorating being so independent, so free. I also kind of enjoyed the thrill of being stranded. The whole trip, we had things planned down to a tee, but it was exciting and felt like real tourism to roam Florence for a couple of days with nothing to do. Eventually, my family was able to wire enough cash to tide me over until the passport situation was finally resolved, but by the time I received my new passport, I didn't want to go home.

"I met a generous family while at lunch on my second day stranded. I barely remember how now, but I think I was flirting with one of their sons. One thing led to another, and they became eager to help me out until my passport situation was resolved. It was surreal and almost scary how nice they were. The whole time I'm thinking, *Are these people going to kidnap me? Murder me?* People just aren't that friendly, but they were.

"Besides sleeping there, the family provided me with meals, toured me around the city, and even taught me how to make real Italian pizza. I've never met such friendly, affectionate people. I couldn't get over it. By the second day, I felt like a member of the family. The father spoke pretty good English, and the rest of the family were passable. They called me poco, or sunshine, since I had my hair dyed blonde at the time. Maybe it's just me, but I feel like that is the most precious name ever. It was a sad goodbye, but I promised to come back."

I could see the interest and intrigue on Ann's face. Stories like Celia's only fueled her desire to travel. She took a couple of trips before she had Will, but she had barely even made it out of the state since then because her husband could rarely get off work. Her eyes glowed as Celia went on. They were fixated on her. Half listening, half imagining, I could sense her yearning. The idea came to me just as the story was wrapping up. If I took Will for a week or two, then Ann could be free to travel! I decided to propose my offer when we had some alone time, or at the very least, I would call her the next day.

"Wow, that's crazy. Did you ever go back to visit the family?" Ann was still rife with bewilderment.

"Regrettably, no." Celia's voice deflated, "I never got the opportunity to head back, but I would like to someday."

"Nick, you should take her!" My head shot Ann's way. She wasn't joking. I just facepalmed. I could see Celia laughing out of the corner of my eye.

"I've got a great idea. How 'bout I just treat us all to a trip there!" I said with enthusiasm.

"About time you used that noggin of yours." My mom was feisty when she drank.

I mulled my drink; the graceful amber glass comforted my hand like a swaddled baby. It was a great evening, but it was getting late, and my mom was getting tired. We were all a little disappointed it had to come to an end.

As things wound down, we found Will in the living room passed out on the couch.

"Five bucks when we wake him up, he says he's hungry," Ann smirked.

"I'll keep my five bucks, thank you."

Sure enough, Ann was right.

We said our goodbyes, and Ann left with Mom to drop her back off at the nursing home. Celia lingered around, waiting till after everyone left.

CHAPTER 16

"Thank you again for tonight. I didn't expect anything less than awkwardness and animosity, but I was completely wrong. And your family is so awesome."

I just smiled back. "It was a great night, and yeah, they're alright. But just wait till they gang up on you." She rolled her eyes at that.

"Okay, so maybe a few drinks are encouraging this, but my counselor told me not to hold back my gut feelings. Uhh…" She let out a long sigh. I had an inclination of what she was going to say based on how flustered she was.

"We feel great together. We just click, and it's been that way the entire time I've been with you. I'm not sure if you can sense it, but I have a hunch that you do. I completely understand if you can't trust me and that was my fuckup, but I would really like to see where this could go. I mean, we know the sex is great. It feels like we can talk about anything, and already meeting the family is tackled. I'm not saying let's jump into something right away, but this shouldn't be the last time we see each other."

She leaned forward. The waft of her perfume knotted between my nostrils. I was moments from breaking my expression, but she retreated back toward the door.

"I've probably said too much, and I'm sorry to just spring this on you." Her eyes searched for an answer or reaction in mine.

"No, no, don't apologize at all," I sputtered out, taking a step forward.

"I appreciate that you were willing to take that leap, and yeah, you're right, I sense it. We connect well, and… you know what, let me grab a drink and gather my thoughts. I'm thinking about too many things at once."

She obliged and followed me into the kitchen, where I grabbed another Captain. I didn't even pay attention to my pour. I just needed time to collect myself. The clink of glass was the only sound between us.

I let out a long sigh as I indulged myself in the pungent concoction.

"Celia, I'm not great at expressing my feelings, and I'm sure I'm gonna forget things I want to say, but I like you a lot. I think you're awesome and exciting, and surprisingly, your past doesn't scare me." I saw a glow appear on her face.

"It's mine." I watched as the glow turned into confusion. "It's my past that scares me. For the past few weeks, months, I've been working hard to change myself. Similar to how you did after I stole from you. The thing is, I really like the new me, and tonight was the first time this apartment's had life to it in who knows how long. You were a part of that, too, and this isn't easy for me, but I think that this should be it."

Words, thoughts, and feelings just rolled off my tongue without my brain processing them. It was like my inner consciousness was speaking, and I finally shut it up as I felt I was starting to ramble.

"You and the drinking aren't bad, but they are parts of my past that lead me into… ahh." I paced around the island. Gritting my teeth and looking anywhere but her, it was hard to explain.

"Do you understand any of this, or am I being a nutcase?" I looked up at her for the first time during my explanation, and she seemed emotionless. Not angry or sorrowful, just plain.

"I completely understand. Completely. I… you're not a nutcase. That was really honest and sincere. Maybe at a different time in our lives, things could've been different. Seriously, though,

Nick, I wish you the best, I'm rooting for you. Don't be afraid to share whatever you're going through. Maybe a phone call every few months just to stay in touch. Friends?"

I gazed at her with an exhausted smile "Friends." She met me from the other side of the counter, and we embraced in a hug.

I could feel her genuineness, and as tough as it was watching her leave the apartment, I knew I had made the right decision. And more importantly, I would wake up with all my things the next morning.

Chapter 17

It had been a while since I had gotten together with Chris, and for the overdue meetup, I decided to get creative. I called him up on a slow day at the office and pitched the idea of driving up to New York and strolling around until we found a place.

"Sounds good! Since when did you become the adventurer?" Chris remarked.

"Since last week. Why? Don't like it?"

"Haha, no, no, quite the contrary. In fact, I'm excited for this shindig."

"Well great! And we ain't stopping at a McDonald's again."

"Oh my gosh! That's malarkey. You know you were happy with that choice! I'll tell you what, we're gonna pick out something as far from McDonald's as possible."

He stayed true to his word.

Stepping out of his duplex, we were met with a chilly breeze as it had gotten late in the season. Chris was bundled up, prepared to get caught out in a freak blizzard. Meanwhile, I had on a light fall jacket, hoping the trek would be short.

The brick stairs leading down to the sidewalk always instilled a sense of sophistication and history. Turning around to look at the aged but charming building, I couldn't help but be a bit jealous. From the west, a stiff breeze stung my face. If it took too long to find a restaurant, I might lose my ears. I already regretted not adding more layers.

Departing after six, we moved our quest from the familiar crowded apartments and small markets of East Village to the even more compact and bustling area of Chinatown. Chris was excited to give me the insider's tour. Pointing out his family's favorite restaurants and delis, sharing tidbits of where crimes occurred. It tickled my imagination when he described a gruesome murder that had occurred at a quaint cobblestone street corner we were approaching. I couldn't picture such a heinous crime in such a setting.

I had been in the area a few times visiting Chris before, but never really took the time to walk around and admire the neighborhood. When I had lived in New York, it had been in Queens. The atmosphere here was much different. It was like a small town where everyone was friendly and familiar, but the neighborhood just happened to be smack dab in the middle of a major city. I'm sure a lot of areas had changed since my childhood, but one remained nearly identical. The buildings started to change along with the atmosphere as we transitioned out of the East Village and into the neighboring borough.

I was hit with a burst of nostalgia. Chinatown hadn't changed one bit. It had been quiet where Chris lived, but the roaring streets of Chinatown were a world of difference. Everyone and everything seemed to be moving faster. At times, it was a challenge to even hold a conversation as we walked down the sidewalk because the noise required Chris and me to nearly yell at each other. The noise was only part of the problem. I had to juke and weave through the crowd like a halfback on a sweep. From other people to street vendors, even inconveniently placed fire hydrants, everything seemed to get in the way. On one close brush with disaster, Chris was in the middle of talking about his son's fight at school. I took my focus off the street for a couple of seconds and nearly leveled a young girl holding her mother's hand. At the last moment, I sidestepped, trying to hop around her. My momentum carried my torso over her. I held the awkward tilt for as long as I could until I had to stumble into her back. I immediately caught myself and reached my arm out for an informal apology. The mom barely looked back.

When I turned around and looked up, I had lost Chris. I scanned the crowd. He shouldn't be too hard to find. He towered above the predominately height-challenged crowd and didn't seem to get the tanning memo.

"Nick, I'm right here." The voice was from behind.

"You think I didn't notice and just kept walking?" he chuckled.

"No, I didn't. Man, this place is a madhouse. You see that woman? She barely broke stride, and her child was a second away from eating through a straw for the rest of her life." I was hard of breath.

A bellow erupted from Chris.

"Don't flatter yourself, Nick. She might have actually knocked your scrawny ass over. Ever hear of something called protein?"

"Is that your nickname for steroids? How is that normal?" I gestured to his thigh and to his neck.

He retreated a little, trying to shield his size with his shoulder. "That's just what beans like you say," he said, a little more gruff than playful.

I smiled, accepting the weak comeback as surrender.

When we got to the street corner, Chris's face lit up.

"There it is," he beamed. His finger pointed in the direction of what couldn't have been more than a shack with a dilapidated sign that read "Gourmet Chinese."

I gave him the "you're joking" look, but he surely was not because he picked up his pace as he approached the establishment. It was a cramped, narrow eatery with four tables, only one of which was occupied. There was one door that led to the back, where the kitchen must have been, and a small stand with a cash register on it near the front. Red paint coated the walls along with paintings of Chinese characters. The tables were generic, and the chairs looked like they would warrant a chiropractic appointment after sitting in them. The place also tried to appeal to Americans with posters of John Wayne, JFK, and Madonna. It was amusing and endearing.

"This place has charm," Chris said, looking around.

Everywhere you looked, there was some new clash of themes, and it didn't instill much confidence in the place. Chris was either ignorant or welcomed all the warning signs and went right ahead choosing a table for us. The place was deserted except for a lone man finishing his meal, not a staff member to be found. Chris was unperturbed.

"Betcha we get a happy ending with each meal."

He cracked himself up with that one, though I was not amused. He gave me a manufactured frowny face and prodded fun at my displeasure.

"Hey, you said nothing like McDonald's, so here we go."

Right then, a head popped out from behind the back door before disappearing quickly. It then reappeared followed by an Asian body. She wore a white apron with smudges of sauce as if she had been both cooking and serving. By her expression, I wasn't sure if she was there to kick us out or serve us.

"Wekom, welcome."

Her tone sure wasn't welcoming. She spoke with a heavy accent and had a problem pronouncing the letter L. She had two glasses of water with her that she placed in front of us. "I give you some time, yes?" She handed us two menus, then rushed off behind the kitchen door again.

Chris gave me an eyebrow and smiled. "How 'bout that service?"

"I think I see something floating in my water," I said concernedly. Chris just rolled his eyes.

We began to scan the menu, and I began to protest.

"We don't have to eat here, you know." I was hoping Chris was leaning that way too, or there would be no convincing him.

"Don't be so quick to judge, Nick. You know what I've found? The best places to eat are often the least you'd expect." He was still unfazed by the place, but his words did little to quell my discomfort. I scanned the menu for something familiar, and I found it with sesame chicken. How had that thought not crossed my mind when at a Chinese restaurant? I had eaten the holy grail of Chinese before, and it held a special place in my heart. All my angst and resistance to the place melted. I needed to get my hands on that chicken.

I must've started drooling on the menu because Chris sensed I was warming up to the place.

"Ahh, you're right, Nick; I think we should go. I'm not finding anything on the menu." He let out a heavy sigh.

"No, no, Chris. I mean, we're already here. Plus, I don't want to be rude, and where else would we go?"

"You found something you like, didn't you?"

"Yes," I admitted sheepishly.

He pulled his menu back up with a smile. No chance he would let me forget it anytime soon. Our waitress came back and asked if we were ready. I went ahead with my order, and then it was Chris's turn.

He took a long pause, furrowing his eyebrows. "I think I'll try the duck," he said confidently. The waitress grabbed our menus and stormed off so fast, I barely had time to question him. He just looked at me and shrugged, "Why stop the adventure at just the restaurant?" He had a good point.

The time we waited was filled largely with catching Chris up on my life. It took quite a while, considering I was usually pretty brief bringing him up to speed. He became extremely intrigued when I started explaining my little love triangle.

"Where did this come from? I never knew you were such a player." Chris gawked when I told him how Celia had come onto me.

"The Nick charm just took some years to mature," I smirked.

He had a good old laugh at that. His laughing was so infectious, it got me laughing, and soon we were bellowing like two drunken idiots. Chris just couldn't get himself to stop. Every time he would try to regroup, he would glance at me, and a new wrinkle would get him going again. I couldn't remember the last time I had seen him laugh this hard. The bellows turned to chuckles as the arrival of our food finally settled us down. Wiping our eyes dry, we quickly shifted gears to consumption mode.

My platter looked heavenly. Golden-brown chicken glazed with sauce and dotted with sesame seeds. On the other side of the table, Chris's entrée didn't look quite as appealing, but it was less gnarly than I had expected. Other than the head, it looked edible. I didn't waste time scanning his meal too long as my stomach's rumbling brought my focus back to the entrée. I reached for my fork.

Where is the silverware? I looked around and couldn't see any on the table. Perhaps the waitress forgot to bring them out.

Just then, she appeared from behind the door and I stared her down. I hoped she came within range of our table, so I could address the utensil dilemma. Chris could read me like a book. I must've looked like a buffoon to him.

"No silverware here, buddy. Only chopsticks." He lifted his pair in the air.

I had never attempted eating a meal with chopsticks before, and, as I imagined most people experienced their first time, I didn't grasp the concept. I couldn't manage to hold the chicken long enough to journey from the plate to my mouth. The pieces always dropped short, and it was beginning to frustrate me. The more pressure I applied, the tougher it got as the sauce would assist the chicken in its escape. I started to despise the meat. It was like it was outmaneuvering me.

I became so distraught and anxious to eat, I used my hands for the first bite, and oh, was it lovely. The caramelized crunchy outside was immediately deflated by my bite, and it gave way to a soft, juicy chicken in the interior. The sweet, tangy sauce coated my mouth and was squeezed to the corner of my lips. A very slight spice emerged in the wake of the sweet, and I closed my eyes in satisfaction.

"Wow."

Chris said what I was thinking, and I looked up to see him mesmerized, eyes closed while chewing. He finally came to, and it looked like he had just come out of a coma. "That might be the best thing I've ever tasted."

"What can I say? You made a good choice," I happily conceded. After a couple more bites eating with my hands, I thought of the genius idea to just stab the chicken. It brought me such joy outsmarting the delicious orange demons.

We devoured our meals, then both relaxed, stuffed and satisfied. The waitress came by to collect our plates. I hadn't noticed the slew of customers that had come in while we ate. It had gone from eerily quiet to rather noisy. Once the table was cleared, Chris caught me up to speed on his family as we waited for the check. His kids were doing great, and the eldest was nearing the end of his football season. He suggested we all hang out soon, and I bring along Will to meet his kids. It sounded like a great idea to me. I could picture Will and them getting along great together.

"Yeah, we will have to make that happen soon. Perhaps another one of your wife's dinners also?" I joked.

Chris half smiled, but his face didn't emanate happiness.

"So… uh… yeah… well, Nick, you might have to settle with my cooking for a while, depending."

I gave him a puzzled look. "Trouble between you and her? I'm sorry to hear that." I couldn't think of any other reason.

"No, no, things are great between us. It's just that Sandra is getting a mammogram tomorrow."

It was a cold glass of water to the face.

"Chris, I'm so sorry. I—"

He held up a hand to stop me. "Let's not get ahead of ourselves. There was just a small lump in her left breast, and we want to check it out. We aren't too concerned yet, but I'll keep you posted."

"Yeah, that makes sense." I sunk back into the metal chair. "Well, let me know if you need anything, and I hope it turns out to be good news."

Chris nodded and seemed to appreciate the gesture. The waitress came with our bill, and the place was dirt cheap. Only

15 bucks for both of us to dine. I made a mental note of the place in case I ever came back. I definitely wanted to.

We left the restaurant to a full moon and dark sky. The street was still pretty well-lit with the multitude of neon signs, but as we ventured farther from Chinatown, things grew dim. It seemed like we were right in the thick of it, and then, all of a sudden, we found ourselves on a dark stretch with no streetlights. I always believed that streetlights were a waste of money until I found myself in an unfamiliar part of the city where they are absent. I clung to the moonlight like a security blanket. I caught a cop out of the corner of my eye, but even still, I was a bit unnerved.

"So, uh, Chris, you know how to get back, right?" I was doubtful.

"You betcha. Just giving you the scenic tour."

"Oh, thanks. I've never seen shadows like this before, simply breathtaking. You know what? I should've brought my camera. I can only see sights like this 12 hours a day. Let's ask that nice gentleman up ahead for a picture!" I exclaimed with enthusiastic sarcasm. Chris's head immediately shot up, his eyes got wide, and his face rigid. He searched the black abyss before us, sprinting and darting his head like a robot scanning for possible threats.

"Gotcha!" I rested my hand on his shoulder and immediately felt him relax. The relaxation was short-lived as he pulled away from my grasp and got gruff with me.

"Shouldn't kid about that stuff, Nick. You'd be surprised at the number of calls we get a night." Chris attempted to shield his embarrassment with a scolding. I wasn't falling for it.

"Oh, but I have a big bad sergeant to protect me." I raised the pitch in my voice, trying to sound like a damsel in distress.

"Grow up, Nick."

"Oh, so you can jerk me around, but as soon as I turn the tables, I'm the regressed adolescent? Okay, Chris." I relented on the tease since it was getting on his nerves.

We continued another block in silence, then started getting into an area that felt familiar. We must have been close.

"You didn't scare me back there. I don't get fazed like that. Walking around at night is serious, though; joking like that isn't funny." He looked down on me like a scolding parent. "Well, maybe it is a little," Chris mumbled the concession so quietly that it was barely audible. I thought about saying something snarky back but instead was content with a smile.

We arrived back at the house, and an offer was extended to come in for drinks. I told him another time. It was getting pretty late, and I still had to drive back.

"Well, Nick, that turned out pretty good tonight. Oh, I have a free ticket for the Yankees game Sunday if you're interested. Got four through work, but Sandra is running the church rummage sale."

"Hell yeah, I am! Sounds awesome. I'll see you Sunday." Even being the Yankees, I couldn't pass up a game.

"Sweet, try to get here 'bout 10 or so." I gave him the thumbs up as I turned and headed toward my car.

"Nick, watch out!" Panic ripped through Chris's voice.

I jumped and whirled around, prepared to see an assailant standing nearby, ready to pounce.

To my relief and embarrassment, there was no one. Chris bellowed behind me, though. I gave him the bird before opening my car door.

"Wait, for real though, Nick, I almost forgot." I felt Chris's voice approach as he moved down the stairs. "I looked into that cop that investigated your dad's murder. Crooked guy was into some stuff with the mob. Sent me down a rabbit hole for a bit, but nothing dirty about your dad's investigation I can find yet. Truth is, he was probably just a lousy detective in that case."

It took me a second for it to register, but once it did, I let out a sigh. "Not sure if that's good or bad, but I'm kinda indifferent, to be honest."

I finally turned around to meet Chris, who was already halfway down the steps.

"You know, I guess there is still the DNA test out there, but after that, I think I'm good. I really appreciate all the work tracking this down, but I think you've gotten me far."

I didn't wait for a response. Simply moved into the driver's side and shut the door.

It was a relaxing ride home.

Chapter 18

Great times started to blend together as time flew. Over the last year, life had only been getting better. Deniece and I had been going steady for about seven months, and I was starting to contemplate asking her to move in, though her daughter Lizzie made things trickier. I loved hanging around with her; she wasn't like most little girls. She had some spunk and was a little tomboy, even showing up Will a bit when we played sports together. Still, I wasn't sure I was ready for that much chaos all the time. I also finally got around to helping Ann get the vacation she needed by taking Will in for a couple of weeks. She indulged with a week in France and then explored Italy and Germany after before arriving home.

She boasted that she had the time of her life, although, in her words, "more time in Italy would've been better." She said the culture and atmosphere were so different that it was intoxicating. She planned for another trip in the near future, this time to Japan. How another part of the world developed so differently than ours was intriguing.

While she was away, Will and Buster became inseparable. Buster had grown out of the puppy stage and turned into quite a brute. Those two were like brothers. Will asked to go to the park with him so often, I started letting them go without me. He was so fond of Buster that I tossed around the idea of getting him his own puppy, though it was doubtful Ann would share Will's enthusiasm.

My mother was home for a while after recovering for a bit in the nursing home, but then she had surgery on her other knee, which landed her back in the nursing home for a couple of weeks. She hated it there, but neither I nor Ann had the time or expertise to care for her. We made it a habit that at least once a month or so, Mom, Ann, and I would get together for dinner or something. It was our measure to keep in touch. Chris's wife had a benign tumor that they removed, and nothing had been abnormal since. That was amazing news.

At one point, I had remembered my promise to Alvin Dupont, and I felt terrible about forgetting his books. I made arrangements the next week to visit him. I even typed out a fake news article disguised as coming from a local paper that I supposedly wrote about him in, along with many more books than he had asked for. I even had to buy my own custom-printed paper to replicate newspaper material. It was quite an ordeal, but I owed him that much. When we met, he expressed that he doubted that he would ever see me again, and I apologized for forgetting about the deal. "No sweat," he said. He was just happy I eventually remembered because the world tends to forget prisoners exist. I asked him about his plans once he got out of the joint.

"Visit my mom and brother up in Attica. My brother's doin' real well for himself. Got the brains like the rest of the family, but not the sticky fingers. Maybe I'll apply for a job, maybe I'll steal something." He flashed me a subtle smile.

I couldn't do much more than sigh and shake my head in disapproval.

"C'mon, I haven't got to snatch more than cigs while I've been here. Gotta brush off the rust." His casual attitude was a little frustrating.

"You read, you're a smart guy, but you're saying that you couldn't get a decent job?" I wasn't going to just accept his regression back to stealing.

"Yeah, employers are drooling to hire a con. I thought you were smart?" His tone turned from playful to serious. "Besides, I've spent so many years in places like this, I know how to live better in here than out there. I get a job, and then what? What do I do with myself? It's always the same. I have a newfound resolve to steady myself in society, but they don't want me. I don't want them. I struggle along until I get bored and dabble in what I do best. I get a little taste, and the thrill brings me back into the fold. Eventually, I slip up or get too risky, and I land back in here. The first few times, I was terrified, but by now, it's more of a comfort. I get anxious when it comes time to be released. So, don't come in here on your high horse and expect to provide me with the epiphany I need to change who I am. I am who I've become, and I can pretend I've changed for a while, but it's not worth pretending anymore."

"Well, Alvin, I wish you the best, man. Enjoy the books, and sorry again about forgetting for a while." He gave me a firm handshake.

"I know you meant the best. Thanks, again. If you're ever in the neighborhood, feel free to stop by." He left me with one last grimace before the guard ushered him back to his cell.

During the ride home, I kept trying to pinpoint where his logic was flawed or he was wrong. I should've brought up family. He loved his family, and that was reason enough to change. If I could've just worked that angle, maybe I could've gotten to him. *Perhaps I'll pay him one more visit before he gets out.*

In February, I decided to leave the firm where I worked because the job was boring me. The pay and hours were great, but the work was so mundane, it was difficult to make it through the day. For years, I had been miserable on the job, but I never mustered the guts or rationale to leave. Deniece finally showed me I needed a change. I needed something more challenging, or I was going to drive myself mad. At the time, I never thought I would. It took a month of job searching before I came across an offer that sounded interesting. After blowing the doors off the interview, I got rewarded with a job offer I couldn't have dreamed up. It was an account managing, organizing/structuring position at a smaller company. They specialized in sending accountants overseas to companies looking to reorganize or expand to global markets.

The job took me out of the country one week a month to places all over the globe but mainly centered in Europe. It paid similar to my last job but was much more demanding. As one might imagine, Ann was jealous of the travel. The job sounded difficult, but I was up for a challenge and took it without a second thought. Once hired, I quickly realized I was in way over my head. The gig was much harder than I anticipated, and it took me a few months to even begin to grasp it. I worked hard, though, and established myself as a reliable asset. It was almost more fun to work than to be at home, but I took precautions so as to not let it consume me. It was also part of the reason I was still kicking around the next move for Deniece and me. I wanted to ensure I wasn't too engrossed in work so that I could leave time for her and Lizzie.

Celia and I still talked occasionally and were comfortable being distant friends. I explained the situation to Deniece, and she understood. It didn't bother her in the slightest, but I imagined if things got more serious between us, I would let my Celia friendship fade.

My life was near-perfect, and I savored every minute of it. I never knew I could be so happy, and I wasn't sure how much better it could get.

And I had *long* forgotten about the DNA samples Chris sent to the lab.

Chapter 19

"Hello?" My voice pierced the dial tone. "Nick at Day One Accounting Solutions, how may I help you?"

"Hey, Nick. Wow, nice enthusiasm," Chris said, taking a jab at my perky greeting.

"Not that type of firm, but there's a reason I make the big bucks." I leaned back, twirling my pen around. "Also, if you're calling about getting together, I got a fancy date tomorrow, I'm taking Will to his football game Sunday, and I'm out of town the rest of the week in Portugal, so we'll have to plan on next week."

"Guess I'll have to get a schedule from your secretary! Man, that's great." A long pause greeted the other end of the phone. "Well, that's not exactly why I'm calling. I have some interesting news for you. Um, maybe I shouldn't say it's *interesting*." His tone turned gruff. "The DNA test came back."

I folded back into the chair as my mouth dried out. The saliva turned thick, and I felt myself feeling the need to swallow. The remaining moisture continued to recede until my tongue dried up like an African well.

I had completely forgotten about the test. It felt like ages ago. I was practically a different person then. I didn't want to know. "Wow," was all I could muster out. My head was a whirlwind.

"I know. I was blindsided too. I… uh… well… I was thinking we would open it at dinner in two weeks, I guess. How about

Mulberry's? That's where this whole thing started anyhow, right? I mean, I don't know what you're thinking. Actually, we should just throw it away. You don't need this result anymore, right? You've moved on." He sounded a little flustered.

"Open it."

"Nick, why do you still want to know? You've put it behind you."

"What does it say, Chris?"

"It's not important, Nick. This shouldn't be done over the phone, either."

"Dammit, Chris! What does it say? You think I can wait two weeks?!"

Silence followed for a few moments, and I took a few deep breaths. I was leaning forward, sweaty hands clasping my desk.

"Nick, relax OK, man, the results aren't going anywhere."

"Chris..." I tried to keep my composure as much as I could, but I wanted to scream. "I want to know *now*, or I'm going to explode."

"Fine."

I heard rustling in the background followed by nearly a minute of silence as he scanned the documents.

"Is it a freaking essay? What does it say?" The phone was pressed so hard against my ear, Chris sounded like he was in my head.

"Dupont didn't do it."

"What?" I asked.

"Dupont didn't kill your dad, Nick." He responded forcefully this time.

"Well damn! Haha, I kinda figured that." I let out some air and turned from the desk. I pivoted toward the window, looking out at the street below. That brought me great comfort and relief.

"I just had this feeling he couldn't have done it. Gonna have to send him a couple more books if he's still locked up." I relaxed, kicking back into my office chair. It was a relief knowing it wasn't him. I mean, I'm not sure what I would've felt if it was. I was friendly to him, even wanted to help him out. And if those same hands I shook had murdered my father, I guess I would've been pretty livid.

"Nick! Nick, you still there?" Chris's voice echoed into my ears.

"Yeah, yeah, loud and clear."

"That's not all."

"What do you mean, that's not all?" I shot upright.

"The DNA test came up with a match."

"What!"

At this point, Chris's voice moved into a dreamlike echo as I tried to process what he had just said. *How is that even possible?*

"It was a female relative, Nick. The test matches your DNA for a female relative. I'm so sorry."

Silence.

"I didn't mention this before, but on the shortlist of suspects was your mother. She discovered the body and even had hand wounds, but the injuries were from a work incident the prior week, which was backed up by work and doctor records. The interviewing officer noted also her genuine emotion of, shock and grief."

I didn't comprehend his response fully. It was like I heard him clearly but couldn't process it past that. I kept playing his words over in my head, but still nothing. My vision was a blur.

"There are other explanations, though. Maybe it happened earlier, and the blood was just left over. Or maybe it happened when they discovered him." He grasped for more, but he knew. We both knew.

He continued rambling, saying things like "I'm here for you" and not to jump to conclusions, but I only listened half-heartedly. Finally ending the conversation with an abrupt "thanks," I put the phone down.

Dazed, I roamed from my desk to the coffee pot by the receptionist's desk. My stomach became twisted and knotted along the way.

"Jeeze, Nick, you look terrible! You're pretty pale." Gloria met my eyes with a ghostly stare.

"Yeah, I'm gonna head home for the day," I barely managed to say.

Reaching for a cup of coffee, I poured a hefty glass, realizing halfway through that my stomach had become too sickened to consume it. I gingerly walked out of the building, taking one piping hot sip before throwing the rest away.

At least the pain meant I felt *something*. I struggled along the sidewalk in a trance, looking down only at the cracks that passed me. After bumping someone, they yelled something, but I couldn't hear them. I felt as though I was going to hurl and ducked into a local restaurant's bathroom to wait it out.

Sitting on the toilet, I began to thaw out. My clouded head began to clear and fill with rage. The anger of almost 20 years began to bubble up as I pictured all the lies and deceit. How I was played and manipulated for most of my life. How could she smile at me? How could she live with herself? "FUCK!" I punched the stall door, ricocheting it off the ceramic wall. When it reverberated back, I kicked at it. I began furiously kicking the door until it hung on one hinge, barely seesawing back and forth with little squeaks. I grabbed the top of the stall and ripped it from its remaining hinge. I stared at it rattling on the floor, limp and defeated.

My mom had betrayed me.

The small explosion helped to quell my anger for the time being. I slipped outside and did my best not to marinate on the subject because I couldn't handle thinking about it too much. My mom got revenge for the adultery and got the life insurance policy and then turned around and lied to our smug, gullible faces, comforting the pain she caused. I continued down the sidewalk, headed toward Cyrus Park. I looked like a madman, talking to myself, angrily speed walking with no regard for those around me.

I couldn't believe it. I was pleading that the whole thing was some cruel, utterly sick joke Chris was playing, but I knew it wasn't. Years of punishing others for their transgressions, and at the root of it all lay her. She took him away from me. What he must've thought knowing my mom was about to kill him and that she would probably get away with it. The thought of his suffering pushed me to the brink. I couldn't have a meltdown in public.

I took a deep breath and broke my solitary illusion, taking in the surroundings. I was near the center of Cyrus Park, populated with moms, day-care clubs, and lots of kids—the typical crowd. And here I was dressed in business casual, sweating feverishly and pale as the moon. No doubt I had already made a few parents uneasy. I needed to take my mind off it.

Spotting a nearby bench, I rested, taking a deep breath as the pine seat creaked and moaned under my weight like it was strained. My leg tapped like a jackhammer. Birds chirped angrily in the fountain nearby, and the sun beamed down on my skin with a vengeance. A child running past tripped and scraped his knee, crying loudly. Apparently, no one cared to comfort him.

As I sat there taking in all the glory that was the park, two moms on the bench beside me were complaining about how it wasn't fair their child didn't make the select team; how it wasn't fair that despite being on a diet, they still weren't seeing results. Suddenly, I felt a sharp, unbearable pain arise from the back of my hand. Recoiling, a bee crawled along the bench. I smashed that bugger so hard, it caused the moms nearby to stop mid-sentence and stare at me. I needed a drink.

I swiftly transported myself to the nearest bar. Being mid-afternoon, the crowd was thin and consisted of some pretty shabby people. I grabbed the nearest stool and caught the bartender's attention.

"Hey, son, what can I get for you?" he asked. He was quite a bit older, and the slow hours were probably perfect for him.

"Whisky on the rocks." I barely glanced up.

He quickly grabbed a glass as bottles clanked together. Within a few moments, the beautiful drink appeared before me. I examined the reflective amber glow and caressed the heavy glass. Bringing it to my lips, I felt the cold radiate down into my stomach and reverberate a warm glow back up. The warmth quelled the harsh sting that followed on my tongue. I calmly placed the glass down and let my muscles and mind go limp. Letting out a deep breath, I felt the last hour momentarily melt from my mind. My body cushioned into the backrest of the stool.

Neon lights glowed dimly in the midday sun. The walls were coated with beer and liquor memorabilia. It was a rather cozy place, a bit drabby, but I could see why it attracted the daytime crowd. I let my problems slip away into the drink and indulged in the bliss that it provided me. For a brief moment, I couldn't be mad at the world, and I simply enjoyed what I had and who I was. Every action inconsequential, every opinion void. All that mattered was what I knew and believed. The bar had that old-time feel that I imagine brought those guys looking for a glimpse of better times. I gave an aged gentleman a smile and nod at the end of the bar. A stone-cold stare greeted me, but he managed a nod. He knew what it was about. I smiled and enjoyed the rest of my drink.

After two more, I decided to head back before I became too inebriated. I left the bar, leaving a hefty tip behind me. The sun had begun to set, and it was a leisurely walk to my car, thanks in part to my liquid sweater setting in. When I arrived back home, I found a loaded answering machine with six messages. I cruised past the counter and popped open the fridge, where a meager selection of beer awaited me. I hadn't gone to the liquor store in a while, and all there was to drink was a malt beer I had gotten as a gift from a coworker. Gross. There wasn't much I could do about it, though. I tried to ignore the sludge that slid down my throat, but it was nearly impossible.

I hunkered over to my recliner and settled in. Buster curled up at my feet like a good boy. Reaching down into the leather side pocket, I felt for the square box. It had been a long time since I had enjoyed a game of solitaire, and I missed it. At least I thought I did. I barely played three hands before it deterred me. *What other game does someone lose so many times? It's all just pointless*, I thought. Heading into my fourth beer, a heavy sadness began to creep in. I tried to shake the feeling by pounding a fifth, but it did nothing to help. My eyes welled, and then tears began pouring down my face. A few sniffles and a whimper eked out, but it was mostly just tears. Lots of tears. Her face was ingrained in my mind, the face when she first comforted me in the hospital. She was so sincere.

I cried for it all. For my dad, for my mom, for my sister, but mostly for myself and the years she took away from me.

What I wouldn't do for more time. I could've had it. What he must've thought to see his spouse bringing a knife into his chest. To comfort his kids with the same hands she used to kill him. No. A switch flipped in me, and my sorrow turned into anger. I wished my mom was in front of me so I could put an end to her.

I slammed the empty bottle on the floor. The shattering sent shards screaming back into my leg, and blood began to funnel into my sock from the sliced skin. Buster scurried away toward the bedroom and broke my blinding anger. I hustled over to the kitchen, making sure to soak and disinfect the wound. I wasn't sure if it even mattered since it was cut by glass with alcohol on it and reasoned it was probably already sterilized. I dabbed at the cuts with a paper towel until the flow of blood subsided and slouched back in my recliner. I felt numb. Flipping through the channels, I found nothing of interest and headed off to bed.

The next few days, the realization continued to fester, but not the fester like you get from a sliver. No, it was like the fester you get running a marathon with Civil War trench foot. Bursts of anger coincided with nausea in a twisted feeling that sucked what life I had managed to build in the last year out of me. Most of my day was consumed with thoughts and memories of my mother lying to me or talking badly about my dad. I felt suppressed by her. I operated through my days in a zombie-like trance. I was functioning, talking, and living, but I wasn't feeling anything. I canceled a date with Deniece and a business trip to Europe.

When I got home on Thursday from work, I tossed my keys on the counter. They bounced off the answering machine. I had ignored my messages and phone calls for a couple of days and finally gave one a listen out of courtesy.

I pressed the button, followed by a beep, and then Chris's voice.

"I kind of figured I would get your answering machine again, and I'm not sure if you have been listening to these, and I don't want to get ahead of ourselves, but have you thought about reopening the case? I mean, I'm sure... ah, you know what? Never mind, that's stupid. What am I thinking? How are you, Nick? I'm worried about you."

I buried my face in the table, my eyes welling up again.

"I can't imagine what must have gone through your head these last couple of days, but I hope you're managing. I know you went to work because I called to see if you came in. Now, listen, Nick, you have to talk to someone about this. I'm here for you, or you can go to a counselor, but you can't do this alone. Everyone needs help sometimes, you know? Well, listen, I will stop the spiel. I probably have your answering machine filled up with how many messages I've left. But I'm gonna stop in this weekend, regardless of whether you want me to or not. Do your best not to think about it too much until we can sort it out. You remember our quote when we were down as teens? 'The only way to suffer is to care, and the only way to live is to suffer.' Love you, man."

The tears that had welled up in my eyes fell down onto my mouth. Their salty tinge graced my taste buds before trickling down onto my arm. Chris's message gave me a moment of clarity. I knew what I had to do. He was right. I couldn't let this nag me forever. I needed to move past the cowardly regret and grief.

I needed to kill her.

I rose from the epiphany, grief-stricken no longer. I grabbed a beer from the fridge, opened it, but left it in the kitchen.

"Nick, you crazy bastard."

It was September 18th; I only needed to wait 3 more days.

Chapter 20

The next couple of days came and went. I was no longer in anguish over my mother's betrayal and instead was rather muted. I called Chris back and thanked him for the message. I told him it really helped clear my mind, and I reassured him I would manage. His voice held such relief when I told him I would go see someone to work things out. We agreed on dinner at Mulberry's the coming Monday. I dropped Buster off at doggy daycare for a week with Ann as the emergency contact.

It wasn't until the night of September 20 that things started to change. My emotions became unhinged again. I lay in bed restless and awoke after barely sleeping a wink. Cold sweat glued my nightclothes to my body. Adrenaline, anger, and sadness gripped me. There was no way I could rest knowing what I was going to do today. I cursed God for my fortunes, for my pain. I rampaged around the apartment, focusing my ire on a family picture found on my nightstand. I brought the pictures into the living room, laying them on the carpet. I couldn't rip up the pictures of my mother fast enough. Her smile was an insult. I smashed them into the floor until I was exhausted. I lowered myself prone, letting my body and mind float.

I played with the fibers of the carpet, the individual weaves unraveling at my fingertips. The softness eroded and ran coarse against my thumb. It stung, but they kept unraveling. The pain turned numb as the red impression on my fingertips deepened.

Eventually, a single strand was left, and I plucked it from its stitching. The cold air caused the exposed raw skin to burn. I stared at the wound in bewilderment. The strand was dead, but it left its mark. My steadfast conviction of the last few days could not elude me in my time of need.

I couldn't let myself get too frenzied, as it was still a few hours before I was to head to the nursing home. Time crawled to a halt as my anger bubbled. I knocked back a couple of drinks and left for the park since I couldn't be cooped up at my place much longer.

Escaping to the park didn't release my tension either. It simply got me more agitated. All these perfect happy, giggling families frolicking like they were in the Garden of Eden, and here my mom murdered any hope of that for me. *These people take it for granted; they don't understand.* I seethed, staring at every happy person. I suddenly felt the uneasy stare of a mom sitting beside me.

It was almost 1:30 p.m., and they would be changing shifts soon at the nursing home. Plus, it was naptime for most residents. I rose from the bench and heard an audible sigh of relief from the woman next to me. I got my first dose of panicked nervousness as I approached my car.

I arrived at the nursing home around 2 p.m. Vengeance had never been so personal, so painful. A nervousness built up in me that I had never felt before. My chest constricted until I could only manage shallow laborious breaths. I took a second to compose myself and push off the lingering thoughts of the consequences. If I let them in, I may not be able to do it. I marched into the front doors, attempting to seem as normal as possible. I had taken a deep breath right before I entered the sightline of the nurses at the front desks, but surely I looked like a madman. I could barely keep a handle on my composure. My legs jiggled their way forward like two gelatin appendages, and I wanted nothing more than to collapse and curl up in the hallway. I checked in and made my way toward her room. I couldn't even call her my mom anymore. I approached, wanting with nearly every fiber of my being to end her. However, there was one strand left, yanking at me to let it go, to forgive her.

No, it wasn't that simple. So many years of revenge taught me it was impossible to do that. This would put an end to it. I crept up to the door, slowly letting myself pass the oak barricade. I took a glance into the dark L-shaped room. I couldn't see her living room or bed, so I wasn't sure if she was down for a nap. The TV was off; that was a good sign. I slid the "do not disturb" sign on the doorknob and gently set my bag down. I started to tiptoe to get a glimpse around the corner. I needed to cut my toenails. They dug into the skin with how much weight was on them.

My head emerged from beyond the jut out in the wall, first seeing the TV and then the recliner. It was empty. I could hear my heart thumping as I continued to inch around the corner.

And there she lay. Covered by a white sheet and on her back, the sight of her produced sheer panic, followed by the gritting of my teeth. She slept so peacefully for what she had done. I retreated to my bag, opened the first zipper and pulled out a large kitchen knife. The same weapon she killed my father with. It glistened with my reflection. The wide body would be difficult to bring deep, but it was sharp. In a short while, blood would taint the clean steel. I trembled terribly holding the weapon as I turned the knife over, letting the grip form to my hand. I returned to the corner of the small living room area to the bedroom. Pictures of my mom, my sister, and I lined her dresser. There were none of my father.

My throat began to dry up, and I had trouble getting air. My panic rose until it felt like my body was about to fail. I was weak and dizzy on the approach. The sweat was beginning to affect my grip on the knife. I inched forward, crouched in the shadows. Every step took me a minute, and each was only forced by another wave of anger. I begged her to wake up, so I could stop the anguish. I couldn't do it.

Finally, by her bedside, I watched her breathing. Inhale… rise… hold… fall gently. With every breath, she let out another lie. She was lying to me, to my sister, to our family. I wanted to demand an answer, but it would be frivolous. I knew. She knew. Money problems, cheating, a flawed marriage. Murder was her ticket out. She thought she had gotten away with it all too, but the past always catches up.

My breathing was thunderous in the quiet of the room. Perspiration leeched from my brow as I stood over her. Knife held above her with two hands, a bead of sweat began to slide down my face. The saltwater bombshell continued until it hung menacingly on the edge of my nose. I watched it, dared it to release itself, undoubtingly waking my mom in the process. My pores had betrayed me.

I reached up with my sleeve, but an abrupt twitch shook the droplet. The oiled concoction entered a free fall towards my mother's face, my mouth agape as the drop splattered violently on her nose and the fragments of its dispersal clung to her cheek. I withheld breathing for what felt like an eternity. Small breaths leaked out to prevent a loss of consciousness, but that was all. I waited in agony, trying to think of what my action would be if she awoke.

Her face twitched, and she brought her hand up to wipe away the irritant. It was followed by a moment of restlessness. Then, probably sensing my heavy breathing or presence, she opened her eyes.

"Nick?" Her face was pure confusion. "Wha—"

I drove the knife down into her chest as her eyes bulged with horror. The knife bore into her body just above the breast. It made a horrific slicing sound as it cut deeper. Blood bubbled to the surface and seeped into her gown, and the silver blade slowly disappeared as it descended. She looked as though she was screaming, but no sound came out. She stared at me, tears running from her cheeks onto the pillow. Blood was beginning to gush from her like I had never seen. Its sticky warmth coated my hands. My firm grip began to loosen as the lubricant slid my palms down. My bottom fingers sliced against the pressure of the metal. Tears streamed down my face. I was frozen in place, only a portion of the knife remained. I could feel her eyes boring holes through me. With a glance, I caught her stare.

It hurt more than I had ever felt before.

Mom. What have I done?

Her eyes were not filled with the anger I anticipated, but instead, they pleaded with me in disbelief and sorrow. They conveyed love. The glistening of the tears refracted the dark dominance of her pupils.

I couldn't remove my hand from the knife, even as I collapsed to my knees. One hand remained on the black plastic, partially out of shock and partially out of fear that she would take it out and assault me in my feeble state. I sensed her growing weak. My grip loosened.

I wanted it all to stop; I wanted it to end.

I collapsed against the side of the bed, slowly sinking to the floor. The mass of my quivering body curled up into a blubbering paralysis. I couldn't comprehend the concept of my action. I lay parallel to the laminate wood flooring. The objects in the room were a blur in my eyes.

A warm drip began on my back. Blood from the bed had made its way down the white sheets. I scooted forward, avoiding the flow.

I'll never hear her again.

My mind echoed over and over as in a canyon. I lay still, my body unable to move. Blood from the bed began to pool on the floor around me. I fell into a state of confusion and shock, losing track of time. I entered a dreamlike state, devoid of object permanence or self-awareness. I couldn't bear to stare at anything but the door that held my gaze frozen. The crimson had consumed my place on the floor.

I remained motionless until a loud noise from the hallway startled me out of my stupor. I blinked furiously, trying to snap myself into a stable consciousness. Scrambling up, I rushed into the bathroom and vomited.

Even after I stood hunched over the toilet, the sickening feeling in my stomach was still present. I felt disgusting. I began to wash off the blood and took off the soiled clothes. All the while, I was realizing there was no going back, no way to get away with this one. Subconsciously, I knew that from the start, but it was really sinking in now.

Examining the wood inlays of my watch as I gripped the sink, the hands pointed to nearly 3:30 in the afternoon. Time had lapsed incredibly fast. I changed into my second set of clothes. I took one last glance at the lifeless, ghostly corpse that lay in the corner of the room. A chill penetrated my soul. I felt her presence looming.

Trying to gain some composure, I looked at myself in the mirror. The cold eyes of Nancy Papperman stared back at me.

Chapter 21

I barely made it to the car before reverting into a nervous wreck, trembling with seizure-like volatility once inside. I only had a couple of hours before they came to get her for dinner and discovered the scene. And only a few minutes after that before they connected the dots.

I needed to tell someone. I needed to tell someone everything. This was my last chance. I couldn't hold in the lies anymore.

My sister. I needed to apologize.

I drove like an utter madman, flying toward my sister's house. I could barely see the pavement outlines between my tears and the images of my mom that summoned a deep pain. I reached Ann's house feeling emotionally numb. I wasn't sure I could absorb any more.

I busted open the door of my sister's house. It flew wildly into the wall, nearly shattering the glass panes in the door. I stumbled into the foyer, my breathing still laborious. Sweat coated my brow, and my eyes were manic. Before I made it down the hallway, my sister popped out from around the corner in a black shirt and shorts.

"Oh, Nick! God, you startled me." She covered her heart. "I thought you were a burglar! You had me worried for a moment."

I just stared back at her. She began to notice my state as I drew closer.

"You look terrible. Are you sick? Is that mom's coat?" She backpedaled away from my march to the kitchen.

"We need to talk." My steel tone cut the mood.

She quickly grabbed one of the kitchen chairs and flipped it toward me.

"What happened?" Concern weighed heavy on her face.

"Just give me a minute… I'm sorry." I couldn't even look at her.

"OK, Nick, well, whatever it is, you're starting to freak me out. I'm gonna grab you something to drink." She scurried over to the sink and grabbed a glass. The clinging and banging of glass finally gave way to the slow fulfillment of its purpose. Once Ann shut the water off, she paused and stared at the mantle in front of her before reaching for something.

"Oh, and you must have left your watch here last week because I found Will wearing it the other day. He was so upset when I took it. He said he wanted to be just like you. Precious, I know. I was gonna drop it off sometime next week but didn't have time." She fetched the watch from the kitchen ledge and placed it on the table beside me, along with the glass.

"So, I'm ready, Nick. Let's hear it." She took a seat across from me.

I took a quick sip of water and collected myself, looking down at my lap. I didn't know where to begin. How do I begin a conversation where I'm confessing that I just killed our mom?

A beam of light reflected onto my eye, and I jerked out of its path. The sunlight entering through the patio window bounced off the watch on my wrist. The watch on my wrist was my watch. I was already wearing my watch. I turned toward the one on the table. It must've been a mistake; maybe it was one of Nate's watches.

"Sis…"

I stared at the watch, perplexed. It looked exactly like mine, but it couldn't be. It had the same wooden inlays with a platinum band and body, encompassed with gold around the border. The timepiece on the table, however, looked slightly more worn. The platinum looked a hue darker, as if it had lost its polish. The gold also suffered from the same neglect. Other than those disparities, they were nearly identical.

Then I noticed the initials. They read J.J.

"Hey, sis, I don't think this is my—" And then it dawned on me. The initials J.J. stood for Justin Jacobs, my father.

Chris's voice echoed in my head. "All that was stolen was cash and his watch." She noticed I was staring at the piece, her eyes then wandering to my wrist.

"Oh, sorry, that's dad's old watch. Just something I kept to remind me of him; I forgot yours is the same." She reached for the piece, but I snagged her arm just as she was about to touch it. She managed a convincing lie, but I had the DNA tests and police records.

"No!"

I turned toward my sister, panic and dread cemented on her face.

"You!" I let her hand retreat.

"Nick, it's not—"

"Why do you have dad's watch!" I demanded. "I know it was stolen."

"It's not what you think!" Her plea fell on deaf ears. I hung my head and squeezed my eyes tight.

"I was so high, and he wanted me to go to rehab, but I just couldn't, and he grabbed my arm, and, and…" Her voice shook so horribly that she could barely get the words out. "I grabbed a knife. I wasn't even thinking, Nick. I just swung it. I wasn't looking, and then the blood was everywhere, and I panicked, I couldn't… I was messed up. I have regretted it every day since. I wake up in cold sweats half the nights because of it." She was almost yelling. "Why do you think my husband is never here? You think he wants to deal with this? I can barely go a day without thinking about it!"

What had I done? What had she done?

"But you killed him," I said, shaking.

I turned away in disgust for the both of us. I killed my mom for nothing. All that love and everything she provided was genuine. How could you? I slapped myself on the head and began pacing the kitchen floor. "You made me do it. None of it would've ever happened, and you are responsible for this…" I mumbled profanities under my breath.

"Nick, you're scaring me." Her voice was distressed. I had slowly approached the counter from behind the kitchen table where I had been standing. I wrapped myself around the breakfast bar. The granite countertop was cold as my hand brushed along its surface. The impurities in the design were what I fixated upon as I maneuvered around the outside.

"Ann, I wish it didn't have to be like this." I lunged toward her, catching her off guard. My momentum pushed us up against the side of the counter. She struggled vigorously to break away and almost did. Her fist was beating against the top of my head. The commotion and yells of the struggle made me conscious that Will might be home and hear this. She managed a few good scratches, cuts, and a gnarly bite, but I eventually subdued her in a headlock. I felt her body give way as she passed out. I quickly moved to search the garage for rope, eventually settling for extension cords and duct tape. I took a kitchen chair, and propping her up, I secured her well, making sure that only a Houdini could escape. At this point, I was too far in to turn back, but the conflicting feelings were threatening my decisiveness. I needed to keep emotion out of the equation the best I could.

She awoke with a splash of ice water. I stood pacing in front of her. Her fog eroded into blistering anger.

"Nick, what the fuck! Untie me!" She was under the illusion that she was still in control. "I know you must be pissed, but what is this? We're family!"

I barely acknowledge her pleas. "You ripped my whole life away from me! Then you spent years lying. Lying to us all until mom took the fall."

"What are you talk—"

"Mom's dead." That sucked the air out of her lungs. She stared at me like I was revealed to be the devil. Her voice was almost breathless. "You… ki… killed mom?" I simply looked away, but she knew. Neither of us said anything for a minute, nor could we look at each other.

"I thought she did it."

"Why would you thin—"

"The DNA from the blood said it was a female relative! I had Chris run a couple of samples, and I was sure it was mom." I let the news sink in. I had been so quick to assume.

"Nick, I didn't take away your life; you did."

"No! Don't you dare! Don't you fucking dare! None of this would've started if you hadn't killed dad. I could've been happy. We all could've!"

CHAPTER 21

"No, we couldn't, Nick! Dad—"

I stretched the roll of duct tape tightly around her mouth, muffling her screams and pleas. It only infuriated her further. I whistled and stood calmly by until she settled. She needed to understand.

"You hid your little secret for years, watched my turmoil over it, pretended like you really cared about him, and you think I took away my own life. Was it my fault that I spent the first months crying myself to sleep at night? I guess it was my fault going through every day begging for something to make me feel, terrified that I may never escape from my depression. Don't you dare say it was my fault! Besides, I only have one more life to take." With that, I reached across the counter for the kitchen knife. She began wildly throwing herself in the chair in a last-ditch effort to break free. Her eyes, racked with fear, fixated on the glistening of the long blade, then at me. She looked at me like I was a stranger, and I was. She didn't know me. Only one person ever did. I heard a crash from upstairs, and instantly, both our heads shot up.

Her fear turned to panic, and her eyes pleaded. I began to back away from her and toward the stairs. I sheathed the knife in my coat and began my ascent. Her frenzied movements increased ten-fold, and I had to return to her and reinforce the restraints. She was exerting every muscle in her body to break the chair. Her muffled screams through the tape could still be heard once I reached the top of the stairs. I stopped in the bathroom, collecting myself with a splash of cold water. There was really no going back now. I moved swiftly to Will's room, taking a deep breath before entering.

Will was lying on the floor of his bedroom, headphones on and a Walkman beside him. Hot Wheels in hand, he was running a race with the lot, complete with sound effects and crashes. The crashes would have been excessive even by movie standards. When two cars collided, they erupted hundreds of feet in the air with a huge explosion. In slow motion, the two cars performed an exploding acrobatic routine before finally falling to the floor with one last boom. I assumed that the drivers of the two vehicles were dead a few times over. He didn't notice my entrance.

"Hey, bud. That the Daytona 500?" He didn't turn. I raised my voice nearly to a yell. "Hey, bud!" His head shot sideways, and his surprise quickly turned to excitement.

"Uncle Nick!" He bolted up and sprinted into my arms. "I thought you weren't coming till tomorrow!" He pulled back.

"Well, I decided to come for a surprise adventure."

His eyes lit up instantly. "What is it?"

"See, I can't tell you. It's a surprise."

"Please, you have to tell me. At least give me one hint. That's the rule." Will tugged at my arm.

"Says who?"

"I don't know? You just have to!"

"Fine, fine." I pretended like he was really cracking my resolve. "Well, it involves hot dogs and a trip to the park."

He looked puzzled. "That's not a good hint."

"That's the best I can offer you, bud." My shoulders shrugged. The furrowed eyebrows and discontent on his face told me I had to do better than that.

"Fine, if you must know, I also have a surprise gift." This was the answer he was looking for, and he raced to the stairs, almost before I could stop him. Ann was still bound to the chair, her screams piercing the duct tape bindings. I told Will I would race him to the car but held his arm back while going down the banister to focus his attention. I loudly talked nonsense, almost to the point of yelling. Spewing on about nonsense and teasing him that I would win. My voice deafened the muddled screams from the kitchen while I ushered Will out the door. A sigh of relief accompanied the exit. I looked back at Ann. This time her eyes were desolate, devoid of the fiery rage a few minutes earlier. I mouthed "I'm sorry" before closing the door on her and heading back to Will.

Chapter 22

Will was already eagerly waiting at the car. "Where is my mom? Is she coming?" he asked.

"No, she's got some errands. It's just us two today," I said as I rounded the hood. Unlocking the door, I couldn't shake the paranoid feeling that Will was going to figure out what I had done. My face told the whole story. I tried to act naturally, but my eyes gave it away. Every time his met mine, I was telling him another part of the secret.

"Uncle Nick, are you okay? You seem a little weird." The line of questioning induced a stiff awkwardness as I tried to appear casual. My unnatural body language was in complete contradiction to my speech.

"Well, I'm just hungry and a little tired. It's been a long day." I was having trouble keeping up the cheerful façade. "Say, how about we stop and grab some dogs and some soda? How about that?" He seemed to like that suggestion and eagerly nodded. I turned up the music. "Paint it Black" played through the radio waves. I cranked my window down, allowing the breeze to blast my face. Will held his head out the window, telling me he was just like Buster, tongue out and all.

We stopped at a small hot dog joint near the edge of town and ordered a couple of Chicago dogs. They were loaded and delicious, but I hardly took notice. I continually glanced at the staff, expecting one of them to report me to the police. Ann had probably summoned Herculean strength and broken free by now, or perhaps her husband had come home early. Maybe she had knocked the phone down and dialed 911 with her nose, and the manhunt was on. Panic pulsed as the plethora of options continued to fray my nerves. I picked napkins apart at our table. I stopped when Will took notice. My eyes darted around, prepared to bolt at any moment if I saw someone looking at me funny. I forced Will to take the dog on the road before he got to his third bite. I told him we were late, and he didn't throw much of a protest. Rushing out of there, we finished our dogs on the road. Before we even got out of the parking lot, a drop of ketchup squeezed out of Will's bun and splattered on the seat.

"I'm sorry! I didn't mean to." He was in a panic. "I will clean it up!" He reached for a napkin and attempted to clean up, but his circular motion just cemented the stain in the fabric.

"It's alright, bud. It won't matter. Forget about it."

He didn't appear to trust the nonchalant response.

Just then, out of the left side of my vision, a cop car came into view. My breath was taken away so fast I nearly choked. My heart lurched against my chest. He was probably on the hunt for me. Had they discovered my mom or my sister? I watched my rear-view mirror for the next mile to make sure we weren't being tailed. Sweat had begun to stick my shirt to my body, and I moved around uncomfortably, trying to air it out. This continued until we were back at my apartment. I hesitated at the door, frightened that a SWAT team was waiting to ambush me.

The detour didn't take long. I grabbed something from my room and left a note on the kitchen counter for when the authorities inevitably came. We soon arrived at the end destination: Glenwood Cemetery. When Will asked how this was supposed to be an adventure, I told him that sometimes, when you least expect something, it can surprise you. I asked him to trust me. He reluctantly obliged, and I brought him in tight with my arms around his shoulders.

"This cemetery is the resting place of my father. And there is a lot of history here. He was a great dad, and it's about time you learned a little about him."

We made our way from the newer section with concrete paths to the grassy area packed with forgotten headstones. The gravestone was fourth from the end, at the peak of a small hill that overlooked half the cemetery. On the walk, I couldn't help but think about how I got to this point in my life. A lot of hate and hurt had formed me into who I was, and while that had started to melt, it came roaring back after the DNA test. I had just begun to grasp happiness when all the years of depression and anger tried to come back. I didn't let it. It blinded me, though it tends to do that. It takes away what you built and leaves those around you hurt. It wasn't going to control me anymore.

We settled down, our backs against the gravestone on a chilly Saturday afternoon, and stared out at the cemetery. There was always an unsettling silence in a cemetery, one that rubbed you numb and made you feel solemn. I had brought a small bottle of Captain and was enjoying generous swigs. The sun was beginning to set, and its peaceful glow was alluring. The colors danced along the horizon and played long shadows behind the gravestone.

"Nick, am I gonna make it to the pros?" Will asked. He amused me with the question.

"You know, kid, I sure would hope so, but you never know what's gonna happen in life. I think you have the heart."

"But heart doesn't hit home runs," Will said bluntly.

"Yeah, you're right, but home runs don't always win."

He started to rattle off the rest of his stats this year, saying that if he kept them up, then he would be one of the best players in the majors. That really entertained me, and I let him go on for a little while before interrupting.

"I think it's time for that surprise, Will." He shot to attention, eyeing me eagerly for my gift.

"You have to close your eyes first, though. No peeking at all, deal?"

"Yes, yes! Fine, I promise!" He extended his pinky toward me. What a sweet boy.

Now that the oath had been taken, I presented a scarf and tied it around his head. I told him he didn't have to put it over his eyes yet. I needed a minute. I re-adjusted myself against the stony backrest. I could feel the letters carved in the gravestone. The grainy stone scraped against my coat. The sun was halfway set, and the bright red and yellow turned to deep crimson red. My eyes welled up. It was a beautiful world.

"Lower it, kid, and sing 'Take Me Out to the Ballgame' loud, and don't stop for nothing or no surprise."

"TAKE ME OUT TO THE…." I took a long pull out of the bottle. Taking a deep breath, I unsheathed the knife from my coat pocket and raised it high.

"BUY ME SOME PEANUTS…"

There was no going back after this. I felt connected to the gravestone, like my father was there with me, taking me back to one of my favorite memories.

We had been out on the front lawn during a blisteringly hot summer day, just wrapping up my birthday in the back. The smell of the grill lingered and mingled with the summer scent. My dad had disappeared around the side of the house for a minute and reemerged with the garden hose, spraying us all lightly. We leaped, ran, screamed, and squealed until he relented. As soon as he did, we attacked in a laughing assault. We mauled him and subsequently returned the soaking, hugging him with our wet clothes. Mom watched, laughing, my father giggling as we tried to inflict damage. We only settled down at the mention of opening gifts.

I ripped through the presents because the only one I cared about was the new glove from my dad. I barely gave the other gifts a second thought before I begged Dad to play catch and break it in. He knew I was going to ask and beamed a proud smile down at his little ballplayer.

On the front lawn, my father had tossed the first ball, a gentle toss slicing through the air. The bright laces spiraled wildly, outlining the rest of the ball against the blue background. It fell perfectly into the web of my glove like it was born to do. I removed the treasure, cocking my arm back, prepared to throw. The laces grooved between my fingers, a four-seamed fastball roaring to go.

"FOR IT'S ONE…"

I brought the knife down, driving it deep into my inner thigh. Blood gushed instantly as pain shot through my body. Unfortunately, the alcohol I drank did little to numb my injury, and I needed all my willpower to hold back a yell and scare Will. The blood began to slide down my thigh. Its warm ooze was a slight comfort before transitioning to a shivering wet by the time it reached the grass. The bitter weather pierced me and sent shivers up my body.

"What's the surprise, Nick?" Will had finished his recital.

Still wincing from the pain, I reached into my coat pocket and shakily pulled out a baseball, giving the all-clear to remove the blindfold.

"It's a baseball signed by every starting Mets player that won the 1969 World Series. It was my father's. He gave it to me, and now I want to give it to you." He looked at me with bewilderment and amazement. I held it there in a tremble as he gazed upon its wonder.

"Now I have to play for the Mets when I grow up!" He reached for it. "Thanks, Uncle Nick. I love you." I smiled and was a little taken back by those words. Those three simple words brought me more life than anything. It was real. I felt it. My soul tingled with what I can only describe as true happiness.

"I was going to wait till your birthday, but I didn't think it could wait." I smiled as he examined the ball with intrigue. A crimson fingerprint lay exposed across the laces. Will paused, trying to process how there could be blood on the ball. It was getting darker, but there was still sufficient light to see. He glanced over at me, looking me up and down until he saw it—my hands. We briefly locked eyes. He was frightened. I began to choke up a little, my throat suffocated by some biological mechanism.

"Are you hurt?" Will turned toward me, leveraging his hand on my leg. Reflexively I grimaced and squirmed, to which he quickly retracted his arm. I could see the fear and concern in his stare.

"How did you—"

"I did it to myself, Will." He just stared at me blankly, like he couldn't comprehend someone hurting themselves.

"I've done some bad things, and I don't expect you to understand or forgive me for a long time, maybe never. But I want you to know I love you, but this has been something building for a long time." I graced him with a smile to let him know it was okay, but he didn't seem reassured. I brought him in for a hug, and he wrapped himself tightly around me. It was firm and warm, which counteracted the freezer that was becoming my body. The sun was nearly set, and the night crept along the retreating shadows of its brightness. Will's hair felt soft against my chin. Its velvet feel radiated comforting heat. I brought myself close to his ear.

"I know you'll make the pros, bud, I know." Tears began forming, and I tried mightily to hold them back. The pain in my leg was virtually gone.

Will looked up, tears streaming down his face, his voice so shaken I could barely make it out. "You're gonna be okay, though, right? You promised we would go to the game."

He sniffled, and I embraced him tightly. "I don't think so, bud. I think they are gonna be one fan short." I buried him in my chest so as not to witness the tears streaming down my face.

"I'm scared." He was sobbing now, and if not for the pressure against my chest and my growing weakness, I would've started sobbing too.

After a minute or so, I was able to pull myself together enough to look at him. I wiped tears away from his cheeks and pushed his chin up so he looked at me.

"Can you make one last promise for me, Will?" Tears continued to well. He nodded in agreement.

"Don't make the same mistakes I made. Don't let it control you. Do you understand?" He shook his head apprehensively.

"It is when you get picked on, and you want to punch that person back; it is when you strike out or make an error, and you want to throw something. Anger, fear; even if something really bad happens, it doesn't do you any good."

"I don't want you to go, Uncle Nick. You're my favorite person." His eyes begged me not to leave. He buried himself further into me.

"I wish it could be different. I just figured it out too late."

"Mom says it's never too late; that's just an excuse." I chuckled to myself because, in a way, he was right. I could've stopped.

I felt myself start to slump, and Will tried to help me upright. He looked down at his hands, now red. It took a tremendous amount of effort, but I was finally repositioned against the gravestone. My back molded into the letters nicely. The sun was down, and the only light remaining was the dark glow from the sun as it retreated and the illumination of the moon. I had brought a phone, a Nokia 1011, and dialed 911, only to be able to mumble, "Glenwood Cemetery. He's safe." I hung up before they got a chance to ask any questions, and almost instantaneously, I could hear sirens flare up in the distance.

"It sounds like help!" Will shook my coat. He sounded almost distant.

"I thought you needed a ride home." I spoke with such calmness it frightened me. It was so cold.

"I'm scared."

"I know, I know." I gave him another embrace. The warmth was surreal. I could feel the youth, the innocence, the love.

"You're cold, Uncle Nick," Will said, concerned. Indeed, the loss of blood was staggering, and I found myself becoming dizzy. "I can warm you up, though." He quickly ripped off his jacket and tossed it enthusiastically over my body, frantically making sure

I was as covered as possible. I couldn't do much but smile and admire his character. *He's going to do good.* The cool howl of the wind ripped against the new barrier.

"I love you, bud, and tell your mom I love her, too." My voice was soft and cracked under the pressure of holding back another wave of tears.

"And Grandma!"

I let out a physical wince. Will's interjection pierced me deeper than any knife could. The full realization of what I was putting him through stung. Someone I loved so much and who was so innocent. I was a monster. I could picture him learning the truth, and it hurt so damn much thinking about it. Worse than my leg, worse than the nursing home, worse than when my dad died. The pain manifested itself so deeply that I felt it grasp my insides until I could barely breathe. It reached the pit of my soul and then dug deeper, lodging itself in the fabric of my being. I couldn't bear the thought.

I turned toward Will. "I'm so sorry, bud. You don't deserve this." I slumped further down against the gravestone and began to sob uncontrollably. The sirens were getting closer.

"Don't cry, Uncle Nick. I'm sure the police will understand if you did something bad. I won't let them take you. I just have to wish on a star, like that time you made that shot on my birthday. I wished for you and it happened."

The sky was dark now, all but the shimmering stars. Will pointed out constellations that they were studying in school. He was fascinated that there was so much out there, and I couldn't blame him. They were alive, but the lights in my head were fading now. I told Will I was going to go soon.

"What about the sirens?" he said. "Am I in trouble, too"?

"Oh, don't worry about them. They are coming to escort you back to your house. I'm going to stay here for a while," I assured him.

He laid his head against my chest as we sat in silence.

"I won't let it get me, Uncle Nick. That thing you said, I won't let you down, I promise."

"You could never let me down, Will. I'll be watching, rooting." My speech trailed off, and my cold turned to warmth. I was finally discovering where people's thoughts reside in the fleeting moments of death. It was youth. The memories of my dad and me, especially on the baseball diamond, flashed vividly before me.

The peaceful visions slowly transitioned to Will and me playing catch, enjoying a beautiful summer day at the Mets game. Dippin' Dots and his secret crush. A smile formed as the lights grew dim. The sirens were close now. Hopefully, my sister would understand. Hopefully, Will would understand. He was whispering in my ear to wake up because the cops were there, but I could no longer respond to him.

I felt something on top of me being ripped away. The sound of Will screaming my name echoed in my head. They were taking him away.

"I forgive you, Anita."

*Special thanks to Mom,
Pat and Scout team player of the year, Luke.*

About the Author

Zachary Daniel is a young, ambitious author whose unconventional career path and approach to life has wielded a story seven years in the making. A story first hatched over a glass of rum and a sunset.

Zachary worked in Nuclear Medicine before starting his own investment practice Digital Edge Wealth Management. All the while keeping focus on his writing. Drawing inspiration from an avid imagination, life experiences, friends, family, Ron Diaz Rum and a tobacco pipe for those quiet evenings.

If you happen to see him out in the wild, expect a warm friendly Midwesterner with an appetite for trying new things. Whether it be gator wrestling or a board game night, there isn't much he can't get behind. He is obsessed with Bitcoin and friends would say he has a propensity for the unorthodox. He prefers to be thought of like an onion, with many layers.